Witherstone

Witherstone

Witherstone

First Published in Great Britain 2011.

Copyright © *Witherstone* J. A. Brunning, 2010

The right of J. A. Brunning to be identified as the author of this work has been asserted in accordance with the Copyright, Designs and Patents Act 1988.

All rights reserved. No part of this publication may be reproduced, stored in a retrieval system, or transmitted in any form by any means, electronic, mechanical, photocopying, recording or otherwise, without the prior permission of the author.

ISBN-13: 978-1466348738
ISBN-10: 1466348739

~

www.witherstone.com
www.jabrunning.co.uk

~

Witherstone

J A Brunning

Witherstone

Even though she wanted me to
dedicate it to the spiders,
this book is dedicated to Hattie,
the best reader a writer could
ever wish to write for.
(oh, alright then, and the spiders...)

Wᵒ Witherstone

1

The Homecoming

I couldn't run fast enough, and knew we wouldn't be able to escape. I looked back and Dad was right behind me, hauling on Mum's arm trying to help her keep up, and he was carrying my little sister as he ran. Mum's face was hidden from me but I knew she was frightened. Catherine was stretching her arms back over Dad's shoulder towards Grandma, and I groaned.

Grandma was already way behind, and I caught only glimpses of her as she fell further and further back. Our pursuer was getting closer, I could sense it, and cold fear sliced through me as I tried to run faster but my feet faltered. I couldn't see Richard anywhere. My brother had disappeared into thin air.

Suddenly we weren't in the village any more. We were in the forest, the trees silent all around us, and I couldn't hear anything as I ran through the dense undergrowth. I looked back in panic, and stopped dead. My family had completely vanished. Terror caught in my throat and I couldn't breathe. I looked wildly in all directions, but I was alone. Alone apart from the figure who stepped silently out of the trees, and I knew then that we had lost.

I woke up gasping for breath. The nightmare again. It was never exactly the same but we were always trying to escape from someone, but I didn't know who. And I was always alone at the end - alone with our enemy, a shadowy figure who filled me with terror. Whenever I tried to see their face, my eyes seemed to slide over them so I could never see who it was. I also woke up feeling horribly guilty because I'd kept running, leaving Grandma far behind and then somehow losing everyone else as well.

It was still dark outside but a pale light flickered across the room, and I turned to see Grandma at the fire. I wasn't the only one to have woken up early. She was coaxing the sleeping embers into life. Her face looked grim, but she nodded to me. It was almost as if we'd both known that something was going to happen that day.

Later that morning, when someone staggered into the cottage, it took me a few seconds to realise it was my brother. He was taller than I remembered, and bone thin and deathly pale. As Richard lurched into the room, Mum flew towards him and Grandma sent me to tell Dad that Richard had come home. That he was alive.

As I ran up the lane towards Thompson's Farm, a cold shiver ran through me. Why had Richard been the first one to disappear in my nightmare? I prayed it wasn't a bad omen as I shot through the stone gateway towards the scattered group of labourers at the far end of the field. I saw my father, stooped over with his heavy mattock levering stones out of the earth. I ignored the faces looking towards me as I passed, and Dad turned towards me, a large stone in his hands.

My breath came in painful gasps.

"R – Rich – ard," I managed, "Richard's - home –"

Dad's face was shocked, and he twitched forwards for a moment, urged home to see his son, but instead he turned towards the man making his way purposefully across the mud towards us.

"Tom?" the man said. "Is there a problem?"

"No, Master Thompson," Dad said at once, dropping the stone into the wooden barrow beside him.

"Eppie just had a message for me, that's all. I'll see you tonight, Eppie," Dad said, stooping for the mattock and turning back to his labour without looking at me again.

The yeoman stood with hands on hips, his impassive face staring down at me. I knew Dad wouldn't be able to come home early to see Richard, even though we hadn't seen him for two years. Even though for the past few days we'd been afraid my brother was dead. Master Thompson was always looking for any excuse to lay my father off work altogether, so I knew Dad would have to wait until tonight to see Richard. But at least he knew my brother was alive.

I resisted the urge to glare at the yeoman, and instead turned back to the gate. As I reached the stone gateposts, I looked over at Dad's bent back, the tall figure of Thompson towering over him. Then I stepped into the lane and my father was lost from view.

At home Mum was trying to persuade Richard to eat some porridge. He managed a little before he slumped over the table, his head dropping onto his arms. Mum tipped the uneaten contents of the bowl back into the pot with a sigh.

"Is Gran'ma fetchin' the laundry, Mum?" I asked.

"Yes," she said, turning towards me. "You should go an' help her, Eppie. Take Catherine with you."

My sister looked torn between staying to stare at the brother she barely remembered, and coming with me. She was persuaded by my opening arms, and launched herself onto my hip with a giggle of delight.

After finding that Grandma had already called at Edward Cowper's cottage, we hurried to Parson Burnett's house. Grandma was coming out of the kitchen door with a loaded basket.

"'Bye, Ellen," she called back, and the Parson's cook waved at us with her floury hands before she closed the door.

"You took your time," Grandma said, giving me a bundle of laundry to carry. Catherine set off towards home at a run, her brown pigtails flying behind her.

"How's your brother lookin' now, Hephzibah?" Grandma asked.

She was the only person who ever called me by my full name. Everyone else just called me 'Eppie'. I guess it was because I was named after her. Knowing Grandma, she probably felt the shortened version was an insult to her.

I chewed my lip. "He looks really ill."

"Well, he must be well enough, to have walked all this way back. When Old Isaac told us the boy was ill, it sounded as though he was at death's door. Trust Isaac Bailey to exaggerate."

I looked at Grandma's thin lips, knowing she'd been as worried as the rest of us since the pedlar told us Richard was ill two weeks ago. Mum had wanted to go to my brother herself, but Dad had forbidden it.

"It's over fifty miles, Martha, an' you're barely over your winter cough. I'll go an' fetch him home. I'll ask Thompson if I can go tomorrow."

"You must tell him how sick Richard is, Tom."

But the next evening Dad had come home from work with a face like thunder.

"Thompson said if I go, I'll lose my job to someone else," he had raged.

Mum's face had drained of colour as she began to weep, and Dad groaned.

"What can we do? We haven't any choice, Martha. If I go we'll all bloody starve."

A sick dread had begun in my stomach then, terrified my brother might die. We had spent the next two weeks hearing nothing, with Thompson refusing to let Dad go to Shipley Magna to fetch Richard if he wanted to keep his job, and Mum alternately weeping and raging in fury, raging as much at Dad as Master Thompson because Dad wouldn't let *her* go. Grandma couldn't go either, with her bad hip. This last few days Dad had been saying he'd have to go to Richard somehow, even if that meant losing his job, but then this morning my brother had come home.

I couldn't imagine how he'd managed to walk all that way, the state he was in. But he was home. He was alive.

Over the next few days, Richard slowly recovered, and I was so glad to have my brother home. There was even an odd satisfaction in him beginning to tease me like he used to. He had often infuriated me when we were younger, tormenting me until I hit him or threw a real screaming fit. Only when he'd succeeded in making me snap would he laugh and leave me alone. Then he'd been sent to work away during a really bad winter two years ago.

It had been a desperate time. Dad had been out of work as Thompson had nothing for him, and Witherstone Hall Farm wouldn't take him on anyway, of course. Dad had ended up leaving Witherstone to look for work, and after many days away had come home empty handed and starving. The second time he had come home with a fever too, and Mum wouldn't let him go again after that.

"What would be the point, Tom? You'll end up dead of fever or starvation, an' then we'll be finished."

She had folded her arms, her mouth a thin line, challenging Dad to contradict her, but he knew she was right. He had ended up doing odd-jobs in the village in return for any scraps he could get, and had to claim Poor Relief from the Parish – which made Dad very bitter - and in return Parson Burnett found Richard the farm labouring job at Shipley Magna. This was the first time any of us had seen him since.

From the day Richard came home, Grandma took me out collecting herbs every morning, then she and Mum showed me how to make a nourishing soup. Catherine insisted on helping too before sitting quietly on the bed to carry on staring at our sleeping brother. The bed I shared with my sister and grandmother had Richard in it now, so Mum and Dad took Catherine back to their bed on the other side of the room. Dad managed to get some extra bed straw and the Parson's cook begged an old blanket from her mistress.

"That was kind of Ellen to ask!" Mum exclaimed.

"Yes, an' that way, *I* didn't have to suffer a sermon on thrift an' clean-living from Mistress Mercy Burnett," laughed Grandma.

Richard slept a lot those first days, despite a few visitors. The most welcome was our grandfather - and Richard's namesake – Grandad Richard Creswell. He had no qualms about waking Richard, who slowly sat up and leaned his head against the wall as Grandad sat beside him.

"What happened to ye' then, lad?" he asked.

Richard rolled his eyes at me, then told us what had happened when he became ill, and how the yeoman's wife had let him stay on in the barn even though he was unable to work, although the master had grumbled about it.

"She gave me some porridge every day, but I was too poorly to eat much," he said. "When Old Isaac called at the farm a few days later, he said he would come on to Witherstone next an' tell you."

"He did," Mum's voice turned bitter, "but James Thompson wouldn't let your dad come an' get you."

Grandad swore under his breath and looked at Dad whose face had tightened, and he refused to meet Grandad's eye. Grandad turned back to Richard.

"Go on, lad," he said.

"Well, after Old Isaac left, the master said I had to get back to work or get out of the barn. He wouldn't let his wife give me any more food until I was workin' again. I managed to get up for the ploughin' the next mornin'–"

He looked at Dad apologetically.

"But I-I was too weak to work the ox or move the plough, an' the master raged at the others for tryin' to help me, sayin' he's not payin' all of us to do the work of one man. He said I had to leave."

Dad stood up abruptly and turned to the fire. He added a log to the flames, staring at the fire as it raged up, his hands trembling. Grandad looked at him but didn't say anything. After Dad had calmed down, he lifted Catherine onto his knee and sat back down. Mum sat white-faced all the while.

"Well, I started for home," Richard went on, "but I couldn't walk far. I had to keep restin'. I was shiverin' with cold, but sweatin' too. When I couldn't walk any further, I laid down under the hedge out of the wind an' tried to get warm. I don't know how long I was there, it felt like days. I thought I was goin' to die. But then Old Isaac found me."

He smiled, leaning his head back against the wall.

"I thought I was dreamin'. Old Isaac was shakin' me awake, then he lit a fire an' made hot soup, an' built a shelter for us in the woods. He looked after me 'til I was well enough to walk. He took me across the moor as far as Dunham, then he went on his way, sayin' I'd be alright to get home from there."

"Thank God for Isaac Bailey!" exclaimed Grandma, and I saw tears running down Mum's face. She left the table and took Richard in her arms.

"God had nowt to do with it!" growled Grandad, as Richard struggled against Mum's embrace. "It was Isaac's own good heart. He's not one for squeezin' every last drop of blood out of a body, to feather his own nest."

"I don't want to listen to any of your blasphemy, Richard Creswell," Grandma said, and got up to see to the flatbread baking on the hearth.

"Well, I don't see what good God has done *you*, Hephzibah Smalley," Grandad replied, "nor your family neither!"

Grandma tightened her lips but carried on scraping ash off the bread.

"Leave it, Dad," my father warned, and I looked from one to the other, hoping a row wouldn't break out. Not with Richard home and everything so good. My brother had managed to get himself out of Mum's arms and was slumped back against the wall, looking tired, and Mum joined Grandma at the table to finish preparing the meal.

"An' as for that bloody yeoman!" Grandad went on, ignoring his son. "Throwin' a sick twelve year old boy out of doors because he's too ill to work! He'd have earned a good profit from the boy's labour for the past two years, in return for a few pennies an' a corner in a rat-infested barn."

"I'm fifteen," said Richard. "*Eppie's* twelve."

"I'm nearly *fourteen!*" I hissed indignantly, and Richard's grin broadened mockingly.

"It would ha' made no difference if you'd been a babe-in-arms!" Grandad went on. "The masters are out for themselves, whether they're grand Squires or yeoman farmers, they all treat us workin' folk no better than dogs."

Mum indicated that I should help at the table, and I got the bowls and spoons ready while Grandad ranted about how the rich and powerful stole the land, the food, the labour, and the lives of the poor, so that we couldn't even feed ourselves without the will of the landowners, who claimed the authority of God, the Bible, and the King, while surely, *surely*, God created us all as equals – in his own image – out of the good clay of the earth, and as such, no-one has a right to set himself above others.

Even while Grandad got up stiffly from the bed, he raged on. Then he turned to my grandmother again.

"You know I'm right, Hephzibah, more than most. Privilege an' the Bible have been used against your own family, an' nearly cost you -"

"That's *enough!*" Grandma cut across him, glancing sharply at myself and Richard, and Dad put his hand on Grandad's arm.

Grandad shook Dad off irritably. "Well, Privilege has made sure it's kept *us* poor, an' that I *do* know."

"I know your Dad used to manage the Hall Farm," my father said, trying to calm Grandad's fiery mood, "but when he died, the old Squire had to get someone in to run the place. You were just a boy at the time -"

"Yes, an' Sylvestre took advantage of that, *an'* my mother's ill-health, to turn us out, with nothin' but the clothes on our backs an' my father's Bible in our hands."

Grandad's mouth was grim as he met his son's eyes.

"Managin' that farm was our livelihood, Tom. We Creswells should be workin' there still, not scattered to the four winds as we are. It weren't the Wars caused *us* to be split up, unlike for a lot of other folk. *We* were always fightin' on the same side – for the rights of the honest labourer to be his own master an' determine his own government an' his own God, without the Masters an' the Preachers usin' *their* version o' the Bible to keep us in our place. You should be answerable to no higher man than yourself, Tom. If you had your birthright an' was managin'

Witherstone

the Hall Farm alongside me, *we'd* be fair to the other men, unlike Sylvestre or that bloody slave-driver Thompson."

Grandad's eyes were blazing as he ranted on.

"If the old Squire thought he was bein' fair, why wouldn't he let me carry on workin' there, eh? I worked beside my dad since I was old enough to walk. But Sylvestre wouldn't let us Creswells live or work on that farm after my dad died, an' it's been the same from that day to this. *As you well know*," he said, jabbing his stubby forefinger at his son.

Dad met his father's eyes but didn't reply. Mum and Grandma were keeping well out of it, preparing the food quietly, but Richard was clearly enjoying Grandad's rant.

"An' it were nowt to do with us fightin' for Parliament, neither," Grandad was almost shouting now, his temper well up. "The old Squire's own son was a Captain in Cromwell's army. No, the Sylvestres set themselves against us Creswells when my father died, an' they do still. That's why *this* poor lad -" jerking his head towards Richard "- has had to work away from home since he was ten years old –"

"Thirteen," interjected Richard, grinning.

"- cos the landowners know they can treat us as they like. They'll be stoppin' us from takin' fish from the river an' rabbits from the fields next. Speakin' o' which," he cried, his voice changing as he picked up his bag from the floor. "I nearly forgot!"

He took a dead rabbit out of his bag and gave it to Mum.

"Thank you, Richard!" she said, laughing, and hung the rabbit from the hook on the door. "Now come an' get your tea before it gets cold."

After we had finished eating, Grandad surveyed our faces around the table.

"It's a shame you didn't name the little 'un 'Martha'," he said, nodding at Catherine, "then we'd *nearly* have the full compliment, along with the two Hephzibahs," pointing at me and Grandma, "an' the two Richards already sittin' here."

He laughed.

"Then we'd only need another one, to be called 'Tom' like his father, to be complete. *An' who*," he turned towards Mum, "might be joinin' us sooner rather than later, unless I'm very much mistaken."

I was confused to see Mum blush. Grandma tutted at him and began to clear the table, and I saw Grandad's smile broaden with satisfaction.

Mum smiled though her cheeks still flamed.

"Well, Richard, we named Catherine after your own sister."

She immediately regretted her comment as Grandad's face darkened.

"That you did, Martha," he said, "that you did. An' I'm grateful to you for keepin' her memory alive."

He looked at Catherine, who was leaning sleepily against Mum now.

"She was just a little 'un when she died, an' it broke my mother's heart, comin' so soon after my father dyin'."

He sat quietly for a few moments, and I held my breath, fearing this would set him off ranting again, but he only sighed.

"Of course, my sister was *herself* named after my Gran'ma Catherine. A woman with strong opinions she was, an' clever too. She taught my dad to read when he was a lad. Young Catherine here has her eyes."

He smiled at my sister before he went on.

"My Gran'ma died even before my father, so I don't remember too much about her - although I *do* remember her workin' just as hard as the rest of us on *our* farm."

There was an awkward pause, but instead of launching into a tirade against Squire Sylvestre and the masters in general all over again, Grandad sat staring into the fire and his past memories.

I felt a chill pass through me as I watched him. I could only imagine how terrible it must have been for him. Grandad's mum had died not long after his father and little sister, leaving him with no family at all before he was even nine years old. He'd survived by labouring for any farm that would take him.

I looked at my family around me, grateful that Richard was home and we were all together again, however hard life could be from day to day.

Grandad stirred from his quiet contemplation.

"Speakin' of my Gran'ma Catherine, there was a tale she used to tell, about old Black Annis..."

The firelight flickered, emphasising the wicked glint in Grandad's eye as he told us the familiar story of the old hag Black Annis, her face covered in blue woad, her wild hair and black eyes and, worst of all, her long sharp fingernails, roaming the wild wood looking for children out collecting firewood. She would catch them and drag them back to her cave, then suck them dry of blood and peel off their skin and eat their flesh, hanging their skins from her skirts and piling their dry bones in her bed.

"Of course, few children are foolish enough to go into the wild wood, with Black Annis there," he said. "So every so often, the old hag gets very, very hungry. An' then," his voice dropped to a hoarse whisper, "*then,* on dark nights ye' can hear them long nails scratch-scratch-scratchin' at the door, then scratch-scratch-scratchin' at the window, an' a scrawny arm with long, sharp fingernails reaches in, further, further, to snatch away the child sleepin' in its bed, or listenin' to their Grandad tellin' them tales by the fire…"

I couldn't resist a quick look at the window and Grandad laughed. Dad was smiling at Catherine's face, barely visible as she peeped from under Mum's arm, her eyes wide. Mum flashed her eyes at me in mock terror while Richard feigned indifference, raising an eyebrow nonchalantly to prove he was above stories told to scare children.

Grandad yawned and stretched.

"Well, I suppose I'd best be off. Thank you Hephzibah an' Martha," he nodded to Grandma and Mum. "It never ceases to amaze me what fine food you Smalley women make from such humble fare."

Grandma harrumphed but I could see she was pleased at the compliment, and I smiled at Grandad's ease for making peace despite his strong opinions.

"Thank *you* too, little Eppie," he said, catching sight of my smile, and he laughed at my scowl at the 'little', making the insult worse by ruffling my hair as he let himself out into the night.

Lying in bed that night, I didn't want to fall asleep thinking about Black Annis in case it set my nightmare off again, but I was haunted nonetheless. My mind kept churning with what Grandad Creswell had said to Grandma, before she had warned him off.

"You know I'm right, Hephzibah, more than most. Privilege an' the Bible have been used against your own family, an' nearly cost you -"

What had he meant? Grandma was a religious woman, so who could have used the Bible *against* her? And what had it "nearly cost" her?

Grandma was my Mum's mother, and her family were a mystery. I knew that Grandma's family name was Smalley, but she never spoke about her own parents. She used to get so angry at my questions that I soon learned to stop asking. Mum told me that she'd never known who her father was, and I knew it was a great scandal to have a child out of wedlock so I was wise enough not to risk Grandma's wrath by asking any more questions on *that* score.

But it was strange that she never mentioned her own parents. Perhaps they had disowned their unmarried pregnant daughter? If so, it was no wonder she didn't want to answer any of my questions. I knew that such things happened, and I shuddered at the thought of my own family turning against me for anything.

Little did I know as I lay there that night that my family would soon be torn apart, and that it would be my fault. My nightmare was about to step over the threshold and into my life. And I had only a few precious days left.

2

An Unexpected Visitor

A few days after Grandad's visit, Richard was well enough to start working at Thompson's with Dad, and I decided to visit my friend Mary Ann. I hadn't seen my best friend for weeks, and I was dying to tell her about Richard coming home.

Once my chores were finished, I asked Mum if I could go out for the rest of the morning. She agreed straight away.

"Of course you can, Eppie," she said, kneading dough at the table. "You deserve a break. I'll take the loaves to the bakehouse if you're not back in time. Where will you go?"

"Oh, I-I hadn't really thought. Probably back down to the river. I think I might have seen bluebells when I was milkin' the goat this mornin'."

Mum paused and shaded her eyes from the sun as she looked at me framed in the cottage doorway.

"It's a bit early for bluebells. You're not goin' to see Mary Ann, are you."

It was a statement, not a question.

"Of course not," I replied indignantly, but I turned away at once, afraid she would see the lie in my face. "See you later!" I called as I fled through the gate.

For as long as I could remember, Mum and Grandma had forbidden us from going to Witherstone Hall, or anywhere else on the Squire's estate for that matter, including the Hall Farm. And I had no idea why. Just because Grandad Creswell had a bee in his bonnet about the Sylvestres, with his family having been evicted from the Hall Farm when he was a boy, I didn't see why Mum and Grandma should join in.

But if I didn't sneak up to Witherstone Hall once in a while I would never see Mary Ann at all. Since she had started working in the Hall kitchens over a year ago, she lived there instead of in the village, and I hardly ever saw her.

I headed across the meadow, checking the small line of boats on the riverbank to see if anyone was around as I hurried towards the coppice wood and the stream which flowed down to meet the river, forming the boundary between the village and the Witherstone Hall estate.

I crossed the stepping stones into Hall Farm Woods, then made my way through the trees round the edge of the farm towards Witherstone Hall Woods. Once I reached the denser woodlands around Witherstone Hall, I could see the tall chimneys of Witherstone Hall and the stone wall surrounding the gardens. I followed the wall round to the back of the house then hoisted myself up a tree far enough to be able to climb on top of the wall, hitching my skirts up to my knees so I could sit astride the stone.

I sat there for a few minutes beneath the shadowy branches, checking the many small leaded-glass windows glinting towards me.

One half of Witherstone Hall was the old Great Hall, said to have been built before the time of Henry Tudor. It had huge oak timbers and a stone chimney and stained-glass windows, bright with sections of coloured glass, reflecting sunlight in flashes of red, yellow, blue and green. The rest of the building had two neat rows of smaller windows glinting over the kitchen garden.

Witherstone Hall was beautiful but I felt a cool chill across the back of my neck as I sat there, feeling exposed despite the shady tree, so once I'd checked the many windows I dropped over the wall and into the garden. Hunched over, I darted between shrubs and crooked apple trees, giving the row of domed bee hives a wide berth as I skirted the neat borders of the kitchen garden, and by the time I reached the massive wooden door to the kitchen I was out-of-breath with nerves more than exertion.

I knocked and asked the kitchen maid who answered whether Mary Ann was able to come. The girl tutted and sighed, but said she would see and closed the door. After a while, the door opened again and Mary Ann's delighted face appeared.

"Eppie!" she whispered, nipping out and pulling the door closed behind her. "I haven't long. Lady Sylvestre is in a vexed mood, an' has some mendin' she wants me to do. I don't work in the kitchens at all any more," she went on proudly, "I'm upstairs now, as her Ladyship is organisin' a huge birthday celebration for young Master William's fifteenth birthday."

"Well, we're havin' our own celebrations," I responded, pausing for effect before adding, "Richard's home."

I was pleased at Mary Ann's surprise, and we stood and chatted for several minutes. I told her about my brother's illness and dramatic journey home, even embellishing the tale to try to eclipse her stories about the lavish birthday preparations going on at the Hall.

"Well, of course, the young Master will become the *Squire* one day, if Sir Henry's brother doesn't come back," Mary Ann said, trying to regain the conversation, "which of course isn't likely as *he's* not been seen or heard of since he went off to fight in the Wars."

She leaned towards me and whispered, "He was fightin' in Cromwell's army - *against the King!* An' against his own father an' brother! Margaret, her Ladyship's *personal* maid, told me all about it. But he got his just desserts," she said with satisfaction. "He'll be rotted bones in a ditch somewhere, or buried in a mass grave on unhallowed ground."

Mary Ann shuddered dramatically, clearly enjoying the scandalous tale and out-doing my news about Richard.

"I know about that," I tried to join in. "My Grandad told me the old Squire's eldest son was a Captain -" but Mary Ann carried on as though I hadn't spoken.

"An' because young Master William will be Squire himself one day, there'll be lots of Lords an' Ladies comin' to his birthday celebrations. Maybe even *the King*."

I raised an eyebrow. She was seriously exaggerating now.

But before I could say anything, the door swung open and a red-faced woman hissed, "Get yourself upstairs quick-sharp, Mary Ann! Her Ladyship has been callin' an' callin' you, an' she's in a high temper now!"

Mary Ann's face drained of colour. She shot back in at once, with a hasty "'Bye Eppie," as the door was closed, leaving me alone on the step.

I sighed. Mary Ann always ended up monopolising the conversation, and I wondered why I bothered. I headed back across the garden, bent over as before, and climbed back up the wall, then sat astride it for a moment to get my breath. I turned to look back at the house and was shocked to see the white of a face at one of the windows, and it was staring right at me. I could see at once that it wasn't Mary Ann.

I leaped off the wall onto the tree, scraping my knee and nearly losing my footing, then scrambled down to the ground and ran back through the woods at full pelt, not slowing until I reached the corner where Witherstone Hall Woods led directly on to the meadow. I was still shaken, and didn't want to walk all the way through the trees past Hall Farm the way I'd come. I just wanted to get home.

The stream was much deeper here than further down at the stepping-stones, but narrower. I leapt across the stream and made my way straight across the meadow as quickly as I could.

As I met the track which leads up from the river towards the lane, my grandmother got to her feet from the shadows of a boat on the riverbank and came towards me.

My stomach lurched and I felt my face reddening. She stopped right in front of me, hands on hips. I hoped she hadn't seen the direction I'd come from across the meadow. I looked back into Grandma's dark eyes as steadily as I could.

"Where have you been, Hephzibah?" she asked.

"Just in the woods, lookin' for bluebells."

Before I knew what was happening, she gave me a stinging slap across the face and I gasped, my cheek burning.

"You've been to Witherstone Hall! Don't you *ever* lie to me," she raged.

I tried not to cry, but the shock of the slap forced the tears and my face crumpled.

"I j-just wanted to tell Mary Ann – that – that Richard-" I sobbed, but couldn't finish.

My grandmother looked at me for a few minutes, until my crying began to subside.

"Perhaps the message will sink in better *now*, Hephzibah Ann Creswell," she said, and turned and walked back along the track towards the lane.

I followed her back to the cottage slowly, still crying, but it was turning to anger now. I hated my Grandma sometimes. When I got back to the cottage, she was preparing food at the table with Mum. Mum looked up to my red cheek and her mouth set into a thin line, but she turned back to the table without a word and I felt worse than ever. Mum knew I'd lied to her.

The next afternoon we were hanging out the laundry. We were tired out. Even Catherine had been helping with the back-breaking work, carrying water from the river, heating it over the fire, then pouring the hot water and lye into the half-barrel we used for the wash. We had carried and boiled and scrubbed and rinsed and wrung the wash since daybreak.

My arms and back were aching as I stretched to hang up the heavy wet linen. Luckily the spring weather was breezy and clear, so we could avoid the unpleasantness of wet laundry hanging all over the tiny cottage for days on end.

After we'd finished, Mum went into the village and Grandma took a complaining Catherine down to the river to cut willow for baskets. We sold most of the baskets we made every year and used the money to buy rye, oats, and dried peas to get us through the winter months. I walked with Grandma and Catherine as far as the meadow, then they carried on towards the coppice wood while I turned towards our goat. She was grazing by the water's edge and I clicked my tongue at her as I approached, but only when I reached her did the creature raise her head and nuzzle at my hand. I dropped some oats into the grass in front of her, then quickly milked her before she could eat them all and move impatiently off.

"Mornin' Eppie."

I turned to see Job Allen making his way down the riverbank behind me. He slid his boat into the water, throwing his oars and net into the bottom and stepping in after them as the boat caught in the eddying waters and swung gently round.

"Tell your mum I'll bring her some fish later," he said, as he began to pull away upriver. "For her help with the baby when Alice was poorly – an' your Grandma's help gettin' Alice well again too, of course!"

I smiled back at the fisherman, and watched as he rowed out of sight round the curve of Hall Farm Woods. *Hmmm... fish for tea!*

Witherstone

I carried the jug back to the cottage and left it in the shade by the door. I fed the hens and collected the eggs and watched the blackbirds taking wisps of straw from around the yard to line their nests. I loved the way they kept a wary eye on me, and told them not to worry, I wasn't after *their* eggs, and smiled into their bead-like eyes as they flicked up their tails almost as though they understood me.

"You know what they say about young wenches who talk to woodland creatures..." said a voice behind me.

I whirled round to see Old Isaac leaning over the gate, his brown face crinkling into a smile. I flung the gate open and threw my arms around the dusty old man. His yellowing cloak and faded brown doublet smelled of mildew and sour sweat but I didn't care. Isaac staggered in surprise at such an affectionate greeting, and his heavy pack clanked to the ground.

"Steady on, Eppie, you'll be breakin' the tonics open all over the cloth!"

I apologised as I helped the old pedlar pick up his bag and carefully inspect the contents. Satisfied there was no harm done, Isaac allowed himself to be led into the cottage, and he took off his cloak and his faded broad-brimmed hat then sat at the table while I added more onions to the stew. Isaac listened as I told him everything that had happened since he was last at Witherstone a few weeks earlier, when he'd come to tell us that Richard was ill.

When Mum came home, she went straight to the old pedlar and laid her hand on his shoulder.

"Isaac," she said, but then couldn't say any more. He patted her hand, and she leaned forward and kissed his forehead, then tried again.

"Thank you for helpin' my son," she said. "Without your help -" her voice quavered to a stop. "If we can ever do anythin' for you, Isaac -"

The old pedlar smiled. "Well, I wouldn't mind a sip of your delicious honey mead to wash the dust of the road from my throat, Martha."

Mum laughed and poured Isaac a mug brimming with mead. He drank it all in long gulps, then put the empty mug down on the table with a satisfied *platt* and wiped his mouth on his sleeve. Mum refilled his mug and we gave him two bowls of stew and several slices of bread.

I suddenly had an idea and whispered in Mum's ear. She nodded, smiling, and I made a thick batter with rye flour, oatmeal, eggs, and some of the creamy milk while Mum hooked a flat griddle iron over the fire. I melted a scoop of butter on the griddle and added dollops of the mixture, which spread slowly into thick pancakes. When the underside was brown, I flipped them over to cook the other side. Isaac had finished his stew and was watching the proceedings with smiling anticipation.

When the cakes were ready, I put them on a platter in front of the pedlar while Mum took a small earthenware jar down from the high shelf. I watched Isaac's smile become even broader as she unwrapped the cloth from the top of the jar and spread thick, buttery honey onto them.

"Food fit for the King!" he exclaimed, eating the cakes enthusiastically and licking the honey off his fingers.

Mum wrapped up the remaining cakes and some bread in a piece of muslin and packed them in the old man's bag. I topped up his mug again while he told us all the news from the road, but after a few snippets of gossip, he said something which made Mum gasp.

"There are rumours that London is sufferin' with outbreaks of the Plague."

I looked at him in shock. I couldn't remember when the Plague had swept across the country when I was a baby, but I'd heard all about it, of course.

"Them that think they need things from London will have to go an' fetch it themselves from now on. I've plenty of trade to keep me busy between Witherstone, Hawbury, an' Shipley Magna for the rest of the year."

He promised to take Mum's thanks to the yeoman's wife at Shipley Magna, along with the willow basket we had made especially for her.

"It's no trouble at all, Martha," he said. "I'm headin' that way anyway. Eppie tells me the young man is back workin' again."

"Yes, Master Thompson has taken Richard on for the sowin', but he may find himself short of work over the summer months 'til the harvest," Mum replied, her lips thin. "He won't be gettin' full pay, either. Thompson said he's not up to much."

"Pah!" Isaac exclaimed, shaking his head. "That boy's got more work in his little finger than that old slave-driver's got in his whole body. But now," he said, getting reluctantly to his feet, "I've got a tonic for Master Cowper, an' two orders of cloth to deliver – some fine muslin for Mistress Burnett, an' a bolt of silk for Master Robinson the tailor. He's makin' a special order for 'er Ladyship at Witherstone Hall. I'll be callin' at the Hall an' the Hall

Farm to see if they're wantin' any knife sharpenin' done too, so I'd better get crackin'," he said.

"Have you any spare muslin, Isaac?" Mum asked. "The coarse weave will do as it's only for cheese cloths. The goat's with kid again so she'll be givin' a fair bit of milk soon."

I watched as the pedlar opened his bag. The myriad of cloth, bottles, string, knives, and bric-a-brac he hawked from place to place were always fascinating. Some were special orders, and some – like the roll of muslin he was taking out of his bag – he always had with him.

Mum selected a length of muslin and Isaac doubled it despite her protestations, then he folded the edge and cut a slit into the corner with his knife, and tore the cloth in a perfect straight line to the bottom of the fold. Meanwhile, I snooped around the things he had put on the table.

I opened a fold of linen and found it was wrapped around the most amazing material I'd ever seen. I realised at once that it must be the silk for Lady Sylvestre's clothes. It shimmered in the light and was the colour of bluebells. Isaac had occasionally had velvet in his bag - rich browns and greens – and the velvet seemed to absorb the light into its vibrant colours. The blue of this silk almost glowed with a light of its own.

After I'd admired it for as long as I dared, nervous that Mum would tell me off, I folded the linen back round the silk, and unrolled the long strip of old leather which held Isaac's selection of knives and spoons. Among his usual collection, I came across a strange object. It was the same size as a knife but had two long metal prongs where the blade should be. The handle had a small shield carved into

Witherstone

it, decorated with what must be a snarling clawed foot raised to strike and bat-like wings arching behind its back.

"What's this?" I asked.

"That," said Isaac, stepping over to me, "is a fork. I came by it a few weeks ago."

He took it out of my hand, frowning.

"A man I met on the road sold it to me, though the Lord knows who I'll sell it on to. He *said* he'd come across it durin' the Wars. There was a fair bit of thievery from some fine houses durin' them dark times, of course, but-"

He stopped, tracing the engraving on the handle with his thumb and still frowning.

"Well, I suppose it's best not to worry too much about what I can't change," he said, "but I'll be glad to pass it on elsewhere just as soon as I can."

He looked at me and smiled, holding the handle out so that I could take it back.

"The well-to-do use a fork, I'm told, to eat their food."

"*What?*" I laughed out loud, turning it over in my hands. "How can you use *that* to eat? The food would just fall through the gap!"

I dipped the fork into the stew and it came out again with just a tiny scrap of onion clinging to one prong, and Isaac and Mum laughed. Then I took a spoon from the table and scooped a heap of stew with a mouthful of the gravy, slurping it noisily from the spoon. Mum shook her head, laughing.

"I expect those that can afford a cut of meat for every meal pick it up with a fork instead of the fingers the Good Lord gave them," she said, and she took the fork and cleaned it on her apron, then put it back on the table with Isaac's other things.

The pedlar packed everything back in his bag, tying the willow basket on top, then he put the money my mother had given him for the muslin into his purse. He threw his mildewed cloak around his shoulders and hoisted his bag over his back as he went out into the yard.

We watched his familiar gait make its way down towards the centre of the village. As he reached Weavers Cottages, he turned and gave us a cheery wave before he knocked at the first door.

I helped Mum prepare the evening meal, telling her about Job's offer of fish.

"How kind of Job!" she said, and we prepared everything with a mind to what would go well with fish for our tea.

Grandma and Catherine came home a short while later, loaded down with willow sticks. Grandma was complaining under the huge bundle that she carried on her back, and Catherine imitated her complaints with her own more modest pile swung over her shoulder. I helped my grandmother swing the heavy wands down to the ground, then, her hands free, she cuffed Catherine lightly for her cheek, and my little sister ran laughing to Mum to show her how many sticks she had managed to carry all by herself. She came over to show me too.

"An' we saw Old Isaac!" she said excitedly. "He'd been sleepin' in the woods by the river. He gave me a ribbon!"

Catherine showed me a thin band of bright red ribbon tied around her wrist.

"It's beautiful, Catherine."

Witherstone

"He said it'll bring me good luck!" She ran back to show Mum the ribbon too.

Grandma helped me to finish the meal preparations while Mum started the cheese-making. Catherine was flat out on the bed, sleeping soundly, by the time Job Allen called by with two fat carp for our tea.

The next day I was helping Mum fold the dry laundry, ready to take back to the village, and Grandma was mending a tear in the collar of Edward Cowper's shirt, her cracked fingers sewing almost invisible tiny stitches in the lace. We were outside in the warm sunshine where there was room to fold the washing without ash from the fire dirtying the clean linen, and Grandma had better light to see by than inside the dingy cottage. Catherine was chasing the hens round the yard and through the hedge into the lane while Mum and I folded the linen between us, Mum humming quietly as we worked. Then Catherine shot back through the hedge and ran into the cottage as we heard footsteps approaching.

My jaw dropped open in surprise when I saw the Parson's wife, Mercy Burnett, coming to our gate. Mum took it all in her stride, smiling politely and wiping her hands on her apron as Mistress Burnett stepped into the yard, holding her skirts to prevent the dust and the mess from the hens dirtying the hem.

I glimpsed a pair of dainty shoes with pointed toes beneath Mercy Burnett's overskirt of purple wool, and once she let go of it, I could see her skirts reached right to the ground, unlike mine and Mum's and Grandma's skirts which reached only to our ankles to keep them out of the way while we work. Mistress Burnett wasn't wearing an apron over her own skirts, and the purple overskirt had a deliberate long slash which allowed her sumptuous red underskirt to be seen. Her doublet was also purple wool, with wide slashes in the full sleeves which showed off the red lining inside to spectacular effect as she swung round to latch the gate.

Mum fetched a stool from inside which she dusted down with her apron before placing it for our guest. Mercy Burnett seated herself and looked directly at me, and I blushed and looked away as I realised I was still staring. She turned towards my grandmother.

"Good morning, Mistress Smalley. I trust you are well?"

"Yes, thank you, Mistress Burnett," replied Grandma, not pausing from her sewing but continuing on with flying fingers.

The Parson's wife turned back to Mum and asked whether the blanket she had sent for Richard had been satisfactory. Mum thanked her for her kindness, and was rewarded with a gracious incline of the head and Mercy Burnett's opinion that as soon as Richard was well enough, he would *of course* be returning to Shipley Magna and the farming position that she and her husband had found for him when the Creswell family had been in dire need.

After a brief pause, Mum replied that Richard would not be returning to his previous employment as she felt he still needed his mother's care.

At this, she received Mercy Burnett's judgement that the sooner the boy left home for good the better, as the cramped conditions at the cottage with six people sharing a single room and living on such meagre wages – with what looks suspiciously like another mouth to feed on the way - was clearly inviting disease into the home. Cleanliness was next to Godliness after all. And we didn't want to be relying on Parish relief again, did we?

I was affronted at Mistress Burnett's tone – she was speaking to my mother as though to a child! - and I looked at Mum for the response I was sure was coming.

I was amazed to see Mum biting back whatever retort was on her lips as her hands flew to her skirt front. My eyes widened suddenly as the full meaning of Mercy Burnett's words sank in. Another mouth to feed? A *baby?* Why hadn't I noticed? Now I was aware, I could see how Mum's skirt was swelling out at the front. That's why Dad wouldn't let Mum walk all that way to Richard. And *that's* what Grandad Creswell had meant when he joked about someone joining the family table 'sooner rather than later' - someone who ought to be called Tom after its father.

I felt angrier than ever at Mistress Burnett as I knew Mum would have wanted to tell me about the baby herself. I turned and glared at the arrogant woman, holding Court in our own yard as though we were her servants and she was Royalty.

Mercy Burnett stood up and smoothed her skirts.

"We need someone at the Parsonage as the kitchen maid has gone home to Hawbury, and Ellen can't manage the kitchen on her own. She suggested that the girl –" nodding towards me "- is a clean and capable body, so I'm willing to try her out and see."

She opened the gate and then turned back towards my mother.

"She can come tomorrow morning, before dawn."

After the briefest of pauses, Mum nodded.

"I'll see about her wages and whether she stays on when I've seen how the girl shapes up. Good day."

And with that parting shot, Mercy Burnett swept back down the lane towards the village. There was a silence in the yard when she had gone. Grandma had stopped sewing and was staring after her. *Even the birds have stopped singing*, I thought.

The silence was broken by Grandma, who exclaimed "Mercy me!"

Mum's face didn't move for a moment but then her blue-grey eyes met mine, and her mouth twitched as she lifted my chin up and spoke in a haughty voice:

"Cleanliness is next to Godliness after all!"

Then all three of us were laughing and laughing.

Mum leaned on my shoulder, holding her stomach as she shook, while I leaned against her, giggling helplessly. Grandma's raucous laughter filled the air, and she put her sewing aside, wiping the tears from her eyes. She stood up from the bench and put her arms round us, and we stood holding on to one another as our laughter rang through the yard.

3

The Little Maid

Early the next morning, I stood nervously at the back door of the Parson's house. I didn't want to be here at all but the money I could earn for my family left me with no choice. A moment later, the door swung open and the Burnett's cook ushered me into the delicious smell of freshly-baked bread.

"Take a clean apron, Eppie dear," Ellen said, gesturing to the basket of clean linen that Grandma and I had returned only yesterday.

I did as I was told and joined Ellen at the large wooden table in the centre of the room, trying not to stare me at the huge kitchen which was bigger than the cottage where my entire family cooked and ate and slept in the one room.

Mary Ann had told me a long time ago that the Parson's family, like the Squire's family at Witherstone Hall, slept upstairs in rooms with wooden beds rather than on straw in the kitchen, and that they had a different room for dining and yet another room – a Parlour – just for sitting in or entertaining guests. I couldn't imagine what they did to occupy themselves if they didn't spend their time in the kitchen. And the Burnett's kitchen itself was almost overwhelming. It had a large fireplace with an iron spit and a small pig already roasting slowly over the fire, plus the brick-built chimney had a bread oven. We took our own loaves to the village bakehouse, although we often cooked flat, unleavened bread on the warm hearth at home.

Ellen was rolling out the most *golden* pastry I had ever seen. She lifted the thick pastry sheet into a large earthenware dish, and got me rolling out more of the pastry while she ladled delicious-smelling chunks of mutton and onions and carrots into the dish, along with their thick cooking juices. She nodded with satisfaction at my pastry-rolling and laid the finished sheet over the top of the pie, then opened the oven, scraped the hot embers to one side and put the pie in.

"Now," she said, turning back to the table, "I want you to make a batch of cinnamon and raisin griddle cakes, Eppie, and make sure you keep an eye on the pig while you're at it."

I made a pile of soft, fluffy griddle cakes full of brown sugar and bursting with juicy raisins and cinnamon within half an hour, and the delicious smell of them was nearly driving me mad. I turned the spit regularly as I worked, to make sure the meat didn't burn.

Ellen bustled over to see how I was getting on and looked very pleased with the griddle cakes, taking one and eating it in a few bites, nodding and sucking air into her mouth to cool her tongue. She asked me to check the roasting pig again, and I guessed she wasn't going to offer me a griddle cake.

While a dozen eggs were boiling over the fire, Ellen showed me how to make a sauce for them, then we peeled and sliced the eggs and poured the hot sauce over them. Ellen sliced the loaves, leaving the blackened lower crusts, and took the pie out of the oven while I put the griddle cakes onto a decorated platter and heaped butter, jam and honey into several dishes.

We carried the huge pie, eggs, bread, griddle cakes, and the other dishes down the passage from the kitchen to a room with a long, dark oak table in the centre. It took us several trips back and forth, and as we were putting the last dishes of food onto the table, the door opened and Mistress Burnett swept into the room. Ellen immediately folded her hands in front of her apron and lowered her eyes to the floor, so I quickly did the same.

Mistress Burnett approached the table to inspect the food, then her skirts stopped in front of Ellen.

"This looks acceptable, Ellen. And how did the girl manage?"

I raised my head as Ellen replied, "Wonderful well, Mistress. I've never had a better girl in my kitchen. The griddle cakes are all her own work, an' lighter cakes I've rarely seen."

"Well, I've yet to taste them."

Mercy Burnett's face was expressionless as she turned and looked at me.

"You will stay for the rest of today, girl. I'll decide about tomorrow when we see how you have shaped up by this evening."

I felt my face flushing with annoyance. I've got a *name*, I thought. I managed to stop myself from glaring at her and lowered my eyes, my cheeks burning.

"Thank you – Mistress," I managed as politely as I could.

As I followed Ellen back down the passage towards the kitchen, we passed Mercy Burnett's son and daughter coming down the stairs. Lucy Burnett walked past me without even acknowledging my presence, even though we'd often played together on the village green when we were younger. Her older brother Adam met my eyes and smiled before following Lucy into the dining room, but my pleasure at Adam's friendliness quickly disappeared.

A dark figure was gliding towards me, its face in shadow, and the skin of my arms prickled. Parson Burnett's sermons seemed to ooze from his silent cloak as he loomed towards me, his approaching shadow endorsing the Demons and Devils dragging all Sinners, Puritans and Parliamentarians down to Hell with them. The air darkened as he swept past me and into the room behind me, and the door closed quietly behind him. I hurtled down the passageway as though the Devil himself was behind me, back to the warm brightness of the kitchen.

Once we finished clearing up after the breakfast preparations, Ellen got us making another batch of recipes, and I realised with a shock that all the food we had cooked that morning had just been *breakfast* for those four people. It was nearly as much food as my whole family ate in a week.

For the rest of the day we cooked and washed pots and then cooked some more. After we'd carried the Burnett's evening meal down the now almost pitch black passage to the family's table, Ellen stayed in the dining room to carve the meat, sending me back to the kitchen to begin the washing up. When she came back to the kitchen a while later, she was tending carefully to one of her fingers.

"Tear me a strip of that muslin, will you Eppie," she said, "and come and help me bind my finger."

Ellen had a deep puncture wound in the side of her finger, but it wasn't bleeding. I helped her to bind the muslin round it, then finished washing the pots while she put out a few pieces of bread and two bowls of the remaining stew from the Burnett's midday meal for us to eat. While we ate at the kitchen table, Ellen laughingly told me how she was using a fork to hold the meat while she carved it at the Burnett's table, but it had slipped and impaled her finger.

"I didn't dare let on to the Parson or the Mistress, especially as the wound didn't bleed. I didn't want to be accused of bein' a witch."

"Why would that happen?" I asked, amazed.

"Surely you know about the Witch's Mark, child? They say that a witch has a mark on her body showin' she belongs to the Devil, an' you only know it because when you prick it, it doesn't bleed."

I looked uncertainly at Ellen, then down at her injured finger. She guffawed when she saw the expression on my face.

"Don't look so worried, Eppie. I'm no more a witch than you are! But when I was a young girl, mind you, there was a witch hanged right here in Witherstone - from the lime tree opposite the church." She gestured out of the window, and nodded at my shocked expression before she continued.

"I remember my mother sayin' that Hannah Pendal had fooled everyone into thinkin' she was a good woman who just knew the old ways, helpin' poor folk who needed a cure for ailments, an' helpin' women bring their babies safely to birth. Yet she murdered the old Squire with witchcraft."

I gasped. *"Murdered the Squire?"*

She nodded.

"Sir Henry's father. I daresay Hannah Pendal suddenly found she had few friends after that. An' those that doubted she was a witch soon changed their tune when her daughter, who was accused along with her, disappeared from the lock-house at Hawbury right from under the gaoler's nose. One minute she was there, locked up with her mother awaitin' trial, an' the next she was gone! The gaoler swore she never got past him, an' the room was still locked an' had no windows. My mother said the Devil had claimed her for his own," said Ellen, crossing herself.

I shuddered, and Ellen leaned forward and whispered.

"Just before the witch was hung, they say she cursed those she claimed were out to do her a mischief. My mother kept me at home for the hangin', but they left the witch up in that tree for several days anyway, with a guard to make sure she didn't get down an' walk off. It was a fearful sight swingin' up there, an' I was terrified she could see me every time I passed, an' would put a curse on me too. After a while, they took the body down an' burnt it, which was a relief I can tell you."

I stared at Ellen, horrified.

I was surprised when her expression suddenly changed, and she flushed and looked away from me, perhaps feeling guilty at the horror on my face.

"Anyway," she said sharply, making me jump. "We've work to do Eppie, an' can't be sittin' around on our backsides all day like we're Gentry."

After I washed the last of the dishes and helped Ellen knead the dough to be left to rise in the hot kitchen for the next morning's loaves, my work was finally finished for the day. I didn't get home until well after dark and I was exhausted.

While Ellen had made sure that I'd eaten a meal at the Parson's house, she also sent me home with two of the remaining griddle cakes and a piece of meat that the Burnett family had left. She pressed her finger to her lips conspiratorially as she handed me the bundle of food, to ensure I kept it quiet from Mistress Burnett.

That night I had my nightmare again. This time, when I found myself alone in the forest and my pursuer stepped out from the trees, the shadowy figure was holding a thick rope coiled in long white hands and I woke up gasping for breath, feeling as though I was suffocating. Grandma hushed me, and I lay there until dawn, staring at the shadowed roof above me, afraid to go back to sleep.

A few hours later I was back in the Parson's kitchen, feeling tired before I'd even started work. After the Burnett family had eaten breakfast, Ellen was happy to let me clear the dining table on my own while she got on with preparing the next meal.

When I was leaving the room with the final few dishes, I had a closer look at the paintings on the walls but found the faces staring out of the frames unnerving. Their eyes seemed to follow me round the room.

The portraits of Adam and Lucy Burnett must have been painted several years earlier. Lucy looked no older than Catherine was now, although her cheeks were rounder and her hair fell in luxurious ringlets on either side of her face. Adam's face looked cold and remote above the full lace collar, his eyes distant. While the painting of Mistress Burnett seemed to look at me more kindly than its original usually did, the portrait of Parson Burnett looked even more sinister than the man himself.

His face loomed a pale oval out of the deeply shadowed background, his eyes seeming to pierce into my inner thoughts just as they did when he gave his sermons, and the hairs prickled on the back of my neck.

I moved away from the paintings quickly, walking over to the oak Court cupboard on top of which was a book. Glancing nervously at the closed door, I placed the dishes on top of the cupboard and picked up the book.

It was bound in fine brown leather and had gilt lettering on the ridged spine. I opened it carefully. The inside cover was beautifully decorated, and I turned the first page of the thick, creamy paper to find an engraving covering the whole page, showing a woman in fine clothing in different rooms. In one she was sitting on a high-backed chair embroidering in a round frame. In another she was instructing a small child, and in yet another was sitting amongst other people at a table heaped with fine food. Above and below the engraving were fine, curling letters.

I turned the page, enjoying the crisp feel of the paper in my fingers and breathing in its paper-and-ink smell, and found the whole of the next page filled with row upon row of small letters and nothing else. The first letter was elaborately curled and set into a decorated square, but there were no pictures to give me a clue what any of it meant.

"Are you interested in becoming a fine Mistress then, Eppie?" asked a voice at my shoulder, and I spun round in shock, the book almost flying out of my fingers.

Adam Burnett was smiling at me, and at the book in my hands.

"Oh, Adam – I mean Master Burnett! You startled me," I laughed, shakily.

I looked down at the book, my cheeks flushing.

"Becomin' a fine Mistress? No, of course not. I–I was just wishin' I could read," I finished lamely.

"Ah," said Adam.

My cheeks blushed deeper and I couldn't meet his eyes.

"Sorry Eppie, I meant no insult," he said after an awkward pause. "I daresay you've no time to be lounging around reading books and pamphlets."

I shook my head but said nothing.

Adam hesitated, then he said, "Look, here it says, '*A Daily Exercise for Ladies and Gentlewomen*'," and he pointed carefully at each word as he spoke it. "This '*A*' here is the first letter of the alphabet – you know what the alphabet is?"

"Yes, that's the name for the Letters."

I looked intently at the page once more, picking out and tracing the lines and flourishes of the large 'A' with my eyes.

"Look," he said, his voice awkward, "when you've finished your chores for the morning, Eppie, why don't I show you some more letters?"

I looked at him with sudden eagerness, but this quickly became confusion.

"Once I've finished washin' the breakfast pots we have the midday meal to prepare, then we have to clear up an' cook the tea, then there's the supper to do, an' the bread dough for tomorrow. I–I don't finish 'til quite late."

"Oh," he said, flushing with embarrassment himself now. "Well, I'd better not keep you, then. We don't want Mother to see you slacking," he smiled, as he took the book and held the door open for me.

I picked up the dishes and took them through to the kitchen, my cheeks still burning. I hated looking so stupid in front of him.

As I helped Ellen wash the breakfast dishes and prepare the midday meal, I wished there was a way of taking Adam up on his offer to teach me the letters. I really wanted to learn to read but knew that finding the time while I was working in the Parson's kitchen was impossible. Even Sundays would be difficult as Adam was always busy then, as his father had him reading the Scriptures when not actually in church for the services. I suddenly remembered Parson Burnett beating Adam right in front of me, one Sunday evening last summer, when he had found his son playing with his friends on the meadow instead of studying at home. It had made me sick to the stomach.

I sighed. There was no way I would be able to learn to read. I tried to bring my mind back to my tasks. I didn't want to get into trouble with Ellen or Mistress Burnett.

Mum was concerned about the length of time I had to work in the Parson's kitchen every day, but as Mercy Burnett had decided I could carry on helping Ellen, the meagre wage she would pay me would be a help to my family.

Mistress Burnett had wanted me on Sundays as well but Mum put her foot down at that, and Ellen said she could manage perfectly well on her own for just the one day. In truth, on my first Saturday in the Burnett's kitchen I helped Ellen prepare as much as we could of the Sunday meals in advance, alongside our usual cooking, and I was grateful to Ellen for making sure I could spend Sunday with my family without having to contend with the disapproval of Mercy Burnett.

As I left the Parson's kitchen late on that first Saturday evening, I was surprised to be met in the lane by Adam. He passed me a folded sheet of paper then slipped quietly back into the house. I hid the sheet under my cloak and hurried home.

When I got to the cottage, I unfolded the thick, creamy paper by the fire and stared at the beautifully-drawn letters Adam had written down for me. I traced the delicate strokes of the first letter.

"*A*," I whispered.

That Sunday I felt so happy to be at home. I knew Mum could feel it too. As we all walked back from the church, I saw her looking at us all with a contented look on her face. Until she caught me looking at her and deliberately crossed her eyes and stuck out her tongue.

While Mum and Grandma cooked our Sunday meal ("*No cookin' for you today, young lady!*" Mum said), I sat in the warm sunshine in the yard studying the sheet of letters. Richard tried to snatch the paper out of my hand, to tease me, but Mum sent him off. A little while later, she came outside and sat down to look at them with me, and I showed her the slanting lines of the 'A'. Mum pointed to another letter.

"This one's 'M' for Martha," she said, "Edward Cowper showed me that one a few years back. An' he showed me a few others," she said, sliding her finger across the page. "This is 'T' for Tom. This is 'R' for Richard, an' here, 'C' for Catherine – an' Creswell! An' this one," she said, tweaking my chin, "is 'H' for Hephzibah."

I looked at the new letters, thrilled.

"Which one's 'E' for Eppie?" I asked.

"I don't know," she laughed, shaking her head.

Then we thought of as many words as we could that began with the letters we knew. The whole family joined in as we sat down to our meal.

"Apples."

"Carrots."

"Turnip."

"Rabbit."

"Goat!" shouted Catherine, who didn't quite get it.

"Meadowsweet."

"Hemlock."

"Agony."

"Marriage!"

"Rye."

"All is grist that comes to the Mill," said Richard, who always liked to outdo everyone else.

"Speakin' of which, we need to take some more rye an' barley to the mill to be ground for flour," laughed Mum.

"- an' Appetite comes with eatin'," said Grandma, "so tuck in."

My family were shocked when I told them how much food the Parson's family ate every day, having several full cooked meals including supper, with at least one cut of meat and a pile of other food at every meal.

We rarely got meat to eat more than once a week, and usually had to make it last a few days. Most of the time we only had a cooked meal in the evening, except in the winter months when Mum would try to keep a pot of porridge simmering for a warming breakfast if we had enough oats. Most days, most seasons, we had a perpetual pot at the fire which had new foodstuffs added to it for every evening meal, making a pottage which was pretty much the same taste from one day to the next.

Sometimes we would cook in the daytime, such as when Richard was ill or when Old Isaac came by, but otherwise we had bread with boiled onions or cheese, or sometimes a pie, during the day. Precious extras, such as the rabbit from Grandad Creswell and the fish Job Allen had brought for us, lingered in the memory long after the last scraps had been eaten.

Now Richard was home I hoped we would have fish more often as my brother had gone fishing regularly before he'd been sent to Shipley Magna. Dad tried to trap rabbits when he could, but as he worked from dawn until dusk every day except Sunday, and work was forbidden on Sundays – even fishing or checking rabbit traps – it was often difficult to get hold of those extras in practice.

Witherstone

My father became tight-lipped when I was telling them about the excesses of food at the Parson's house, and he soon asked me to stop talking about it. He said that on no account should I tell Grandad Creswell. The old man was belligerent enough about our own situation compared with wealthy folk.

"Let alone with *Parsons*," Dad muttered.

Perhaps it was just as well Grandad hadn't come that Sunday as he would have had another one of his rants without a doubt. It was too far for him to come and visit us every week, but I knew I'd still rather listen to Grandad ranting than not see him at all, and I missed his stories.

It was left to Mum and Grandma to tell us tales that night, and Mum told us about the water-witch Jenny Greenteeth, hiding in the weeds in deep water, her slimy hands waiting to grab the ankles of unsuspecting children if they strayed too close to the water's edge, and pulling them down into a watery grave.

"An' sometimes, she'll creep under your boat... *an' tip it over so she can get you!*" she said, grabbing Catherine's ankles and making my sister shriek.

Dad said that Richard's rowing would be to blame for the boat going over, and even Richard laughed. Dad sang a ballad about star-crossed lovers after that, and he held Mum's hand when we all joined in the last verse. I slept deeply and dreamlessly that night.

The next day was Monday, so it was back to work for all of us. I'd settled into the routine of being at the Burnett's house from dawn until after sunset every day, so my usual jobs fell to my family to do instead.

Witherstone

Grandma was taking Catherine down to milk the goat and showing her how to tend to the hens, but the new week also brought in another load of laundry. Mum and Grandma were still busy with it when I got home that evening, putting the linen to soak in lye overnight, and I was worried about how they would manage it all.

We did a regular batch for the Parson's household and for Edward Cowper during the summer months, plus the occasional basket for other villagers too, so I knew it would be a much harder task for Mum and Grandma without my help. And when Mum gets closer to having the baby, which she thinks will be early summer, it will be hard on her to be doing so much.

Richard and my father were out labouring so they couldn't help, and Catherine was too small to do anything more than the lighter jobs.

Mum tugged my chin and told me to stop worrying.

"Me an' my mum have been doin' the wash together since before you were born," she said, "so we'll hear no more frettin' from *you*."

The very next day, however, something happened which gave us all much more to worry about.

When I arrived at the Parson's house the next morning, I found Ellen in tears.

"What is it, Ellen?"

"It's my uncle," she said. "He - he's ill. We – we think it might be the Plague," she finished in a rush, and my jaw dropped in horror.

The Plague? *In Witherstone?* Ellen's uncle was Edward Robinson, the village tailor, and he was also Mary Ann's grandfather. I did as much of the breakfast preparations as I could as Ellen was finding it hard to keep her mind on her work.

After we'd served breakfast, Mistress Burnett in a heightened temper and overly critical as she inspected the food, Ellen took herself off into the garden for a breath of fresh air while I washed up the pots.

After I'd finished, I could hear the Parson and Mistress Burnett talking as they walked up the passageway to the parlour, so I went to clear away their breakfast things. It took me several trips on my own, and as I was carrying the last of the dishes into the passage, Adam was suddenly right in front of me without warning, and two of the dishes tumbled out of my hands and crashed to the ground. Adam and I stared in horror at the shattered pottery as Mercy Burnett came hurtling down the passage towards us.

Adam tried to say it was his fault, but she sent him away and turned to me. When she'd finished shrieking at me for my clumsy and slovenly behaviour, her normally disdainful expression contorted with rage, she said the cost of replacing the dishes would be taken out of my wages. Then she turned on her heel and marched back down the passage.

The Parson's dark figure was standing at the far end of the passage, his face inscrutable in the shadows. He stepped into the parlour behind his wife and quietly closed the door.

As I struggled to pick up the shards of pottery from the floor, I was shaking and in tears. Adam appeared again and bent down to help me, my swimming eyes blurring his face and I wiped my eyes on my sleeve.

"I'm so sorry, Eppie" he said. "Mother's upset - worried. In case this business with Robinson *is* the Plague.

She doesn't often fly into a rage. She does cold condescension much better, as I'm sure you know," he grinned suddenly.

I was still too upset to smile back, and his grin disappeared as quickly as it had come.

"It's best to just leave her to it when her Humours get the better of her," he said, and moved away so that I could take the shattered pottery down to the kitchen.

At home that night I told my family about Edward Robinson, and Dad said that one of the other labourers at Thompson's hadn't turned up for work that day. We speculated about whether the Plague had really come to Witherstone. Catherine seemed to be unsettled by the gloomy mood that evening, clinging to Mum and sucking her thumb, which she rarely did now she was four.

Later, I told Mum about the broken dishes as quietly as I could, but Dad heard me. He said that if Mistress Burnett was going to take the money for the dishes from my wages, then I wasn't to go back to the Parson's house any more.

"You stay an' help your mother tomorrow, Eppie," he said, "an' if Mercy Burnett wants you she knows where to find you, then your mother can put her straight on *that* matter. The woman pays you a pittance as it is, an' you're worth more to us here, helpin' your mother, than slavin' over *her* Royal banquets."

I had trouble sleeping that night, nonetheless, worrying about going back to the Parson's house, and worrying about not going. By the time the sky had begun to get light in the morning, I'd barely slept and felt exhausted. Dad and Richard got up quietly to go to Thompson's, and before he left, Dad leaned over me and told me to go back to sleep as I was to stay at home. After that I fell asleep at last.

I woke with a start to find the sun shining through the open door and the sound of chopping at the table. I heard a small sound coming from my parents' bed, and turned to see Mum leaning over Catherine. My sister's face looked flushed and clammy as she stared up at Mum with sombre eyes.

"Oh, Catherine!" I exclaimed, and shot up from my blanket and over to my sister. Catherine stared up at me, but she looked languid and ill. I smoothed her damp hair.

"You're best to keep away from your sister for the time bein', Hephzibah," Grandma said from the table, "but you can do her some good if you help me here."

I stared at my sister for a moment, then hurried over to the table.

"Crush the wild garlic an' mix it with a good handful of each of these herbs, but chop them fine first," she said briskly, indicating the earthenware jars set out on the table.

I set to work, and after a few minutes Mum came to help. When we'd finished, Grandma put everything into the pot and we left it to simmer, and once the broth was ready, Mum sat my sister up and tried to get her to sip the steaming liquid from a spoon. Catherine wouldn't take very much, so after a while Mum laid her down on the bed again and bathed her face with the herbal brew.

Grandma swept the loose straw from the floor out into the privy at the back of the yard, then scattered several handfuls of herbs onto the floor of the cottage and over both of the beds. We all avoided saying what we feared.

Before mid-morning, Ellen came puffing up the lane to see why I hadn't come to work. I'd forgotten all about the Parson's house. When I told Ellen about Catherine, she took a step back from the doorway.

"My uncle is proper bad, now. His neck is all swollen, an' his skin's turnin' black. My aunt is ill too – an' their daughter's child."

"Not Mary Ann?" I exclaimed.

Ellen nodded.

"You were always together when you were younger, you two," she said, "'til Mary Ann went off to work at the Hall. Lady Sylvestre has sent her home – an' she sent two of her cooks away too, they say. I think they both come from over Hawbury way so I don't know how they'll get home if they're as bad as poor Mary Ann. I only saw her from the doorway, but - oh," she said suddenly, as though remembering something.

"Mary Ann was anxious that I should give you a message. She said to tell you that '*She knows it was you*', *an' she's really angry*', an' that ye' must be careful. It seemed to be worryin' her a lot. I don't know what she means, do you?"

I shook my head, wondering about Mary Ann's message. Did she mean that my grandmother knew I'd been to see her at Witherstone Hall? Well, I knew *that* already. It was a strange message, but I had enough to think about at the moment.

Ellen looked back through the doorway at Catherine. Mum was trying to encourage her to take little sips of broth again.

Ellen stepped back towards the gate.

Witherstone

"I'm sorry to see Catherine so poorly, Eppie. I'll tell Mistress that you'll be stayin' away for now, shall I?"

I nodded. "Yes."

"Hope she gets well again – soon," she added, flushing. "She's a good little maid."

She closed the gate. "Oh, an' Mistress said not to worry about the bowls. Let me know if you need anythin', Eppie," she called back as she hurried away.

Catherine had a raging fever by late morning, and Mum had a difficult job persuading her to sup any broth or water at all. My sister seemed unable to recognise any of us or understand what we said to her.

Then Dad and Richard came home, even though it was barely midday. Dad looked furious.

"Both of Thompson's boys have it, an' when I told him about Catherine, in sympathy with the man, he blamed *us* for givin' it to his sons an' sent us away!" he said angrily. "His lads had been workin' alongside the man who didn't turn up yesterday, so if anyone on that farm passed it on to his boys, it wasn't us."

I watched Dad pacing around the small room and out in the yard, while Mum bathed Catherine's hot face and neck to try to bring down the fever. At last, unable to stay cooped up in the cottage feeling like he was doing nothing useful, Dad took his axe and set off down to the coppice woods by the river to gather wood for the fire.

After a few minutes, Richard and I followed him, taking the smaller axe with us. As we walked, my brother said he might borrow Edward Cowper's boat in the morning and see if he could catch us a nice fat fish for our tea.

I listened to him describing the best place to try for a fish, and the best way to cast the often I got the chance to be alone with him, even though he'd been back from Shipley Magna for a while now. He'd spent several days with Mum fussing over him, and since he'd got well again, he'd been working at Thompson's with Dad nearly every day.

I felt shy suddenly, as I looked up at my brother. His blue-grey eyes twinkled through his dark blonde hair as he caught me looking at him. He looked so much like Mum, although her hair was always tied into a neat bun beneath her linen cap while Richard's was unruly, curling down past his collar. Since he had come home, he'd started wearing it in a pony tail like Dad did, although his hair often escaped from the tie and flopped in front of his eyes as it was now.

My hair and eyes were much darker, darker even than Dad's, whose eyes were hazel-brown like Catherine's - except hers seemed to change colour with her mood, shifting from greenish-brown to smoke when she was angry. Mine were as dark as Grandma's.

Richard pulled my plait as he stopped talking about his fishing plans and looked at me with sudden amusement. I laughed and looked away.

"You seem older, Eppie," he said. "You'll be fourteen soon, won't you?"

I nodded. "On the first day of May."

"But are you too old to run?" he shouted, and set off at a sprint across the meadow towards the woods.

Laughing, I leapt forward and ran as fast as I could after him, determined to catch him up or even beat him to Dad, striding into the trees ahead of us. Richard won, of course, which I wouldn't have minded so much if he hadn't then spent the rest of the afternoon teasing me that I was getting as old as Grandma. He didn't seem to get bored of acting the gross caricature of a crooked back and gnarled fingers beside me as I carried the branches I collected. I knew he wouldn't dare do that in front of Grandma.

As we were thinking of returning to the cottage, we saw a large fallen branch just on the other side of the stream in Hall Farm Woods. The other side of the stream was the Sylvestre estate, of course, and the villagers were not allowed to collect wood there. Dad thought that he and Richard could drag it back between them, if they could just get it across to our side of the stream quickly. He asked if I could manage the branches we were already carrying by myself.

"Of course I can," I said, ignoring Richard's mocking grin.

I balanced my own branches on my shoulder, then Dad and Richard laid theirs on top. My shoulder felt crushed by the weight. I was aware of my brother watching me and kept my expression clear of effort. Then, while I kept a look-out, Dad and Richard crossed the stream to get the large branch and bring it back over to the meadow before anyone came.

I was really nervous while they struggled over the stepping stones. They seemed to take an age. They finally managed to get the branch across and dropped it to the ground with an enormous thump. I left them splitting it with their axes and set off home with the heavy pile of sticks balanced on my shoulder, my arms curving over them from either side to try to steady them.

By the time I made it across the meadow and back to the cottage, I was grimly desperate to put the wood down. But I'd made it this far, and I refused to give Richard the satisfaction of seeing the branches anywhere other than stacked neatly on the woodpile behind the cottage. I made it to the woodpile and lowered the branches with trembling arms, managing to roll them off my shoulder and onto the pile with barely a stick dislodged.

I straightened up, satisfied, knowing Richard could have nothing to say to *that*. Rubbing my arms and shoulder to soothe my trembling muscles, I walked across the yard to the open doorway, anxious now to see how Catherine was. As I reached the threshold, I could see Mum and Grandma sitting on the bed by my sister, just as they had been a couple of hours earlier. I also realised they were arguing, and stopped in surprise. They rarely disagreed about anything.

"I don't think we have any choice, Martha," Grandma was saying. "I don't know enough. She's the *only* person who might know what to do – how we can save Catherine. The child hasn't got the swellin' yet, so there might still be time."

"But it's too dangerous," Mum hissed back, "*especially* with what happened before. She'll be an old woman by now, even if she is still alive, an' she might not be able to do anythin' to help. An' it's far too dangerous for Eppie – for all of us! I'm not goin' to risk losin' two daughters -"

She stopped suddenly and spun round as my grandmother hushed her, looking at where I stood in the doorway.

Mum looked at me intently, trying to determine how much I'd heard.

I knew I had a big decision to make. Should I pretend I'd heard nothing? I looked from Mum to Grandma and back again, then at my sister lying on the bed between them, the thin band of red ribbon vivid against her pale wrist.

I stepped forward into the room.

"What's too dangerous?" I said.

4

The Wild Wood

I walked towards Mum. She watched me approach and then looked down at my sister lying on the bed, shaking her head.

"No," she said.

"Tell me what I can do, Mum," I pleaded. "We can't just let Catherine die without doin' everythin' we can to try an' help her. We'd *never* forgive ourselves."

"I'd never forgive myself if I lost you too, though, Eppie." Mum looked up again and our eyes met. "An' *that's* what we risk."

"Why don't we tell Hephzibah, an' then let her decide?" said Grandma. "She's old enough to make her own decisions by now, I reckon."

Mum shook her head firmly.

"No. This is *my* decision."

She gently wiped Catherine's face. My sister was neither awake nor asleep but seemed in a stupor, her eyes half closed and focused on nothing.

Grandma looked at the back of Mum's head, then she looked at me.

"There's someone who might be able to help your sister," she said, ignoring Mum's face swinging back round to glare at her, "who might know somethin' we could try - a herb or cure I don't know about."

I waited for her to carry on but she was glaring back at Mum now, both of them with determination on their faces. I looked from one to the other as the silence stretched out.

"Well? Who?" I asked.

"A – a woman who used to live in the village, but – but left some years ago," Grandma said, and Mum made a noise of frustration.

"So where does she live now?"

"*Enough!*" Mum shouted, and Grandma sighed heavily and went to tend the fire.

After several minutes of angry silence, Grandma sloshed some of the herb broth into a bowl and went over to the bed. She squeezed Mum's shoulder and passed her the bowl.

"Shall I do that, Mum?" I asked.

Mum smiled at me.

"Yes please, Eppie. I need to stretch my legs a bit."

She passed me the bowl and went to lean against the open doorframe, watching as I lifted Catherine into the crook of my arm and tried to get her to take some of the broth. It was hopeless, and after several minutes, I gave up and laid her down again. Suddenly Grandma was at my elbow.

"*In the wild wood*," she whispered, her dark eyes looking at me intently.

I looked at the doorway, startled, but Mum had gone out into the yard.

"If she's still alive, that is," Grandma went on hurriedly. "I haven't seen her for a few years, an' she was an old woman *then*. You'll need to follow the stream through the woods, up past the waterfall an' over the crags, an' then follow the stream a fair few miles into the deepest part of the wild wood. I haven't been able to get up there since my hip got bad. It would take you a good while to reach where she lives, an' even then she may not be there. Or still alive."

She paused.

"Or you might get lost in the forest."

I would be lying if I said I wasn't scared. No-one ever went into the wild wood. It was said to be haunted, and some folk said there are still wolves in there. And I couldn't help thinking of the scary stories people told about the wild wood. Like the one about Black Annis.

"Mummy?" came a whisper from the bed beside me. "Head's hurtin', Mummy."

"I'll go," I said, "I'll go."

Grandma nodded briskly, her mouth a thin line, then she moved round the room quickly, gathering several things and packing them in a large canvas bag, glancing at the empty doorway every few seconds.

"There's a bag of oats in here, an' a small loaf," she whispered quickly. "I've also packed my tinderbox an' five beeswax candles. Make sure you give them all to – to – *her*. The old woman. I'll leave the lanthorn by the hen house tonight with a smoulderin' match cord. Blow on the cord before you leave to make sure it's still alight, but it's best not to light the lanthorn until you're in the wild wood on top of the crags. You can't be seen from the village when you're up there. I've also packed some bread for you to eat on your way. You'll be fine for water as you'll be followin' the stream all the way there. If you stay by the stream you can't get lost, remember that."

She glanced again at the doorway.

"It won't be easy, Hephzibah. It'll be dark, an' you're sure to be scared. There are noises in the woods at night enough to turn anybody on their heels. But there's nothin' there to harm you." She hesitated. "An' if you do find the old woman, she – well, she can be scary too. But she'll do you no harm either."

She looked intently into my face, and spoke more gently.

"Are you *sure*?"

I swallowed, then nodded.

"Well, if you change your mind, I'll understand, but come an' help me with these herbs while I tell you everythin' you need to know."

We sat on opposite sides of the table, and I was surprised when my grandmother took my hand and squeezed it. She wasn't one for showing her affection. She told me that above all I must make sure I wasn't seen by *anyone*. And I mustn't let Dad know either, as he would be sure to stop me.

"You'll have to go up through the woods behind Witherstone Hall. I know you know a good route *there* without bein' seen, after all, even in broad daylight," she smiled, her eyes flitting to the doorway again. "An' you're not scared off easily. I'll give you that. The moon'll rise about midnight, so make sure you get well beyond Witherstone Hall before that."

I swallowed, more scared by the minute. How would I know which way to go in the forest?

"The track is hard to find in the wild wood, even in daylight," Grandma went on, "so you'll need to light the lanthorn then. Whatever happens, you *must* keep to the side of the stream the whole time, until you come to a deep, round pool. That's where the old woman lives."

"In-in the pool?" I asked.

"Don't be soft, girl!" Grandma snorted, "She's not Jenny Greenteeth."

Then her head whipped round to check Mum wasn't back yet before she went on.

"She lives nearby. If she wants to see you, she'll let you know. There may be a black Carrion Crow nearby. That'll usually mean the old woman's there. Tell her I sent you, an' why, an' she'll help us if she can."

Grandma hesitated.

"Trust your instincts, Hephzibah. I know you have good instincts, as I have," she nodded, looking intently at me.

I wasn't sure what she meant. Did she mean like when she somehow knew I'd gone up to Witherstone Hall to see Mary Ann, and like when we both woke up early the day Richard came home? Just that subtle feeling that *something* is happening? I didn't see how that would help me find my way through the wild wood.

"Take care not to be seen on your way back home, either. If anyone does see you, tell them your grandmother sent you to find our goat who has wandered off. I'll go an' hide the goat in the mornin', so we'll say the same if anyone comes to check."

"Why would it matter?" I asked.

"It matters," she said flatly, then looked at me thoughtfully before she went on.

"Folk round here would call the old woman a witch. So it would be bad news for us - an' for her - if anyone knows she's there, or sees you there."

My mouth fell open in shock, but before I could ask anything more, we heard the sound of voices and then Mum laughing. Dad and Richard were coming back with the wood.

Grandma quickly stowed the bag under my blanket by the wall, and I could hear the wood being stacked on the pile outside. Grandma gave me a rare but reassuring hug before pushing me towards the bed, just as my brother came into the cottage.

I ignored Richard's smirk when he saw Grandma's hug, and went and sat by my sister. Her face was clammy and her eyes half open. Mum and Dad came straight over to Catherine, Mum putting her arm round my shoulders and pressing her warm cheek against mine for a moment. Then she tweaked my chin gently.

"Thanks for bein' so good, Eppie," she said.

That night, I lay in bed in the flickering firelight, my stomach churning with nerves as I waited for everyone else to go to bed. I was still undecided about what to do. I'd told Grandma I would go, but I was scared to death at the thought of walking through the wild wood, let alone in the middle of the night. And then there was Mum. She had forbidden me to go.

I lay facing my parents' bed where Mum was tending to Catherine. She looked over to me in the shadows and smiled, but I could see she felt more like crying. I knew she was worried sick.

Witherstone

Grandma went out to the privy in the yard then came to bed, signalling me to move over to the wall. As I edged backwards, I could feel the contents of the bag pressing against my back and felt a sick rush of nerves. Grandma lay down beside me, settling into her blanket then turning her back to me and facing the room. After what seemed an age, Richard and Dad got up from sitting by the fire, Dad placing turfs of peat onto the embers to keep the fire smouldering for the morning while Richard went outside for a few minutes before he came to bed. If my brother was surprised that he'd be lying next to Grandma instead of me, he didn't say anything but bundled himself up in his blanket beside her.

After Dad had been in bed for a while, he and Mum stopped their murmured conversation and Dad's breathing gradually deepened. I lay listening to the quiet sounds of my father's sleep for a long time. The only other thing I could hear was the erratic, increasingly panicky beating of my heart, which sounded like it filled the room.

I knew my decision had been made, and that I couldn't put it off any longer. I sat up slowly and looked over to where my parents and sister lay. The room was almost fully dark, the faint glow of the fire hidden beneath the peat, but I could see that Mum and Dad were both asleep. I eased myself up until I was standing on the bed, lifting the packed bag up with me. I stepped carefully across my grandmother, who quietly moved her legs out of my way, then over my sleeping brother and on to the floor.

Heart pounding, I looked back at Grandma's eyes glittering towards me in the firelight, then I turned and walked quietly to the door. I took my cloak down from the hook and picked up my shoes before lifting the latch and letting myself out into the night.

The night was cold, and very dark. I felt for the bench then sat down to put on my shoes. It was hard to see to tie the laces. I was already dressed, having sneaked beneath my blanket fully clothed when I went to bed earlier, pulling the blanket up to my chin.

I stood up from the bench and took my linen cap from my apron pocket, then put it back again, realising my dark hair would be much harder to see at night, and following on from that thought, I unlaced my apron, glowing palely down from my waist, and stuffed it into the bag, along with my white linen neckerchief. Now only a pale strip of the neckline and cuffs of my shift could be seen, outlining my dark woollen doublet, so I tucked these in behind the doublet as best I could, put on my cloak and hefted the bag over my shoulder.

I crept across the yard to the hen house, feeling around for the lanthorn quietly. I didn't want to wake the hens in case Dad came dashing out, thinking there was a fox after them. I found the lanthorn and blew on the match cord to keep the red embers smouldering before winding it carefully inside the lanthorn to keep it safe, then I opened the gate into the lane.

I looked down towards the village, checking the coast was clear, before setting off in the opposite direction towards the meadow. Once in the meadow I kept to the line of the riverbank as far as the coppice, figuring I'd be more difficult to see against the black water and the shadowy trees than I would crossing the largely featureless meadow. I could see where the geese were roosting for the night, huddled together on the bank, and gave them a wide berth in case they woke up and set up a racket.

The dark sky wore vast swathes of stars, sweeping a bright arc above me with occasional pale wisps of cloud drifting silently across them. There was no moon yet so the coppice wood was dark. I crossed the stepping stones and followed the line of trees bordering Hall Farm into Witherstone Hall Woods and round to the back of the Hall, and on past the spot where I usually climbed over to visit Mary Ann.

Oh, poor Mary Ann, I thought, remembering that she too was ill, then a chill traced its fingers down my spine as I suddenly remembered the white face at the window, and Mary Ann's warning came into my mind.

'She knows it was you, an' she's really angry'.

I couldn't help glancing over my shoulder at the house. It was dark and silent, the windows blank eyes, and I walked more quickly until I could hear the sound of the stream again, at the far side of the Hall.

I reached the stream and began the steady climb up through the woods and out of the valley. It was very dark and I had to go carefully on the rough ground, unseen branches catching at my hair and clothes. I kept so close to the stream that I was more in danger of falling in it than losing sight of it. After a while, the track was getting much steeper, and I paused in a small clearing and looked back while I got my breath. The trees through which I'd walked were traced with pale light. The moon had risen, its bright circle complete but for one blurred edge. I began climbing again, the moonlight turning the bubbling waters beside me to quicksilver.

After climbing the steep path for a while longer, I was hot and took off my cloak, rolling it up tight and stuffing it into the bag. I wished I could take off my woollen doublet too, but knew the pale linen of my shift would be more easily seen moving through the trees. Instead I scooped handfuls of the cold stream water and splashed my face and neck to cool myself and drank deeply, the intensely cold water making my teeth ache. I rested for a few minutes, sitting on a rock by the stream, then I slung the bag over my shoulder and turned back to the path.

As I started to move up the track once more, I suddenly heard the murmur of voices ahead and froze. At that same moment, the voices stopped and I saw a man crouched down by the stream up ahead, his face turning towards me in the moonlight, and I glimpsed another figure melting silently into the shadows behind him.

"Who's there?" a man's hoarse voice demanded, and he stood up and walked down towards me.

I knew I'd lost my chance to run. Everything slowed down, and it felt like my nightmare. The man stopped in front of me and tried to make out my face, hidden in shadow as the moon was behind me. His face, on the other hand, was fully lit. His skin was lined and weathered, and he had a deep scar running down his face, slicing clean through one eyebrow and carving a gouge down the length of his cheek and into his bearded jaw.

"Well, well, what have we here?" he said, his voice mocking now, rather than – what had it been? Fearful?

I said nothing. My mind was racing, yet I was frozen to the spot as I stared up at his face. He spoke with an accent I'd never heard before.

"Cat got your tongue, young Mistress?" the man asked more kindly, seeming to realise the effect his appearance was having on the girl in front of him as he turned his scarred cheek away from me slightly and took a step back.

"Don't worry, I mean you no harm. I was just wonderin' what a young girl is doin' up here in the middle of the night?"

My throat was dry. I swallowed before I answered, but my voice still came out in a childish whisper.

"I'm lookin' for our goat."

The man laughed.

"Oh dear," he said, "I hope that weren't the goat we ate yesterday."

Then he seemed to think he had said something he shouldn't, and stopped laughing abruptly.

"Where're you from?" he asked, a harder edge to his voice.

"The village," I gestured behind me. "Witherstone."

The man nodded yet his eyes narrowed slightly. He looked at me intently for several moments as though he was considering something.

"So, you're just wanderin' through the woods after a goat? At night?" He paused. "In *these* woods? Aren't you scared you'll get lost?"

"N-no," I answered, then improvised quickly. "The goat always goes to the same place, just up here a way, so I often have to run up an' fetch her. I-I didn't wait 'til the mornin' as I know where she'll be, an' I work in the Parson's kitchen early so won't have time then -"

I stopped, a sickening lurch in my stomach as I realised I'd said far too much. He could easily find out who I was now. The man looked at me for a few moments, his expression impossible to read.

"What's your name?" he asked.

I hesitated. I'd already said enough for him to find out exactly who I was so it seemed best to stick to the truth as much as possible, in case he decided to check up on me. I felt sick to the core at the thought that he would ask about me at the Parson's house.

"Everyone calls me Eppie."

"Well, Eppie, you'd best be off after your goat."

He stepped to the side of the path, gesturing me though with a sweep of his arm and an extravagant bow.

After a moment's hesitation, I forced myself to walk up the track and past the man, my legs trembling so badly they felt as though they would give way at any moment.

As I climbed past him, I felt his eyes following me and suddenly realised that the bag over my shoulder would give the lie to my story about the goat. I swung it quickly off my shoulder and into my arms as I passed, and then was immediately angry with myself for my panicked stupidity as this would only have drawn his attention to the bag.

I quickened my pace and carried on walking up the steep track as fast as I could without actually breaking into a run. I expected his hand on my shoulder at any moment, and the skin on my back prickled with goose-bumps. Then I risked looking behind me and was shocked to see no sign of the man at all. The empty path stared blankly back at me. He had slipped into the shadows as though he had never been there.

I ran then, flying up the steep track in terror, my hands grabbing at anything to help me climb. After several minutes of frantic scrambling, I was forced to slow down as my feet stumbled and slipped on the rocks and tree roots of the narrow path, and branches were scratching my face and arms. I also realised I'd been making a huge amount of noise and forced myself to stop and listen.

I stood there gasping for breath, my eyes staring back down the way I'd come and every fibre of my body rigid with tension, and then I started to hear noises all around me. A scrabbling sound over there. A rustle of movement at my back. My eyes strained in every direction as I tried to see what might be in the shadows around me, until finally I nearly screamed at myself to *stop! Calm down!*

Forcing myself to turn my back on the dark path and climb up the track once more, I moved as quickly but as quietly as I could, listening for any sound of pursuit as I tried to calm my terror. I kept on climbing, my hands hauling myself over the craggy rocks, but looking back over my shoulder every few moments to check I wasn't being followed. As I climbed higher, I gradually began to calm down, although fear seemed to have been a constant companion since I'd left my bed hours ago.

No, I thought ruefully, *since I'd agreed to do this at all.*

I tried to concentrate on finding the safest route across the rocks, and as I climbed I gradually realised there was another sound. A steady roar had been getting louder as I climbed. I had been hearing it for a while but the blood pounding in my ears had masked it. I must be getting closer to the waterfall. It sounded like the river after heavy rain turned its usually placid flow into a churning and dangerous force of nature. Only much, much louder.

The sound increased as the minutes passed, the stream to my side becoming wilder and noisier as it dropped further away into a deepening gorge. Eventually a huge boulder blocked my path, and I leaned against it for a moment getting my breath, then I climbed up the grey stone and emerged into a deafening roar, staring in awe at the sight before me.

The moonlit waterfall fell straight down from high up in the crags, bright with moonlight and mesmerising, the thunder as it fell into the churning foam at the bottom filling my head, and covering my face and hair and clothes with spray in seconds. I began to shiver and turned to look at the stark cliff face, trying to find the route up over the crags.

I looked for what seemed like an age but finally, I saw it. A steep track moved diagonally up and across the sheer wall of rock, curving round towards the falls before passing up over the top of the crags only feet away from the waterfall itself. I stared in horror. Surely, that couldn't be right. How on earth was I going to climb that? I carried on looking at the rest of the cliff face, but there was nothing else, so it must be easier than it looked. My grandmother wouldn't have sent me if it wasn't safe. How could she have managed to climb it herself otherwise?

I picked out my route by sight, then I made my way across the boulder to the foot of the cliff. I pushed my bag further behind my back to keep my arms free, then I stepped up onto the narrow track and began to climb.

Witherstone

As I moved steadily upwards across the front of the crags, it quickly became clear that this was the most dangerous part of my journey so far.

The surface of the rock was wet and slippery, and to one side of me there was nothing but the plunge down into the roaring pool below. It took all my concentration to keep myself focused on the climb. My hands gripped tightly to every handhold I could find, and I pressed as close to the rock-face as possible for each careful step. The track took me steadily higher and closer to the waterfall, and I was soon soaked to the skin and trembling.

By the time I reached the section of track where it climbed up over the top of the crags, the thunderous cascade was plunging past just a few feet away from me and my feet were struggling to find a firm hold on the slippery and increasingly narrow ledge. My movements were becoming more and more restricted until finally I came to a standstill, my fingers clinging desperately to the rock and my toes practically pressing through the soles of my shoes to get a firmer hold on the treacherous ledge.

I steadied myself against the cliff face and looked at the crag in front of me. Then I knew with a sickening jolt that what I had taken to be the last part of the path over the top of the crags was nothing more than a fracture in the rock. It had been given the appearance of a deeper track from the path below by the stark light and shadow of the moon. I was hanging from the cliff face just feet from the waterfall, directly above the roaring chasm below, and there was no way over the crags. I was stuck.

The longer I clung there, my hands gripping onto meagre handholds on the rock and my cheek trembling against the wet stone, the more terrified I became. I knew that if I didn't force myself to move soon, I would lose my grip and fall.

I tried to turn my face so I could see how best to turn my feet carefully around on the ledge to make my way back down again, but I could barely move. I was terrified that any movement would cause me to topple over backwards, plunging me into the abyss.

Fear froze my muscles to stone. I closed my eyes then opened them again in panic as my head swam. I groaned aloud in terror. Staring ahead of me frantically, I saw that the narrow ledge I was perched on sloped down past the shadowed fissure in the rock, and just a few steps further on it widened slightly and appeared to open out behind the waterfall itself where the force arced out over the crags. It looked like the ledge there became a deeper scoop out of the rock which might just be wide enough to turn around on. With no other options, I shuffled along the ledge a few careful steps down and forward into the gaping shadow behind the waterfall.

I pressed gratefully into the back of the tiny cave, allowing myself to be engulfed by the colossal roar of the falls which was louder in that hollow than any noise I could have imagined. For several long minutes I stayed in that brief sanctuary, my trembling body and thudding heartbeats my only existence. Eventually I calmed down enough to turn and climb back out onto the ledge and attempt to make my way back down across the cliff face.

With a dry throat, I slowly eased myself out onto the narrow ledge from behind the wall of water, steadily retracing my steps across the slippery rock. After what seemed an age, I finally made it back down to the large boulder at the bottom of the falls.

As my trembling body climbed back over the rock, I saw what I had missed earlier. The original track turned sharply away from the falls *below* the boulder, the track lying unseen in the deep shadows. That's why I'd missed it and climbed up over the rock instead, leading myself to the false path across the cliff face.

I leaned against the boulder, shaking with exhaustion and the terror I'd been through. I had to force myself to move, back onto the path and the steep curve away from the cliff and up the side of the crags. Thankfully, the track here was wider than the false path on the cliff so I could climb safely. I still had to be careful where I put my feet but it was a relief to be away from that terrible drop, and after a short while, I reached the top of the crags at last. Hauling myself up and planting my feet firmly on the rock, I turned to look below me.

The view was staggering. The silver waterfall dropped out of sight into the gorge, and the world fell away into the valley below. The bright, steady moon traced the woodlands tumbling down and spreading in a widening swathe towards the river, gleaming and twisting its way through the dark valley far beneath me. The river shimmered as it wound across the valley, then blackened as it coiled away towards the distant horizon, seeming to absorb what light there was into its depths.

Down below me, I thought I could even make out the tiny, dark huddle of Witherstone, nestling into a loop of the winding river and hedged in by the wild moors on one side and the looming hills on the other. Smooth pockets of pale meadow and the black-edged farm fields ran towards the woodlands which extended its arms around them, as though protecting the tiny village from the moors and crags which dominated the shadowed landscape.

Arcing over the whole valley was the sky, moonlight tracing the thin wisps of cloud stretching towards the horizon in copper light. The moon felt like a friend, lightening the shadows. I'd never been this far from home before, nor so high, and had never realised how big the world was. After staring at the shadowy earth spread out before me, I turned my back on the valley and looked into the forest.

Encroaching to the edge of the crags, the ancient trees towered over me like giants, and it seemed impenetrable, the bright moonlight making little headway into the dense shadows. A shiver ran through me, as, taking a deep breath, I stepped into the wild wood.

It was so dark and overgrown beneath the ancient trees that it was impossible to make out any path at all. I took out the lanthorn. The end of the match cord was still dotted with dull red embers and I blew them carefully, then held the match to the candle and blew gently until the wick began to glow and a tiny flame took hold. The relief was so strong that I wanted to look into that flame for the rest of the night. I coiled the match around the base of the candle and closed the lanthorn window. The candle grew brighter, and I turned it to face the direction I needed to go.

The light from the lanthorn was weak but it did push back the intense darkness, bathing the trees around me in a pale, ghostly light. It was still hard to make out a path, but I started walking through the trees in the direction the stream must flow from as it headed towards the waterfall.

The silence of the forest seemed a palpable thing. I walked into the stillness and it was unnerving. After several minutes I realised why the forest seemed so suddenly and so absolutely quiet. It was because I was moving away from the crags. I had left the immense roar of the waterfall behind.

It was difficult to make my way across the ancient forest floor. I was no longer climbing, having reached the top of the crags, but the trees were huge and close together and rocks and fallen branches were hidden beneath a thick carpet of springy moss, making me stumble all the time. And it was so very dark beyond of the feeble glow of the lanthorn. The moonlight rarely found its way into the dense forest, and it was difficult to keep a sense of direction, moving along in a bubble of light through the dark trees.

As I walked on and there was no sign of the stream, I began to be afraid that I'd headed in the wrong direction. I turned slightly, moving more parallel with the crags, and carried on walking further, and yet further, but still I didn't come to the stream. Panic started to poison my breath and I turned even more, fighting the urge to run. I knew hidden rocks and branches would trip me, and I might have turned too far and end up running right off the top of the crags. Or I would lose any sense of direction, and be lost in the forest forever. Instead, I forced myself to stop and listen.

Silence.

Except for the blood roaring in my ears.

I listened harder. The forest around me was still. No. There were sounds. Tiny movements here and there, night creatures about their business, and the sighing of leaves as the wild wood breathed around me. But that wasn't what I was listening for, so I picked through the noises I could hear.

There. Was that the faint sound of water? It was almost imperceptible, but I was sure I could hear it.

I released my pent breath and began moving steadily towards where I thought the sound was coming from, listening all the while. The water grew gradually louder, and I kept my course as straight as I could through the dark trees, and then - there it was. Relief washed over me as I stumbled down the stream's mossy bank.

The stream was silver where the moonlight caught it through the trees. I drank the cold, delicious water, then wrapped myself in my cloak and sat and rested for a while, eating some bread and trying to get warm. I couldn't stop shivering though, so I picked up my bag and the lanthorn and carried on walking. I knew the only way to get warm was to keep moving, and I followed the stream as it led me deeper into the wild wood.

I tried to walk as fast as I could on the treacherous ground, despite the constant obstacles. Several times I was forced to move away from the stream as huge trees blocked my way, felled by age or wind who knew how long ago, and in having to go round them I was afraid I would lose the stream. When I came to smaller brooks, flowing into the main stream, I leapt over them, and as I walked on, my guide became steadily narrower and shallower as I moved upstream of the small rivulets which fed it as it flowed down to the crags.

I walked for a long time, the moon slowly overtaking me, passing overhead to lead me on my way. The intense dark was alive, scurrying and rustling all around me, and as the trees loomed towards me like pale figures out of the shadows, I tried to keep thoughts of my nightmare out of my mind. Occasionally I heard the eerie call of an owl, and once or twice the cry of a small animal, caught by the owl or another of the night hunters, and I pulled my cloak more tightly round my neck. The snuffling of a hedgehog foraging in the undergrowth brought me out in a cold sweat, and the yelp of a fox, like a woman's scream in the night, shuddered down my spine.

As the sounds of the wild wood followed my footsteps, I began to feel as if someone or something was there, keeping pace with me and watching from the shadows, and I tried to keep my eyes focused on the way ahead.

Then I was sure I heard the sound of a bigger creature moving stealthily through the trees away to my left and I froze, eyes and ears straining into the gloom, searching for the shape or sound of man or wolf, for the glint of eyes turning towards me in the darkness. But I could see nothing, and once again I had to force myself to move on, to walk deeper and deeper into the wild wood, and I felt like I was trapped in a version of my nightmare.

I kept my focus on the light cast by the lanthorn and the moon and the stream guiding my way, trying to stop my terror from taking over, but the night and the forest seemed as though they would never end, and I felt I had always been walking in the dark wood.

Then, without warning, I found myself in a small clearing, and there were two moons in front of me. One was hanging low in the sky, just above the trees, and the other was reflected from the depths of a large, flat pool at my feet.

I stopped dead as soon as I saw the pool, my heart thudding. The water lay broad and still, in the shadow of a grove of ancient oaks, and the surface was a black mirror set with the face of the moon like a precious stone. Around the black water the trees stood in silence, and I could see no sign of a house or dwelling of any kind.

As I stared around me on all sides, raising the lanthorn and trying to cast its pale light further into the shadows, I could see only the still pool and the silent trees stretching away into the darkness. There was no house. *There was no house*.

I felt the panic taking over. I can't have followed my grandmother's directions properly. I'd made a mistake about the false path on the cliff face. It *had* been the true path after all and I had allowed my fear to force me back, leading me instead deep into the forest by the side of some other stream, to some other pool. And leading me as far away from finding any help for Catherine as ever.

"*No*," I groaned out loud. "*No*."

I sank to my knees in the shadows and closed my eyes in despair.

5

The Witch

I collapsed into the darkness, my arms across my chest as I rocked back and forth and hopelessness washed through me. I struggled to pull myself together but I was lost for a while, and just let it come. After what felt like an age, I finally lifted my head and looked at the pool and the ancient trees around me.

I shook my head, feeling a kind of anger welling up. This must be right. *It must be.* For Catherine's sake. There had been no way over the crags from the cliff path – no path either me or Grandma could have taken anyway. Grandma had said to follow the stream to the pool. And she had said to trust my instincts. This *must* be the right pool. I would have to wait for dawn to come so that I could see better. There must be a house in the shadows somewhere in the forest around me. There just had to be.

I sat by the pool, huddled in the pale light of the lanthorn and wrapped in my cloak against the chill air and my own fears, and waited for the dawn. The wild wood was completely silent. Even the rustling and scuttling shadows had fallen still, as though the forest were listening.

I huddled deeper into my cloak as I sat there, listening back. The sky and the stars and the shadows beneath the trees waited too, seeming unchanging. The only way I knew time was still moving was the slow but steady descent of the moon, its bright orb gradually sinking into the depths of the pool. I had never wished for the dawn to come more than I did now.

By the time I could no longer see the moon, the blanket of stars had faded until I could see only the bright morning star shining in the pale sky. I leaned forward and blew out the candle.

It was still deeply shadowed beneath the trees, and I waited on. The forest birds were waking, the clear, thrilling sound of a blackbird and then a growing chorus which gradually swelled to fill the whole forest. I realised I could see the birds darting between the trees, engaged now in the urgent business of finding food for their young, and I suddenly felt very thirsty.

I stood up, legs trembling, and walked the few steps to the black pool. Kneeling on its bank, I scooped the cold, peaty water and drank. Then I sat back on my heels and stared for the thousandth time into the wild wood around the clearing. The forest beneath the trees was light enough to see reasonably well now, and I looked and looked but still couldn't see anywhere a person could be living. No hut or shelter. Nothing.

As I stared around me, the hairs on the back of my neck prickled. I had the sensation that I was being watched. My eyes scanned beneath the trees again, and began to search higher into the branches of the trees around the pool. Then my heart jolted as I saw a large, solitary black crow sitting in one of the ancient oaks on the other side of the pool. It appeared to be looking right at me.

I stared at the crow and the crow stared back. I thought I must be imagining it. Surely the bird couldn't be looking at me as intently as I was looking at him? Then I remembered. Grandma had said something about a Carrion Crow - that the old woman wouldn't be far away. Heart beating more quickly, I stared at the bird, sitting black and still with his head cocked to one side as he regarded me, then I stared into the forest beneath him.

After several minutes, as the shadows beneath the trees grew steadily lighter, it began to dawn on me that a small, rough triangle of black was remaining stubbornly dark while the shadows around it were dissolving into the growing light. I stared at the shadow. It was close to the ground, among a tumble of fallen, moss-covered branches beneath the ancient oak in which the crow was sitting. I tried to make out what it was, why it stayed so resolutely black when all around it was becoming lighter - and why it drew my eye so insistently. As the detail of the forest became clearer, the shadows faded but the shape remained, dark and silent.

Gradually a kind of sense seemed to attach itself to the dark shadow. It seemed to be formed by a small space between the trunk of the old oak and the fallen, moss-covered branches tumbled against it. It was almost like a window, except it was too low to the ground – almost in the earth itself. It was even lower than my face as I sat by the edge of the pool, so it would only be at the height of a person's shins at most. Someone walking through the clearing probably wouldn't even see it.

After hesitating a moment, I got to my feet and walked slowly round the pool towards that strange patch of darkness. As I got nearer, I crouched down to stare into the resolute dark, trying to see whether it really was a window of some kind or was just a shadow beneath the fallen branches which my imagination was twisting into something else. Despite the morning sun spreading through the whole forest now, I couldn't make out anything at all in the intense darkness of the strange shadow. I knelt on the thick moss, leaning my hand on the trunk of the tree as I moved forward to peer into the gloom.

A horde of spiders and beetles swarmed out of the opening just in front of my face, scuttling out over the mossy branches and teeming towards me, and I gasped and pulled away in shock. Long gangling legs and scuttling bodies were pouring out in all directions, and they just kept coming. Hundreds of them. My senses were so heightened I was sure I could hear the scurrying footsteps of each tiny creature.

On they came, bodies glinting in the dawn light as they swarmed across the branches, crawling all over one another in their rapid exodus before gradually disappearing into the cracks and crevices of the bark and mosses all around the opening. Finally, the last few creatures trickled out and disappeared, and I sat there open-mouthed and trembling as the forest fell silent once more.

"Well are ye' gonna sit out there all day, or are ye' comin' in?" croaked a voice, just a breath away from my face.

I shrieked and shot backwards onto the moss.

Then what appeared to be a haphazard mass of fallen twigs and mosses to the side of the shadow lifted open like a curtain, held aside by a withered arm which seemed to be coming out of the earth.

"Come on in, me dear, I shan't harm ye'," the voice rasped.

Trembling, I ducked beneath the arm and stepped down into the dark.

The flap dropped back into place and I was in complete darkness for a few moments. As my eyes adjusted to the small amount of light coming in the tiny window, the first thing to emerge from the gloom was the oldest woman I had ever seen. She was stooped just in front of me, her crooked back forcing her to twist her face upwards as she peered at my face.

I cringed back from her, then tried to relax my defensive posture. The old woman's face was ancient and creased and sunken, and as weathered as though carved from the gnarled wood of the tree beneath which she lived.

The glinting black eyes peering out of her creased face were studying me intently. She smelled of damp and mildew, and her dirty grey hair was woven into a thin plait hanging down over her shoulder. Her shift and bodice were filthy, and her stained apron and dark skirts disappeared into the gloom at her feet as though she were growing out of the earth.

Smiling to herself, the ancient woman turned and rummaged in the darkness behind her before emerging with a stout log which she placed down beside me.

"Sit yourself down, me dear," her voice rasped, unnaturally close in the tiny room, and she squatted down onto another seat hidden in the shadows.

"Thank you," my voice quavered.

I sat down and looked at the old woman, still regarding me intently. She didn't take her eyes off me as she settled her back against the tree, and I knew she had sat us in what little light the window had to offer so we could see one another's faces more clearly. But her silent scrutiny was unnerving, and I looked away from her glinting black eyes at the tiny house, etched into the gloom around me.

It was a clever den built beneath the mass of fallen branches which leaned against the huge oak, occupying a deep scoop in the earth and right into the heart of the ancient tree where its massive trunk had hollowed through time and rot into a natural cave. The fallen branches leaning against the trunk above the hollow extended the cave out in a wide arc, and any gaps in the walls were filled with smaller branches and moss, making the tiny house impossible to see from the outside as it blended seamlessly with the blanket of mosses growing all over the wild wood.

In the centre of the room was a flat-topped boulder, which served as the old woman's table, a mug and a wooden platter sitting alongside a bowl with a spoon and an old, worn knife. The thing that stood out most, though, was the small pile of bones heaped up in the middle of the table, a millipede weaving in and out of the pale ribs.

After staring at the bones dry-mouthed for several moments, I forced the stories of Black Annis out of my mind, reassuring myself that they were from a small animal, probably a rabbit, and I made myself look away from them at the rest of the strange house.

There was a smaller rock away to my left, opposite the tree, a fire nestling in its slightly hollowed surface beneath a three-legged cooking pot. A gap at the top of the sloping roof, where it leaned against the tree, allowed the smoke to run up the inside wall before escaping and flowing up the truck of the tree, making it more difficult to be seen from the outside.

In the hollowed base of the oak a few blankets were piled on top of a deep bed of moss, and as my eyes skidded back to the bed, I realised I was making sure the pale, rumpled blankets were not the dried skins of children lost in the wild wood. Of course they were just blankets. I looked away from the old woman's bed again but daren't meet her gaze, which I could feel on me all the while. I didn't want her to see what I'd been thinking, and I carried on looking round the room, trying to look more relaxed than I felt.

Opposite the window, a large water jug sat beneath bunches of herbs and shrivelled roots hanging from the ceiling, along with a young rabbit. Despite the homely effects in the room, I could feel the rigid tension in every nerve of my body. Not just because of the thoughts of Black Annis, which kept coming into my mind no matter how hard I tried to push them out, but because the old woman's cave was alive.

Over and under and between everything in the room, spiders, beetles, woodlice, millipedes and earwigs were scurrying and crawling everywhere I looked. A fat spider was scuttling across the stone table towards me and several earwigs nestled in the bowl, while the millipede was still coiling round and round the pale bones.

I shuddered as a large beetle scuttled across my hands tightly clutching one another in my lap, feeling each of its claws on my skin with every quick step. I tried not to think about the creatures I could feel crawling all over my ankles, or whatever it was tickling its way across my hair.

And in those few short moments which seemed slowed into an age as I looked round the tiny cave, I could feel the old woman's eyes burning into me. Drawing in a shaky breath, I turned and looked at her.

At that moment, a dark shadow suddenly filled the small window right next to my face, and I gasped. It was the crow, its sleek body filling the entire frame. I let out my breath shakily, trying to steady my nerves as the bird sat on the sill unruffled, and cawed once, its voice filling the tiny room, and its raucous tone was echoed by the harsh rasp of the old woman as she leaned forwards and spoke to him.

"Master Nalgah," she said, her sunken mouth gaping.

Then she crooned softly to the bird as she leaned closer, a spider held between her bony fingers. "I'll be needin' ye' later, I'm thinkin', but best be off at present as ye're scarin' our guest."

The crow pecked the spider from her fingers then lifted off the windowsill and was gone. The morning light flooded back into the cave, picking out whirling dust motes disturbed by the bird's wings which rose like tiny stars for a moment before being eclipsed by the shadows. I could hear the crow's wings as it flew back up into the branches outside.

I looked at the old woman, sure that she must be able to hear the hammering of my heart as clearly as I could, then her harsh voice spoke again.

"Well, I take it ye've come all the way up here to ask me somethin', Hephzibah Ann Creswell?"

My jaw dropped in shock and I stopped breathing. The old woman's croaking laugh filled the tiny cave, her toothless gums shocking in the grinning mouth.

"H-how do you know my name?" I asked, terrified of the black eyes gleaming at me from the shadows.

"Well now, that'd be tellin'," her harsh voice replied, gums still grinning while a large beetle crawled steadily across her bodice.

"Are – are you a witch?" I asked, before I could stop myself.

The old woman's mouth snapped shut and the humour dropped from her face in an instant. I stared at her, horrified at myself. The silence stretched out between us.

"Maybe I am, an' maybe I ain't," she rasped eventually, "that depends what ye're askin'. But them that use *that* word are usually up to no good."

She narrowed her eyes.

"I know ye' because I know ye' Gran'ma. An' ye' mother too, though I've not seen ye' mum since she was a girl. Ye' don't look much like ye' mum, mind you, but ye' do look just like ye' Gran'ma did when she was your age, so I'd ha' known ye' anywhere. An' no-one but ye' Gran'ma would have sent ye' up here to me."

She leaned towards me.

"Now then, ye'd best tell me why ye're here, Hephzibah, 'cos I know ye' Gran'ma wouldn't have sent ye' to see me for nothin'."

I took a shaky breath and then told the old woman about Catherine, and our fears that it might be the Plague. I opened the bag my grandmother had packed and put the gifts on the table.

The old woman nodded at the things as they were taken from the bag, putting the bread and oats into storage jars and leaving the candles and tinderbox on the table.

Then she put her hands to her neck, armpits, and groin, and said, "Has ye' sister got lumps or boils here or here?"

I shook my head, sickened by the thought.

"She hadn't when I left last night, but a man in the village has because the Parson's cook told us yesterday that her uncle has swellings on his neck, an' his skin is blackened."

The old woman sucked in her breath sharply and got to her feet.

"That's the Plague," she said. "We've no time to lose."

Then she spat onto the ground.

"The Parson's cook, ye' say? That'll be Mary Robinson, then, an' a bigger busy-body there never was."

"N-no, it's Ellen," I replied, "an' she's been very kind to us."

"Ah, Mary's daughter," the old woman nodded. "My mother delivered that child, though she must be a grown woman by now, of course. She's kind, is she?"

She sniffed. "You watch out for them that claim to be kind. I'm surprised at ye' Gran'ma, lettin' ye' have owt to do with anyone from the Parson's household. But then, maybe I'm not. Parson Cowper was kind enough to her, from what she told me, despite –"

She stopped and her eyes bored into me.

"What has ye' Gran'ma told ye'?"

I looked at her. Did the old woman mean the mysterious things that Grandad Creswell had alluded to? It was a mystery I knew nothing about, other than that it was *something*.

"Erm, nothin'. But the Parson's not called Cowper," I said at last, wondering whether the old woman was confusing Edward Cowper with the Parson. "I know Gran'ma doesn't like it when Mistress Burnett – the Parson's wife – is tellin' us how we should run our household, but she doesn't mind that I'm workin' in the Parson's kitchen -"

"*Burnett!*" she exclaimed. "What happened to Matthew Cowper?"

"I-I don't know, it's always been Parson Burnett as long as I can remember."

"An' ye're workin' *there*? In the *Burnett* house?"

She sounded horrified. I just nodded. The old woman stared at me and muttered under her breath, but she didn't say any more. I thought about asking her what my Grandma was keeping from me. I was sure the old woman must know something about it. I swallowed, but then she turned away and was busying herself at the fire and I said nothing. That I was terrified of her didn't help, but there were more pressing things than mysterious events from my family's past right now.

A wave of fear ran through me at the thought that Catherine might be dead before I even made it back home.

"Do you think you can help us?" I asked. "Help Catherine?"

"*That* I *can* do," she said, as though also referring to – and simultaneously dismissing – the things she couldn't help.

"Ye'll need to go out an' collect some things for me to use, though, Hephzibah. I'm an old woman now, an' can't be climbin' up after bees, or trekkin' half way through the wild wood."

Apprehension traced through my stomach, and I looked at the old woman's hunch-backed figure as she built up the fire, wondering what on earth I was going to have to do. She turned back to me.

"Has ye' Gran'ma had ye' collectin' honey from the bees? Have ye' ever been stung?"

I shook my head.

The old woman tutted and stooped to pick up a tiny earthenware pot from among an assortment of jars in the corner. She beckoned me nearer as she uncorked the jar and placed it on the table.

I leaned across the boulder towards her, and before I had any inclination of what she was going to do, a bony hand shot out and grabbed my wrist and pulled my arm across the stone. I cried out and tried to pull away but the old woman's grip was like iron. My arm was held fast, and I stared at the creased leathery face inches from my own as the old woman whipped something out from her apron.

She bent over my hand, and I could see the thin grey hairs growing out of her scalp and lice scurrying through her hair. Suddenly she jabbed the back of my hand and I gasped as I felt a pin stabbing into my skin, and I struggled, trying to pull free.

"Hold still, girl!" the old woman rasped, and she turned my hand towards the light from the window and peered at it for a moment, then she used her filthy apron to wipe away the bead of blood which formed, then again as another bead shaped itself straight away. The next bead was slower in coming, and she stared intently at my hand as she wiped away the third red dot.

"There," she said. "Do ye' see that?"

She pointed at the small puncture wound on the back of my hand. The bleeding had stopped but the wound was still open, leaving a tiny, clean hole.

"Yes," I croaked, terrified.

The old woman dipped her bony finger in the jar and dripped a tiny bead of liquid from her filthy fingernail onto the pinprick. The wound immediately began to sting and I tried again to pull away as it began to burn.

"Stop it! You're hurtin' me!"

The old woman kept her unbreakable hold on my arm and stared intently at the pinprick for several moments, then suddenly released my wrist.

"It should ha' been done a lot earlier, but it'll have to do. A bit of bee venom, to ward off a fever in case the bees sting ye'."

I rubbed my hand. The hole had closed but the pinprick was still throbbing painfully.

"I've no snake venom, though, so ye'll have to be careful there, I'm thinkin'."

"*S-snake* venom?" I gasped, not even flinching from the spider which had suddenly dropped down to dangle in front of my face.

"I'm just teasin' ye', child," the old woman laughed wheezily. "Maybe the bees'll seem a bit friendlier now, eh?"

She patted my shoulder and poured me a drink of water, and I tried to stop my hand trembling as I drank, the old woman staring at me intently all the while.

"Ye' feelin' alright?" she asked eventually.

I nodded. She nodded back, satisfied at something, then she lifted the entrance flap and beckoned me outside. I left my bag on the floor and ducked beneath the dangling spider as I climbed up into the clearing after her, rubbing the painful area on the back of my hand.

The clearing looked a much friendlier place in the warm sunshine, although the black shape of the crow was still sitting in the tree, watching us.

"Ye' must climb up there an' get the Queen's comb," she said, pointing high up another massive oak near the pool.

After a few moments of looking up into the tree where her bony-knuckled finger was pointing, I saw a hollow in the tree's trunk and a dark mass clearly visible inside it. It was impossibly high off the ground. I stared at the hollow.

"The Q-Queen's comb?"

"Ye' have to cut out the middle of the bees' hive to get the Queen's comb. That's where she broods, ye' see. Dead centre of the hive. An' while ye're about it, ye' can bring back some of the bees for me. If ye' can get the Queen herself, so much the better. She's the biggest bee, so ye'll see her well enough."

I looked at the old woman. Her ancient form was so gnarled and stooped that she was no taller than me, her dark eyes on the same level as mine, but there was one crucial difference. Her eyes were black and glittering mischievously while I knew mine were darkened with fear.

"There's no snakes up there," she said mockingly, "just the bees. But ye'd best leave them 'til later, I'm thinkin', to let the venom work into ye' blood for a while, an' most of the bees will be out of the hive an' about their business later in the mornin'. First of all," she said, her black eyes glinting, "ye'll need to fetch the Devil's Cup."

I closed my eyes for a moment. This just couldn't get any worse. I opened them again to see the old woman nodding, but her mischievous glint had vanished.

"That's the most important of all," she rasped, "an' it's the hardest to find."

She looked at me appraisingly, and I looked back at her, trying to hide my fear. She grinned again suddenly. She was still enjoying herself.

"We'll also need Hemp Agrimony, but there's plenty o' that growin' right here," she waved her arm towards a patch of greenery at the side of the pool. "An' we'll be needin' some bread mould – but *that's* easy enough to find," she chuckled. "Pick some o' the Hemp leaves, an' dig up a Burdock root. You know Burdock?"

I nodded.

"Well, get crackin' then, Hephzibah, we need to be quick for ye' sister," and she disappeared back into the cave.

Catherine.

I turned to the pool quickly, scared about what tasks I would have to do after I'd gathered the herbs. Bees were bad enough, but what did the old woman mean about having to get the Devil's Cup?

I was also more tired than I'd ever been in my life. I'd never stayed awake an entire night before. I felt thick-headed, and my hand was still throbbing painfully. How on earth was I going to be able to climb that tree, *and* take on the bees, without being stung or falling?

I glanced up at the hive involuntarily as I leaned over the boggy ground by the pool. I was more afraid of what would happen to Catherine if I failed to get home in time, though, and I shifted my concentration onto gathering the Hemp Agrimony.

6

The Devil's Cup

The peaty water of the pool was wriggling with tadpoles, and water beetles scuttled across the surface. As I picked the thin green leaves, a newt moved through the water next to me, its body and tail curling and flicking with each stroke. Then, as my shadow crossed the water, its sinuous figure swam down into the dark water and out of sight.

I found a clump of Burdock not far from the pool, among bright wildflowers busy with the hum of bees and even the surprising flicker of early butterflies, like bright jewels in the sunshine. The root was buried deep, and I used a stick to help me dig the root out, shiny red worms still clinging to it, and I shook them off and carried the root and the Agrimony leaves back to the old woman.

It seemed dark and claustrophobic in her cave after the sunshine of the clearing, even once my eyes had adjusted to the gloom. The old woman had cleared the stone table of everything except her bowl and knife, the five candles, and several woodlice.

"Now, Hephzibah, ye' must go an' find the Devil's Cup. I'm thinkin' ye' won't know it?"

I shook my head, my heart picking up speed.

"Ye'll need to head north, an' walk for a good while 'til ye' come to a hill above the wild wood set with pine trees. Do ye' know pine?"

"No," my voice whispered.

"They're tall, straight trees, an' have long thin needles instead of leaves, an' they smell different – kind of sharp. Ye' need to walk into the deepest part of the pine forest to where they grow close, then look in the shadows beneath 'em. Spring's well on now, so the Devil's Cup should be up out of the earth. Some folk call it the Ebony Cup, as it's as black as can be, but some call it the Devil's Cup as it holds the Devil's spit, an' he don't take kindly to us takin' it so ye' need to be careful."

My stomach lurched and I couldn't keep the fear out of my face any longer.

"Ye'll know the Cups when ye' see 'em, child, don't worry," the old woman said, her mocking smile knowing full well that finding them wasn't what was worrying me. "Before ye' touch 'em, though, ye' must walk round 'em three times - sunwise, mind, not widdershins – then dig five up an' put 'em in here."

She gave me a leather pouch and put her bony hand on my arm, patting me to emphasise her points while she went on.

"Ye' must be careful not to touch the Cups themselves, mind, pick 'em up by their roots. An' if ye' hear anythin' behind ye' as ye're leavin', don't look back but keep on walkin' as fast as ye' can."

Her black eyes were serious now, her mouth set in a grim line and her fingers gripping my arm fiercely. My mouth was completely dry as I nodded, and I drank the rest of the water before I followed the old woman outside. She pointed out the direction I needed to go through the forest, following a line north beyond her ancient oak.

"Make sure ye' don't get lost, Hephzibah. There are few parts of the wild wood more difficult to find the way back from, so mark ye' way well. An' keep an eye on the sun. It must be on ye' right goin' to the pine forest, an' on ye' left comin' back. Only don't take too long or the sun will be too high to tell, so ye' need to be quick. If ye' can't find the Devil's Cup by late mornin', ye'll have to come back without. The forest spreads for many, many miles, child, an' ye' won't find ye' way back here if ye' don't take care."

Her bony fingers bit into my flesh.

"The Devil leaves his Cup in few places in the wild wood, but I've found it there beneath the pines in the spring, so it's a good time to look," she croaked encouragingly, and then she gave me a shove into the forest.

I walked past the oak in the direction the old woman had indicated and then looked back, but she had already gone. The clearing looked as though it was the last place on earth anyone was living. I shivered, suddenly feeling very alone as I turned and walked into the forest.

No-one had been this way for a long time. I tried to be aware of where the sun was as I walked, and take notice of markers among the trees around me. But the wild wood soon became a blur of similarities so I began placing occasional fallen branches across the path to mark my way back and walked in as straight a direction as I could, checking the sun whenever I could see it through the dense forest. It was still low in the sky but climbing.

The wild wood was a beautiful place in the morning light, bright with spring leaves and thick with moss, golden beams slanting between the trees as I walked and the birds singing as they darted through the forest. I laughed at myself for having been so afraid in the night. The route had been pretty straightforward after all, just as my grandmother had said. Just long. And dark. *And terrifying*, I admitted to myself. I thought about the cliff path I'd mistaken for the track, and shuddered despite the warm sunshine.

Then I suddenly remembered the strange man. I'd forgotten about him during the rest of my terrifying journey the night before.

Who was he? He'd nearly frightened me to death, especially with his scarred face and his questions, yet he had realised I was afraid and had tried to be kinder. Had *he* been scared? There had been *something* in his voice when he first called out. And I was sure someone else had been with him, slipping silently into the shadows almost before I'd known he was there. What were they doing in the woods above Witherstone?

After I'd been walking for a long time, the ground began to climb. The sun was still rising on my right and fairly high now, heading towards mid-morning as I climbed on. The hill became steeper and the forest trees grew closer and closer together, and I realised there were less birds singing and the lush mosses were left far behind, only a few plants here and there were struggling out of a thick dull carpet stretching on through the forest. The light seemed different, and the air was strangely still.

I stopped and looked back.

Stretching away down the slope and into the distance, the wild wood spread out as far as the eye could see, its leaves sighing in the breeze. I turned and looked into the grey silence of the forest above me. The trees were close-growing, their canopies high, blocking out the sun. Instead of leaves, long thin points lay like a dark hoar-frost along the stark branches. I knew this must be the pine forest.

I marked my route back down into the wild wood then turned back to face the dark forest, the air cool against my skin.

The pine trees stretched ahead of me into the grey shadows, and as I began to walk beneath them, a cold chill crept over me. The sun didn't shine in this part of the forest, and the shadows became steadily darker and cooler until it was as though the morning had turned to dusk. The air smelled dank, and it was almost completely silent, the almost imperceptible tread of my muffled footsteps the only sound. I realised I was holding my breath and let it out shakily. I looked around me and it was all the same, in every direction. It would be all too easy to get lost in this forest.

The thick mat of dead needles absorbed my footsteps as I searched the ground beneath the trees for the Devil's Cup. A chill crept across my neck. No, the *Ebony* Cup.

I looked behind me every few steps to make sure I was keeping as straight a direction as possible, but it was difficult to tell. The sun was blocked out by the pines, and the forest looked the same in every direction, grey trunks extending into the gloom.

I began to scuff my feet through the dead needles to make obvious footprints, and after a while I could make out the path I'd taken stretching faintly into the shadows behind me.

As I searched the grey forest floor beneath the still trees, I could see no sign of the Ebony Cup and began to feel that all-too-familiar panic stirring. I was losing all sense of time in that strange forest where nothing broke the monotony. I could see nothing in the shadows but the featureless grey carpet and my own dragged footprints fading away behind me. I walked faster, my eyes searching the shadows as my feet marked time into the forest floor. I knew there was no point in going back without the Ebony Cup. The old woman had said it was the most important thing of all.

I tried to stem the panic threatening to bubble over at any minute as the muted drag of my shoes and my breathing made the only sounds in the forest. Then suddenly I saw a movement out of the corner of my eye and jerked round to search the shadows.

What was it? A bird? I could see only trees stretching on and on into the gloom. But wait. Was that a splash of green, set among the grey monotony?

As I stared, every nerve taut and my breathing shallow, I realised I could see a face, pitted and creased with deep cracks from its rugged brows to its long beard. Below the face a withered body leaned, its arm resting on a thick staff. The figure was a gnarled tree stump, twisted with ivy, a brief swathe of green relieving the grey forest. It looked like an old man, standing in the gloom. And he was looking right at me.

Heart thudding, I stared. The more I stared, the more the tree stump looked like an old man, and the more he stared right back at me. My scalp tingled.

After several long minutes, staring into that ancient face, I finally looked away and into the forest around me. My footprints faded into the gloom, everywhere grey and shadowed - everywhere except the green figure to my left. I looked back at the rugged face. He was still looking right at me.

As I stared, irresistibly drawn to this one bright spot in all that grey, I became aware of something else. A black crow was sitting in the shadows just above the ancient face, on the lower branch of a pine tree. I looked at the bird. Could it be the old woman's crow? What had she called it? Master Nalgah?

I tried to call to the bird but my throat was dry and made no noise. After hesitating a moment, I left the path and walked slowly towards the crow and the crooked stump, looking from one to the other as I approached. I stopped a few feet away from the ancient face. I daren't go any nearer.

The gnarled stump was clearer now, and I could see the face very well. The rugged brow, ivy-shaded eyes, and the long crooked nose and face was dressed by a straggly beard of ivy. The arm and staff were fallen branches against which the trunk was gently leaning. But the face looked at me with deep-set eyes, and appeared almost to be smiling.

I swallowed, mouth dry. The crow suddenly cawed above me and I nearly jumped out of my skin. The bird was looking down at me. It must be the old woman's crow. I licked my trembling lips.

"Master Nalgah?" I said, but my voices was a dry croak, and I nearly laughed to think how I must have sounded more like the old woman than myself.

"Master Nalgah," I croaked again, "can you help me?"

The crow just looked at me, of course, and I began to feel stupid. After staring at the crow and he back at me, I looked at the ancient face once more. The weathered creases still seemed to be smiling benignly at me. I shook my head at my stupidity. I had failed to find the Ebony Cup and now I would have to turn back before I got lost in the forest.

Turning away from the ancient tree stump and the crow, I took one step then stopped and stared at the ground in amazement. A cluster of small, shiny black cups were right at my feet.

I gasped and crouched down to look more closely. Several black mushrooms with deeply scooped caps were pushing up from beneath the pine needles, and they were thick with a shiny, glutinous liquid. I must have stepped right over them when I walked towards the ancient figure.

I reached out to touch them then stopped, remembering what the old woman had said. I stood and walked sunwise three times around the cups, legs trembling, then faced the withered stump once more. It no longer looked like a benign face, friendly in the gloom, but an empty, weathered old tree stump, dull and grey in the shade of the pines. The forest seemed cold and silent once more.

I looked up. The crow had gone and the shadows around me seemed darker.

Feeling panicky, I opened the leather pouch with shaking fingers and scraped the earth away from beneath the black cups without touching them, carefully lifting five of them, complete with fine tangled threads and bits of soil clinging to them. I dropped the cups into the pouch and tightened the cord, then, with a last glance at the dull tree stump, hurried back to the path, the hairs on the back of my neck prickling, and by the time I reached the path a moment later, I was running and slipping on the pine needles, following my footprints back through the pine forest as fast as I could.

Then I heard it. A twig broke behind me. I stifled a scream, wanting to squeeze my eyes tight shut, but knew that would be fatal on this treacherous forest floor as I hurtled through the trees at breakneck speed. My cloak snagged on twigs as I shot past, and a whine escaped my throat as I flew faster, terrified of unseen hands snatching at me as I ran. I didn't slow down as I went skidding down the slope towards the wild wood, its lush green undergrowth beckoning me back to the bright sunshine on the lower slopes of the hill. I felt a rush of relief as, skidding and tripping, I hurtled down the hill and into the wild wood once more.

Birds cried out in alarm as I shot through the trees. I ran deeper into the green forest, and only when the grey pines were far behind me did I finally stop running, doubled over with stitch and panting hard, my lungs burning. I leaned against a tree and tried to recover my breath.

Since I'd left home the night before, I seemed to have spent far too much time running away from things in the forest. I daren't look behind me, my fear an echo of my nightmare. I knew it was stupid, but I was unreasonably afraid that if I looked over my shoulder I would see that silent figure stepping out of the trees behind me. But I had to look. There was no-one there, of course, just the green forest.

I retraced my path back to the old woman's house quickly, running when the way was clear enough, and arrived back at the clearing before midday. I was pleased to see the old woman's surprise when I lifted the mossy doorway aside and stepped down into the cave.

She hung up the rabbit she was in the middle of skinning and wiped her gory hands on her apron, looking at the full pouch at my waist.

"Sit ye'self down, Hephzibah," she said, "an' have a drink an' a bite to eat before ye' take on the bees."

I suddenly realised I had a raging thirst, strong enough to put the thought of the bees to the back of my mind for the moment, and I threw off my cloak and drank the water greedily, its peaty tang cool and delicious. As I leaned back against the wall, there was a flurry of wings and a familiar shadow appeared at the window.

"Ah, ye're back then, Master Nalgah?" the old woman said.

I looked at the crow hunched in the window, his eye looking back at me. He was black all over, including his beak and feet, but his bright bead of an eye was the blackest of all. His feathers were smooth and gleaming, but they glowed with a deep blue sheen where the sunlight caught them.

I reached my hand towards the crow who promptly pecked it, but it was a gentle peck, and after he delivered it he set his head to one side and looked at me with that bright eye. I knew for sure he'd been up in the pine forest, somehow showing me where to find the Ebony Cups.

The old woman picked a large woodlouse off the bark of the tree and gave it to the bird. He took it and was gone, the swoop of his wings the only sound he made as he flew up to his perch outside.

I untied the leather pouch, and the old woman placed her iron cooking pot on the table and watched me carefully empty the pouch into it, stooping to inspect the shiny black cups and roots without touching them. She nodded and placed the pot with the Ebony Cups gleaming inside into the centre of the table, where a beetle was scurrying across the stone. She had a twinkle in her eye when she looked back at me.

"Find 'em easy enough?"

I didn't know how to answer, sure she knew exactly what I'd been through to get the Cups. Finally, I just nodded, and the old woman's laughter wheezed around the tiny room.

"Ye'll do," she grinned, "ye'll do."

The old woman took a dark loaf out of an earthenware pot and placed it on the table. It was thick with green, powdery mould. I grimaced as I watched her cut the mould off the outside of the bread, placing the crumbling pieces onto the table. Then she cut a thick slice of the remaining bread and gave it to me to eat. It was sour and bitter, and I washed it down with plenty of the peaty water.

While I ate, the old woman took the candle out of the lanthorn, then stuffed handfuls of lichen and moss and small twigs inside and closed it. She held the match cord in the flames of her fire, then blew the glowing point before tying the cord around the handle, leaving the lit end hanging down on the outside.

"Ye'll need to put the match to the tinder when ye' reach the hive, but mind it doesn't flame up an' burn through. Ye' need to make it smoke as much as ye' can, Hephzibah, lettin' it blow all over the hive an' up into the entrance. That'll calm the bees so they'll let ye' take the Queen's comb."

I nodded, suddenly finding it difficult to swallow, and washed the last clog of bread down my throat with more water as the old woman went round the room picking up a bundle of things, including a battered broad-brimmed hat, a length of muslin, and her knife. Then she hobbled out of the cave, and I followed, avoiding the large beetle making its way outside with us.

The old woman gave me a canvas bag with a drawstring opening.

"When ye' come to the hive, put ye' hand inside the bag an' use it like a long glove while ye' reach in an' cut out the centre of the comb. An' if ye're quick, ye' can pull the bag inside out, trappin' the Queen's comb an' plenty of the bees inside."

I hung the bag across my shoulder and the old woman handed me the lanthorn and the knife, then she put the old hat on my head and wrapped the muslin round it.

"Once ye' reach the bees, light the tinder in the lanthorn an' get it smokin' well, then pull the muslin down over ye' face, tuckin' it into the front of ye' bodice. Move nice an' slowly around the bees, even if they sting ye'. Don't panic an' start flapping round else they'll get angry an' sting ye' even more. Cut out the middle part of the hive, makin' sure ye' get a big piece of the comb an' plenty of the bees in the bag an' tighten the string quick. If ye' get the Queen too, then all well an' good," she said, her eyes glittering.

She looked at me for a moment.

"Well, off ye' go, then," she said.

Legs trembling, I walked to the tree and looked up to where the hollow waited, high above my head. I looked over my shoulder but the old woman had already disappeared back into her shelter. She was good at that.

I stared up at the black dots of bees zooming in and out of the hollow, and tried to see the best way to climb up. The crow swooped up to a branch just above the hive and sat there, head cocked as he looked down at me. I hung the lanthorn on my wrist, keeping the lighted match away from my sleeve, and tucked the knife into my waistband. Pressing the hat firmly on my head, I hitched my skirts up over my knees and started to climb.

It wasn't the easiest tree I'd ever climbed. I had to cling to nothing but gnarls on the trunk at times. My arms and legs were quivering before I'd got even half way up. I climbed in a steady corkscrew round the tree until I was crouching on a thick branch just below the hollow.

The number of bees around me had increased. There were loads of them now, although they were still ignoring me and going about their business in and out of the hive just above my head. Holding tightly to the trunk, I stared in horror into the hollow. I could see now that it was so dark in colour because it was alive. A dark mass of bees covered the entire structure, endlessly moving.

Steadying myself against the trunk, I opened the lanthorn and blew on the match cord. The embers glowed and I pushed the match into the heart of the tinder inside and blew gently. As soon as it began to smoke, I took the match out and quickly closed the door to stop the draught of air. I watched anxiously, scared the tinder would burst into flames and be burnt out in just a few seconds. Smoke began to pour out of the gaps in the lanthorn, so I quickly pulled the muslin down across my face and tucked it inside my bodice, then held tightly to the trunk and reached into the hollow with the smoking lanthorn.

The grey coils quickly filled the hollow, swirling all over the bees. I slipped the knife out of my waistband, then opened the linen bag and put my hand in and pulled the bag up my arm like a sleeve. I gripped the knife through the canvas and tried to keep the steady stream of smoke pouring over the hive as I reached in and began to cut.

The buzzing changed in tone and the bees started flying around me, clearly agitated. I forced myself to reach further in, sawing the knife through the resisting wax to reach up towards the middle, cutting a broad arc and scooping the central comb down out of the hive. As I pulled my arm out it was alive with so many bees I couldn't even see the comb I was holding.

There were thousands of them, moving all over my hand and arm, and I was frozen for a moment and sick with panic. I quickly hauled the top of the bag down over the bees, smoke from the lanthorn half-blinding me, and as soon as my hand was free I tightened the drawstring and lowered the bag to hang at my side.

I felt the first sting on my wrist as soon as it was exposed to the open air, and had to steady myself against the reaction to pull away quickly. The sting was burning, and I was terrified that all the bees would begin stinging me. They were buzzing and flying and crawling everywhere, and some of them were battering themselves against the muslin over my face.

I remembered the smoke and brought the coiling tendrils closer to wash over the bees, pressing my shoulder against the trunk to try to maintain my precarious balance. But the smoke was thinner now, the tinder nearly used up, and still more bees were coming out of the hive, flying at me and crawling all over my arms and body. I felt another sting, and then another, and I wanted nothing more than to get away from the bees.

At that moment, the old woman's crow swooped down and landed on the branch next to me, and helped himself to several of the bees on my arms before flying away with a loud *kraaaak*.

I climbed back down the tree as quickly as I could, barely able to see past my skirts and the veil across my face, and the bees crawling and buzzing all around me. I didn't want to raise the muslin so I hitched my skirts out of the way as best I could and peered grimly through the veil as I climbed down. I had several stings now, my hands and arms throbbing painfully, feeling hot and stiff and making it even more difficult to hold on properly.

I practically fell the last few feet, the muslin ripping away from my face as I scraped down the trunk, trying to slow my descent. As soon as I hit the ground I was up and running towards the pool.

The old woman was already hurrying towards me with a smoking bundle of twigs and mosses, and she expertly removed the remaining bees from my arms and body, and inspected the stings.

"Come on, child, I've a salve for them stings," she said, hurrying me inside.

I sat there shaking while she dabbed a thick ointment on the stings. It smelled of honey and wild garlic, and the burning began to ease, and within half an hour the stings weren't anywhere near as bad. I was still trembling, and felt sick and incredibly tired. I'd been awake now for two days and a night, had walked – and run – for more miles that I could think, and had spent most of my time in a state of fear.

Arms still tight with the heat of the stings, I lifted the humming bag over my head and passed it to the old woman, then I collapsed back against the wall, physically and emotionally exhausted.

The old woman opened the bag beneath an upturned grass-weave basket, keeping her hand inside as she felt around the honeycomb. Her frown suddenly disappeared and she smiled as she carefully pulled her hand out of the basket, bringing a handful of honeycomb and surprisingly few of the bees. She put the honeycomb into a bowl and slid a flat slate beneath the upturned basket, which still contained the bag and the majority of the bees and honeycomb, then carried it outside. A few stray bees buzzed around the room then zoomed past me and out of the window.

The old woman reappeared again and her bony fingers began picking out the few bees still clinging to the sticky golden mass in the bowl, dropping them into a jar. There were three long cells on the comb which the old woman carefully opened, removing the white larvae then scraping the surprisingly pale, milky honey from these cells onto a dried leaf shaped like a tiny bowl. She then scooped out each of the smaller cells, adding the darker honey to the milky liquid.

I shuddered as she dropped all the larvae in the jar with the other bees, covered it with a scrap of muslin and put it back with her other storage jars. She moved the small leaf across the table, placing it close to where I was sitting by the window. I stared at the swirls of honey in the leaf, milky pale and dark gold, and felt waves of tiredness washing over me. The old woman spoke, her voice seeming unnaturally loud.

"Ye' can chop the Hemp Agrimony, Hephzibah, an' crush the Burdock root, but mind ye' keep them separate."

She gave me the knife and I wearily pushed myself away from the wall and chopped the Agrimony leaves with trembling fingers, and the old woman scraped the bright pieces into a small clay bowl and placed it on the table next to a long, thin white twig which looked like stripped willow.

I was so tired I was past caring whether the endlessly scuttling creatures were climbing into my clothes and hair as I crushed the Burdock root with a stone mortar and pestle on my lap, leaning against the wall behind me as I worked the pieces into a thick, fibrous paste. My head was throbbing and fuzzy now, yet everything the old woman was doing seemed to take on a strange intensity, every detail etching itself into my mind.

She scraped the mould she had taken off the bread onto a spoon, and placed the heaped powder on the table close to the fire. She scooped the crushed Burdock paste onto a flat stone which she placed next to a smooth brown pebble at the other end of the table, nearest to the hollowed oak. She poured water into a bowl and sprinkled a few drops onto the chopped Agrimony leaves before setting the bowl next to the leaves on the farthest edge of the table from me, halfway between the tree and the fire. It was almost like the old woman was setting places for guests.

She placed a handful of pale powder next to the honey-filled leaf close to me, then wiped her knife and placed it in the centre of the table, next to the iron cooking pot.

Inside the pot the Ebony Cups gleamed as though lit by their own light. The old woman lit the five wax candles Grandma had packed, placing each candle next to each of the ingredients arranged on the stone table. She held the flame of one candle to the small pile of powder next to me for a few moments, and it began to smoke. I could smell Rosemary and bitter Wormwood, and something else. A pungent smell which reminded me of the pine forest.

As the old woman lit the candles, all the light in the room seemed to be drawn into the table's rough circle, despite the bright sunlight streaming through the window. The surrounding walls melted away into the shadows and the candles drew my eyes to their flame, and I stared at them, unblinking.

The old woman turned towards me.

"Well, are ye' stayin', or are ye' goin'?"

I turned to look at her. My head felt heavy, and the pungent aroma of the incense drifted around me.

"But – but I can't go 'til you've made the cure for Catherine."

The crow's shadow suddenly filled the room as the bird appeared at the window, seeming to make the candlelight brighter still, then he hopped past me onto the table. I looked at the crow, and at the old woman's black eyes.

"Well then," she rasped as I remained slumped against the wall, "ye're stayin' then, I take it," and her ancient face grinned humourlessly. "Touch nothin', an' say nothin' - an' ye' can't leave, no matter what ye' think ye' may see or hear."

Then the old woman picked up the knife, hobbled over to face the hollow trunk of the oak tree, and began to mutter a strange incantation.

1

Master Nalgah

I realised with a shock that the old woman was indeed a witch, and my body went cold. I wished I'd realised what she'd meant about me leaving. I thought she'd meant having to set off back home to Witherstone, not leaving her dank cave while she – while she did *this*.

The witch had finished her incantation towards the hollow oak and was now walking round the table, the knife held outwards and pointing at the ground, her lopsided gait echoing my erratic heartbeats as she made an ungainly circle round and round the room. Her hoarse voice was still muttering a rhythmic pattern of words which made no sense at all. It was like hearing another language.

The light from the candles seemed to burn brighter as the old woman's shadow moved across me. I shrank back against the wall as she passed.

After three hobbled circuits of the stone table, the crow and I watching her progress round the tiny room, the old woman's chanting fell silent. Then she walked round the table more slowly, stopping at each of the ingredients and turning outwards with raised hands as though offering a gift.

She began next to me, cupping the smoke from the incense in her hands and releasing it into the air while muttering. This time I thought I heard her scratched voice say, *"Blesséd Air an' Guardian Spirit, Hail an' welcome."*

The fragrant smoke seemed to hang in the air, forming a long swirl which moved gently in the spring breeze coming in the window, caressing my cheek as it stirred before me. The witch moved on, raising the candle before the fire and muttering, and the flames brightened and sparks and grey smoke came billowing out into the room. She moved to the water, sprinkling drops from the bowl and casting a tall rainbow shimmer in the air, and as she raised the brown pebble at the head of the table, the shadows in the hollow of the tree seemed to stir in the flickering candlelight. In the centre of the table, a millipede coiled itself round and round one of the legs of the pot as it began to climb.

The witch turned, placed her knife back on the table and her voice rasped, unmistakably clearly,

"The Circle is cast."

I was terrified, but unable to tear my gaze away.

The witch picked up the slender willow twig and the crow hopped up onto the rim of the iron pot, his feathers sleek with a bluish light.

The old woman reached above the crow with her scrawny arm, pausing for a brief moment, then began to chant once more as she drew the twig down from the air towards the incense and briefly touched the swirls of light and dark honey close to me. Without pausing, she moved across to touch the chopped Agrimony, moving straight on towards the tree and briefly touching the pulped Burdock root, then back across the table to brush through the bread mould near the fire, before finishing back in the air above the blue-black crow where she had begun.

She held the willow twig poised in the air for a few moments longer, still muttering her spell, and then the witch began the ritual once more, passing to each of the ingredients in turn, her chanting growing more insistent, hoarse whispers filling the room. The rhythmic words and movements seemed to go on and on. Strangely, my terror began to lull and I started to feel like I was dreaming. Exhaustion washed over me, and the witch's voice filled my head.

The incense breathed its heady tendrils across my face, and the candlelight flickered. The crow's blue-black feathers glimmered and his beady black eye glinted, drawing my eyes into its depths as it seemed to grow larger and larger, filling the room. The wavering candlelight above his head shimmered like a golden crown. The shadows lengthened and he seemed to grow taller and taller, holding a gleaming sword in his hand. He pointed the sword upwards then down into the iron pot, touching the shining black cups inside, edged with silver. He opened his mouth and spoke with the old woman's voice.

"As above, so below. By fire an' water, by air an' earth, an' by that which binds an' holds them, I charge thee to banish the evil scourge, I charge thee to heal an' mend, binding spirit to body, an' body to spirit. So may it be."

The old woman was leaning over me. Her voice seemed to come from far away.

"Ha, she's sleepin'," she said.

I woke slowly, wondering where I was. Then I remembered as I found myself slumped against the wall of the witch's cave, my cloak thrown over me. Stiffly, I sat up, my head thick and muddled.

The candles had been snuffed out but still sat in their places on the table. I knew I couldn't have been asleep for more than an hour as the sunlight was still streaming in the tiny window and onto the far side of the stone table, where the witch was grinding the pestle in the iron pot. The crow was nowhere to be seen.

"Ye'll need a drink of water an' a bite of food, Hephzibah," she rasped, nodding towards a cup and a thick slice of bread on the table next to me.

Shakily, I drank the water and chewed the bread, unable to tear my eyes away from the witch's face, her black eyes glinting at me as she worked. I felt unrefreshed and more tired than I had ever been in my life, but the bread and water helped me to feel more myself and less dream-like.

The witch had emptied all the ingredients into the iron pot, and was pounding them together into a grey-black mash, and as she worked, her black-eyed gaze was on me all the while but she said nothing.

I watched her and thought about what had happened before I'd fallen asleep. Or had I dreamt it? And I thought about what Ellen had told me what felt like half a life-time ago, but had only been a few days earlier. Plucking up the courage to speak, I cleared my throat.

"Wh-what's your name?" my voice croaked nervously.

The old woman continued to stare at me for a while before she replied.

"Ann," she said, finally.

There was a moment's pause.

"Ann what?"

Witherstone

The old woman carried on pounding the mush in the pot.

"Just Ann."

"Are – are you Hannah Pendal's daughter?" I asked, before I could stop myself.

She stopped dead, her eyes unblinking as she stared at me, then she ground her gums together. They sounded as hard as teeth. I flinched as the old woman leaned forward, her black eyes glittering as they burned into mine.

"Yes, I'm 'er daughter."

Then she went back to her work, smiling in a strange, sly way.

I didn't dare ask her if it was true what Ellen had said – that Hannah Pendal and her daughter had killed the old Squire with witchcraft. The witch carried on mixing and pounding with the pestle, her black eyes still looking into mine and that half-mocking smile on her face.

I was too scared to say anything else so I just sat and watched her as she worked.

After a while she stopped pounding the mush and began to squeeze a thin, blackish liquid from the mixture into a small earthenware jar, crushing the pulpy mash with her bony fingers to get all the liquid out. When she'd finished, the only thing left in the pot was a dark, fibrous mush.

She wiped her hands on her apron, then unrolled a narrow strip of muslin and lit a candle at the fire, dripping hot wax all over the cloth then rolling it quickly and wedging it into the neck of the jar, dripping the hot wax on top of the cloth and the jar mouth to seal it, then she put the jar on the table to let the wax cool and set.

She spoke suddenly and I jumped.

"Ye' remember what I did with the pin?" she asked, pointing to my hand.

I nodded, swallowing.

"Well, ye' must do the same to ye' sister, here, here, an' here," she said, pointing to her heart, forehead, hands and feet.

"Just one drop, mind. It's powerful stuff so ye' need to take care. Make sure ye' drop the potion on after the blood stops, but before the hole closes. An' if she has the swellin' on her neck or anywhere else by the time ye' get home, ye' must pierce them too. Do this five times a day for three days. If she's still alive by then, ye' know it has done its work."

She leaned towards me.

"Be sure nobody sees ye' do it, mind, leastways nobody ye' don't trust with ye' life. An' tell no-one ye've been to see me or there'll be trouble for both of us. Now," she said, dismissively, "ye' must be on ye' way, Hephzibah. It'll be dark by the time ye' get back to Witherst'n, an' ye' must do one more thing before ye' get home."

She looked at me and grinned suddenly, her toothless gums bare.

"Ye' must go into the churchyard, to the dampest corner – the north corner is best – an' get a good handful of earth from a grave."

My eyes widened in horror but the witch carried on grinning, her mouth gaping.

"Make sure it's the clean earth below any weeds, but it *must* be from the grave. Ye' needn't dig *too* deep, mind, so don't worry," she mocked. "Take the soil home an' mix it with five parts good clean water, let it sit by the fire to warm through, then give ye' sister a cup of the water every day 'til she's well."

I felt sick and opened my mouth to protest, but then closed it again. I was in this way too deep. I knew I must do as the witch said. She picked up the small jar and passed it across the table. I took it with trembling hands and tucked it safely inside my bodice.

The witch gave me a shrivelled apple and a slice of bread. I put them in the bag, along with my cloak and Grandma's tinderbox, then I cleaned the lanthorn and set a candle inside, and made sure the match cord was smouldering before carefully lying it around the unlit candle and closing the lanthorn door.

"Ye' be sure to come back an' see me, if ye' ever need any help again, child," the witch said, then I followed her outside.

It was mid afternoon, and the bees glinted with gold light as they busied themselves among the bright flowers around the pool. I thanked the old woman and lifted my bag over my shoulder, looking for a moment into those glinting black eyes which seemed to be smiling, but whether with friendliness or mocking me I couldn't tell. Then I turned and walked past the dark pool to rejoin the stream where it emerged from the peat-black water. Here the stream was no more than a shallow trickle as it began its journey down to the river in the valley far below.

I looked back to where the witch was standing. The black crow was sitting on her stooped shoulder while she fed him insects, and two pairs of black eyes watched me as I tentatively raised my hand in farewell. The old woman nodded and I turned and walked into the trees.

Witherstone

Following the stream back down through the wild wood, I was amazed I'd found my way up there in the dark, with only the lanthorn and the light of the moon to help me. The forest was crowded with huge trees, tall, broad, and fallen amongst the thick brambled undergrowth. Only the stream, glinting now with sunlight, had kept me safely on track, and I shuddered to think of what would have happened if I'd lost this vital beacon in the dark.

Was it really only last night I'd made my way up to the witch's clearing? It seemed like half a lifetime ago. I checked that the small jar was still upright in my bodice, keeping the precious liquid safely inside.

I walked back through the wild wood quickly, weaving between the ancient trees as I followed the stream, desperate to get back to Catherine with the precious potion. An image of a bright red ribbon against her tiny wrist rose in my mind and I prayed I wasn't too late as I hurried towards home.

The sun moved steadily lower, turning the stream to gold as I followed it down towards the crags. The birds were in full voice, and none more so than the crows, flocking from one tree top to another in raucous mood. I wondered if Master Nalgah was among them.

The crows flapped and called across the deepening sky as I walked on through the wild wood, finally emerging at the top of the crags into the red-gold light. I walked carefully towards the edge, the stream urgent beside me now as it raced over the falls with a roar and tumbled out of sight into the gorge, the thunder of the waterfall rising up from its depths.

The world spread out before me looked very different beneath the radiant sky, which stretched on forever, a glowing mantle over a shadowy earth. The sun was setting and the valley darkening, but the sinuous coils of the river were blazing with gold. The shadows reached towards me as the sun sank beneath the earth, the fierce sky quickly fading to yellow then a strange, clear green, before moving into an eternal blue, darkening above and behind me towards the coming night.

With a sudden feeling of apprehension, I turned and quickly picked my way across the cliff top until I found the track down the side of the crags to the valley below.

It was almost fully dark beneath the trees by the time I emerged by the boulder at the foot of the falls, and the birds had fallen silent. I stopped to put on my cloak, the evening air chilly now, then carried on down through the woods as quickly as I could, though it was frustratingly difficult in the dark. My route up to the crags the night before had been lit by the moon, but it had not risen yet tonight.

I debated with myself whether to light the lanthorn, deciding against it for secrecy, but soon had to stop and light the candle as it was too difficult to make my way safely on the steep track.

The pale glow of the lanthorn cast its ghostly circle onto the trees around me, and I made better progress after that. It was a few miles yet before I would reach the woods behind the village, so I figured I should be able to use the lanthorn for most of the way down before I'd have to blow it out to avoid being seen. And the moon should have risen by then.

When I reached a certain steep part of the track, about half way down from the waterfall, I abruptly slowed, remembering that this was where I'd met the scarred man.

I was suddenly nervous and walked on quietly, eyes and ears straining for the slightest movement or noise. The night creatures of the forest were all around me, of course, and I refused to panic at their rustlings, but I couldn't escape the feeling that I was being watched again. But the small jar with its precious cargo bumping against my heart was strangely comforting as I moved at an almost reckless speed, and when I reached the bottom of the slope and passed into the woods stretching towards Witherstone Hall, I blew out the candle.

I made my way through Witherstone Hall Woods as quietly as I could, every nerve tingling. As I passed the back of the Hall its windows were staring towards me, dark and silent, and I was suddenly afraid I would see that face again, gleaming palely towards me through the dark, and quickened my pace.

At the edge of the Hall woods, I looked out across the meadow. The moon had risen, full and bright, but still low enough in the sky to mark out long black shadows across the grass. I hadn't forgotten what I needed to do.

I turned my back on the river and made my way up beside the stream towards the front gates of Witherstone Hall. Stopping at the corner, I looked carefully around, held the jar firmly to my heart and left the shadow of the woods. Darting quickly across the bridge, I dived across the corner of the moonlit meadow, crouching low as I ran to the churchyard wall. I paused there for a moment, heart pounding, before scrambling over the wall and dropping down into the graveyard.

I ran, bent low, towards the north corner then stopped, still crouching down, and strained my eyes into the gloom, looking for a suitable grave. Slowly my eyes scanned the shadows until I saw, in a damp and neglected corner, a tilted headstone leaning over a patch of nettles. I ran over and squatted down and began excavating the earth under the nettles, praying that the long-dead soul whose mortal remains lay beneath my trembling fingers would not take offence at my appalling act.

I was terrified of being found here. I knew that what I was doing was desecration. I scrabbled at the soil, scraping up enough to make a good handful and compressing it tightly into my hand.

As I shifted back onto my heels and raised my head, I gasped as I found myself face to face with a grinning skull, just inches from my face. It was carved into the gravestone, and its features were lit by the strengthening moonlight. For a moment it looked almost familiar, its bare, hollow-eyed grin echoing the face of the witch.

Sickened with fear, I started to pull the nettle roots back over the bare patch of ground to hide my crime, but then I stopped dead. I had heard a noise behind me.

Scarcely breathing, I turned my head. The moon had risen higher in the sky and I was no longer in shadow, the details around me were clear in the silver light. I knew my crouching form would be easy for anyone to see, but I could see no-one else in the graveyard, and the only sound was the gentle rustling of the leaves in the trees. Then a man emerged from the church door.

I daren't breathe as the figure slipped quietly into the shadow below the church tower. I could barely make out his outline as he merged into the dark, but I was terrified he would see me in the strengthening moonlight. A moment later, a second figure came out of the church, putting on a broad-brimmed hat as he joined the first man. His tall figure made him look for a moment like Parson Burnett, but I realised from his build that he wasn't the clergyman, and slowly released my breath.

The two men stood in muttered conversation, and endless moments passed as I crouched by the grave, scarcely breathing, the handful of earth clutched tightly in my fingers. I stared at the two figures in the shadows, trying to make out who they were and praying that they wouldn't see me.

Both men looked towards the lychgate and I thought for a moment they would leave, but they seemed to be arguing, even though their voices were nothing more than a faint murmur. The first man shook his head urgently and tried to grab the second man's arm, but his companion pulled away and walked purposefully towards the gravestones nearest the church door and stooped close, as though reading the inscriptions.

Clearly not finding what he was looking for, he moved on to the next gravestone and then the next, making his way quickly along the row of graves and then stepping across the grass to the next row, moving steadily closer to where I was crouching among the nettles, rigid with terror.

After a few moments, the first man left the shadow of the church and joined his companion, moving on to the next row to examine the headstones there. I realised they must be looking for a particular grave. Perhaps the second man had been praying in the church – or looking at the gravestones inside, perhaps. But those buried inside the church are eminent people, not the ordinary village folk whose remains lie in the graveyard. The Sylvestre family vault is inside the church. I know which one it is, even though I can't read the inscriptions, because it has a magnificent monument carved from pale stone, glowing with a ghostly light in the gloom of the church. A Sylvestre Squire from long ago lies silently beside his wife, holding a long sword and a shield across his chest – Richard used to admire the Knight when he was younger, stealing in to stare at the long sword whenever he had the opportunity.

I was always more drawn to the silent form of the long-dead Lady Sylvestre, her carved face as smooth as a living cheek although ice cold to the touch, and her expression sad as her blind eyes stared at the beamed roof of the church as though longing to see the sky.

I mentally shook myself, amazed I was practically day-dreaming whilst crouching there in terrible danger. Living on my nerves for the past days and nights without sleep was clearly affecting me.

The men had moved away from me and back towards the church as they worked their way along the graves. The moon was slowly dissolving the shadows, and once they reached the end of the row they would move on to the next and make their way back towards me. I knew that if I didn't move right now, they would certainly see me on their way back.

I knew my only chance was to creep backwards through the nettles and hide behind the leaning gravestone, in the shadow of the churchyard wall. My legs had begun to cramp, even while I was trembling from head to toe, and I began to edge myself back slowly, still clutching the grave earth in my hand.

I'd barely moved when suddenly one of the men bounded across the grass towards me, grabbing my wrist and yanking me to my feet. I gasped with pain and terror, and saw with a shock that it was the scarred man from the crags. I was looking up at him in bright moonlight once more.

I struggled, trying to pull my arm away, but his grip tightened and he grabbed my other wrist as I tried to free myself.

The man recognised me and seemed shocked, but then his eyes turned to anger and his grip tightened.

"*Who are you?*" he asked in a hoarse whisper.

I couldn't speak. I was terrified. The other man had frozen to the spot where he was, his face beneath his hat in deep shadow.

"*Answer me!*" the scarred man hissed, his fingers digging into my wrists and his face moving threateningly towards me. I looked back at him, my whole body trembling in terror.

"I-I'm j-just Eppie. Eppie Creswell."

"Well, 'just' Eppie Creswell, why are you following us? *Who sent you?*"

"N-no one sent me. I'm – I'm – just -"

I stopped. What could I say? I'm just stealing earth from a dead man's grave because a witch told me to use it for a Plague cure? That would be incredibly stupid. I would be hanged for witchcraft. But at that moment the man realised

I held something in my hand and twisted my arm round so that the moonlight shone onto my clenched fingers.

"*What's this?!*" he hissed, then he gasped and held my hand away from himself, staring down at the disturbed grave beside us but keeping his fingers gripped tightly around my wrists so I couldn't run.

"*It's somethin' from this grave!*" he said, his voice horrified.

I struggled to free myself but the man's grip was like iron.

"Let me go!" I gasped. "*Please!* I'm doin' no harm!"

Suddenly a black shadow flew between us, flapping and screeching, and the man cried out in fear, releasing my wrists as he raised his hands to protect himself, and I ran.

I reached the graveyard wall in moments and scrambled over it, dropping onto the grass and running pell-mell across the moonlit meadow towards the river.

I was still clutching the handful of earth in one hand and holding the jar in my bodice as I ran, the sound of the bird's loud caws retreating behind me. I darted a glance over my shoulder to see if the second man was following me, but saw no-one. I kept running, flying across the meadow towards the boats on the riverbank and diving into the shadows between two of them, then crouched there, panting and shaking as I looked back towards the churchyard.

The cries of the bird had stopped and the graveyard was eerily silent. Then, thudding heartbeats later, I saw two shadows steal quietly over the wall and drop into the meadow. I tensed, ready to pull a boat onto the river if necessary, but the two figures, crouching over as though not wanting to be seen themselves, ran alongside the wall away from me towards Witherstone Hall Woods.

I watched them until they crossed the stream and disappeared into the trees, then I turned and made my way quickly along the shadowed riverbank in the opposite direction, towards the track and home. I desperately wished I was already there. Safe.

Once I reached the point where the track began to move away from the riverbank, I crept up into the shadow of the trees and waited, hardly daring to breathe, and looked over towards the woods where the two men had disappeared. I scanned the tree-line down to the river, listening intently. I could see no-one and hear nothing – nothing but the yelp of a fox deep in the woods behind Witherstone Hall. There was no movement in the trees, no sign that the men were waiting for me to show myself.

But the shadows in the woods were dark and easy to hide in, waiting, watching. So I stayed put, watching the shadows, and all the while my mind was rushing over what had happened in the graveyard and I felt sick, cursing myself.

Why did I tell him my name?

Both times I'd met the scarred man I could have lied, but instead I'd told him how to find me. *Idiot.*

Suddenly I saw something and my heart lurched. A shadow moved on the churchyard wall. Then it grew larger, coming towards me at great speed, and I realised it was the crow, flying on silent wings. The shadow swooped and the bird landed on my shoulder, his claws gripping me through my cloak. I turned my head awkwardly to see him.

His black eyes glittered in the moonlight as he regarded me, and I lifted a trembling hand and stroked the crow. His feathers were smooth, firmer and sleeker than hen feathers. I smiled, realising I had been watched during my journey back down from the wild wood after all.

"Thank you, Master Nalgah," I whispered, shakily, wishing I had a fat, juicy spider to give to him.

The crow pecked my fingers gently, then he took off and flew across the meadow towards Witherstone Hall Woods and was gone. As soon as his shadow disappeared into the trees, I ran out of my hiding place and onto the track towards home.

8

Home

I almost fell into the cottage, bursting through the door so fast I staggered. The room was a frozen tableau of shock, my father and brother turned towards me from their stools by the fire, Dad half risen, and Mum and Grandma staring open-mouthed from the bed where they were tending Catherine.

I was flooded with a mix of emotions. Relief that Catherine was still alive, surprise that my family were not sleeping at this late hour, and fear that my sister's fragile state of health was why everyone was still up. I darted over to the bed and my fear was confirmed. Catherine was alive but she lay very still, her eyes closed and her skin flushed, and she had grotesque, bruised swellings on her neck, lifting her face up strangely.

I threw my bag to the floor, feverishly groping for the small jar in my bodice. As I began breaking the wax from around the top of the jar, using my teeth as well as my free fingers, I realised the grave soil was still clutched in my other hand.

I abandoned the potion jar on the table momentarily, grabbing the water jug and clumsily pouring some of its contents into a bowl on the table until I judged I had about the right amount left in the jug to make up the five parts needed for the soil. I dropped the compressed earth into the jug, using the soiled hand to break it up and mix it round quickly.

"This water's for Catherine, so leave it for her – she's to have a cup full every day," I said, placing the jug by the fire before darting back to the table.

My father had picked up a knife and cut the wax from the jar, and he silently passed the jar to me. I pulled out the stopper and peered inside. The black liquid glistened in the firelight. I ran to the bed.

"A needle!" I realised. "I need a needle!"

Grandma moved quickly, rummaging on the high shelf then passing me a needle, and Dad strode over to close the cottage door before coming to the bed. Mum moved over to allow me to sit beside Catherine, clearly relieved to see me, but I could see from her expression that she would have something to say to me later for disobeying her.

But I was less worried about that than the fact that Mum looked pale and exhausted. She looked ill. I felt a jolt of fear as I tore my eyes away from her face and leaned over my sister.

I shakily pressed the point of the needle against Catherine's burning forehead. When I took the needle away again I hadn't even broken the skin. This was impossible. How could I deliberately injure my own sister?

I looked at my family around me, Richard having joined the group around the bed, all of them watching me silently. Grandma's lips were tight and thin, and Mum was pale. My brother's face was impassive. Then I looked up at Dad. He looked sickened and afraid, and wouldn't meet my eyes.

Whether that was because of Catherine's illness or his fears about what I was doing, I couldn't tell.

Taking a deep breath, I pressed the needle harder into my sister's forehead. A bead of blood appeared. I quickly wiped it away and looked closely at the pin-prick. I wiped away another bead of blood, and another, then the final red dot, and I leaned closer, the jar trembling in my hand, and poured a shaky splash of the black liquid onto the tiny puncture wound.

It was too much, and I quickly wiped the excess liquid from my sister's face. I pricked her hand with the pin firmly, wiping away the beads of blood then dipping the needle into the jar and allowing a small drop of the witch's potion to fall from the point into the wound before it closed. I did the same thing to her other hand, and then over her heart.

When I turned my attention to the grotesque swellings, dark and bruised, on my sister's neck, I felt sick. The liquid which oozed from the puncture wounds was not clean blood and I shuddered. Silently, Mum uncovered Catherine's arms and I was appalled to see the growths in her armpits, and I pierced those too.

Once I'd dripped the precious ointment everywhere the witch had told me to, I sagged suddenly, utterly exhausted. I had done what I needed to do. I passed the jar and the needle to my mother and lay down next to my sister on the bed, falling asleep almost instantly.

When I woke up the next day, I found everything almost exactly as it had been when I'd returned home in the night. Mum and Grandma were nursing Catherine, and Dad and Richard were sitting brooding by the fire. My father's face was angry, and he still refused to meet my eyes. Richard looked warily at me, his expression difficult to read.

I got out of bed shakily, still exhausted, and took the needle and the witch's potion and pierced my sister's skin once more, dripping the precious fluid into each wound. I poured a cup of the water from the jug by the fire, the soil dark and murky as it shifted in the bottom, and passed the cup to Mum for Catherine.

Mum was trembling as she eased my sister into the crook of her arm, and she tipped the liquid into Catherine's unresponsive mouth bit by bit until the cup was empty. She passed the cup back to me with a thin smile, and, as I placed it on the table, I saw that someone had been down to the river to fill another jug with fresh water for the rest of the family to use.

I also realised that, apart from myself last night, no-one had said a word since I had come home.

For the rest of that day and the next, the whole focus of the cottage seemed to be concentrated on what I was doing for my sister, and on not talking about it.

The only thing which distracted my own attention was my growing concern for Mum. It was clear that she was ill, and that she was refusing to give in to the illness.

By the time Grandma had prepared a stew with the dwindling supplies of food the second day after I'd got back, I could see that Mum was losing the battle, her shoulders drooping as she leaned heavily over the table, barely touching her food. After sitting like that while everyone else ate their meal, our eyes silently on her hunched form, Mum sighed and went and lay down next to

Catherine. My father pushed away his bowl and leaned over the table, his face in his hands, his position echoing that of Mum's just moments earlier.

When I'd administered the next dose of the witch's potion to Catherine, I turned hesitatingly towards Mum. After meeting my gaze with resigned eyes, she smiled weakly and held out her hand for the needle. I heard Dad walk out of the cottage, closing the door behind him, and felt the anxious eyes of my grandmother and brother on me as I set to work.

All the next day, Grandma and I tended to Catherine and Mum. Dad couldn't bear to linger in the cottage and spent most of the morning out setting traps for rabbits. It had been days now since he and my brother had been sent home from Thompson's after the yeoman blamed them for his sons being ill, so in the afternoon they went back up to the farm to ask about returning to work. The food situation was becoming desperate, and Dad knew he must swallow his pride if we were to eat.

They returned several hours later, tired but with food. Thompson was now ill himself, and Mistress Thompson had asked my father and brother to resume their work. At least we would be able to buy food again.

Grandma made a hearty soup for that evening, careful rationing no longer such a desperate necessity, but it was hard to be hopeful when the two sick family members were unable to eat any of it, in spite of our best efforts. I felt a terrible sense of dread, and when my eyes met my grandmother's I could see she felt exactly the same.

I had the nightmare again that night. I didn't know where we were, and this time only Richard was running beside me, with Catherine crying in his arms. Then suddenly the sky turned the colour of blood and they were both gone, and I found myself alone in the silent forest as our enemy stepped out of the trees.

When I woke in the morning I couldn't shake the nightmare away, and it sat around me like a cloak. It was Sunday, and Grandma set out to milk the goat and gather herbs as soon as it was dawn while I administered the potion to Mum and Catherine and gave them some of the graveyard water. Then when Grandma got back, she looked after them while the rest of us went to the church.

We had the pew to ourselves that morning, and other families seemed to be clustered together in little groups, everyone afraid of catching the Plague. Parson Burnett's pale eyes kept flickering towards us during his sermon, and I felt strangely chilled.

When we got back home, I took over at the sick bed while Grandma made a broth with the herbs, and Dad and Richard went to borrow Edward Cowper's boat to go fishing. This they would have to do furtively, with it being a Sunday, but they knew that Edward would be sympathetic to our situation.

I managed to coax my sister to sip some of the graveyard water, but Mum was too feverish to drink properly and most of the murky water in the cup was spilt. There wasn't much left but I quailed at the thought of having to go out and get more soil from the graveyard, and of course I wouldn't be able to get any more until it was dark anyway.

I helped Grandma to freshen the bed straw with some of the herbs she had picked, and we tried to coax Mum and Catherine into drinking the herbal broth. Catherine did sup a little of it, the first food she'd taken for days, even though she was not fully awake and soon slipped back into a deep sleep. I felt a tinge of hope as my sister's skin seemed less clammy, but we couldn't rouse Mum from her feverishness.

She was moving into the worst part of the fever, as ill now as Catherine had been when I'd set off to see the old woman in the wild wood. I checked the potion in the jar and was relieved to see we had plenty left. I just prayed it would do its work.

Early that afternoon, Grandma went back down to the river to refill the fresh water jug, leaving the door of the cottage open to let the warm spring air into the room. I administered the potion to Catherine first, dropping the needle into the jar before placing it on the floor next to the bed while I examined my sister's swellings. Did they seem to be smaller and less inflamed? And not so darkly bruised, perhaps? She was sleeping deeply, but I was sure her skin seemed cooler to the touch.

As I laid her hand back on the bed and turned to Mum, my grandmother suddenly flew into the cottage, her eyes wide with terror, and slammed the door behind her. I leapt to my feet. Grandma stood there for a moment, looking wildly around the room as though uncertain what to do.

"*What is it, Gran'ma?!*" I gasped, and my voice seemed to spur her into action.

She shot forward and dragged me across the room, shoving me onto the other bed and throwing a pile of blankets over me before spinning round to face the door just as it burst open and flew back against the wall with a crash which made the whole cottage shudder.

My face was not completely covered by the blankets and I could still see a part of the room with one half-exposed eye. I saw Grandma facing the door, shielding my body from the tall, black-cloaked figure who had appeared in the doorway.

Sunlight and shadow flickered, then a broad-brimmed hat was looming overhead as the figure strode into the room. I shrank back in terror as the intruder moved past my grandmother over to where my sister and mother lay on the other bed. I couldn't see his face. After a few moments of stilled silence, a paper-white hand reached down from the folds of the black cloak and picked up the jar containing the witch's potion from where I'd left it on the floor minutes before.

The intruder peered into the jar. My heart was beating with sickening thuds as the white fingers slowly drew the needle out of the black, glutinous liquid, and I heard a grunt of satisfaction as the figure straightened and turned back to face my grandmother.

"Hephzibah Smalley," said a smooth, sonorous voice I recognised instantly. "In the name of Almighty God, you are hereby accused of Witchcraft."

There was a stilled moment in which the world had lurched to a halt. Golden dust motes floated lazily in the sunlight as it streamed in through the doorway and there was a roaring in my ears. Then the dust-motes vanished as more figures stepped into the small cottage, and then they were gone, taking my grandmother with them.

I stared at the empty doorway for several long moments in a kind of dazed horror, then I threw off the blankets and ran out of the door. As I ran through the gate and into the lane, I could see Grandma being walked down towards the village, her arms held tightly by the men either side of her.

Ahead of my grandmother, the tall figure of Parson Burnett strode purposefully on, his black cloak billowing out behind him.

When my father and brother returned later that afternoon, carrying a good catch of fish, their raised spirits evaporated immediately at the sight of my face. With a cry, Dad reeled past me over to Mum and Catherine on the bed. When he found his worst fears unrealised, that my mother and sister were still alive, he pulled me round to face him.

"What is it? What's the matter, Eppie?"

I looked at Dad, and he looked back at my stricken face. How could I tell him? He pulled me tightly to him for a moment, then held me at arms length, stooping a little to face me as he shook my shoulders gently, encouraging me to speak.

"Eppie?"

Then I told him what had happened. As I spoke, my father's face froze. He let go of me, his arms dropping to his sides as he stood up straight, and his lips tightened as he looked at me. When I'd finished speaking, he turned and walked out of the cottage. Without a word to me, Richard ran after him.

Before half an hour had passed, they both returned. Richard came in and leaned against the wall by the door staring at me, while my father threw his hat and cloak into the corner of the room and strode to the fire. He stood there with his back to me.

"Your gran'ma has been taken to Hawbury gaol to await trial. It seems she was seen in the meadow behind the churchyard gatherin' herbs early this mornin'. In the company of a large black crow. It was sittin' on her shoulder, an' she was talkin' to it."

He swung round to look at me. My eyes flicked to Richard's impassive face then back to my father.

"That – that – *foul potion* you brought back for Catherine, an' the needle, has given them all the evidence they need. An' worst of all," Dad went on, "a grave has been desecrated in the churchyard. God knows *what* has been taken from it. They think *she* did it."

I stared back at him wordlessly. This was all my fault. I should have hidden the potion. I should have made sure I left the grave as I found it. And telling the scarred man my name was the worst thing of all. Stupid. *Stupid*.

"Is that what *this* is?!" Dad roared suddenly, pointing to the nearly-empty jug of murky water.

Shocked at his sudden rage, I nodded and began to cry in gulping sobs. My father stared at me grimly for a few moments, then he picked up the jug and walked out of the cottage. I heard the smash on the cobbles of the yard a moment later, and then the sound of my father striding through the gate and away down the lane. Richard looked away from me as he moved over to the fire and sat down, staring sullenly into the flames, and I hated him for not comforting me as I wept.

The next morning, Dad and Richard left for Thompson's farm without a word to me. Richard glared at me before they left, but Dad couldn't even bring himself to look at me.

I sat helplessly on the bed next to my mother and sister for most of the day, unable to do anything to help them other than try to persuade them to eat. I had nothing else to offer them. I collected the eggs but daren't go down to milk the goat, and felt bad for her discomfort. I was too scared to go out. Numbly, I gutted and filleted the fish and hung them over the fire to smoke.

I was able to rouse Catherine enough to drink a little of the soup as she had the day before, but then she lay still, sleeping deeply, for the rest of the day. There was no doubt that her swellings were smaller, but Mum was worse. Her face was clammy and flushed, and her half-open eyes stared into nothing. Dad had leaned over her before he left for Thompson's, stroking first her cheek and then Catherine's, then he had turned on his heel and strode out of the door as I crawled out from beneath my blanket.

By that afternoon I could see the swellings beginning on my mother's neck, and I cried with helpless anger. I could do nothing to help her. Or Grandma. I couldn't bear to think about what my grandmother must be going through in Hawbury gaol. Or what was going to happen to her.

I tried to block out the horrible images Ellen had conjured when she'd told me about the witch who had been hung and then her body burnt in the village, but they just kept coming and my mind whirled with the horror of it. Hannah Pendal.

I almost laughed, bitterness rising like bile. I had brought this trouble onto us all by going to see that very witch's daughter! No matter that it had been Grandma's idea. It was my stupidity which had put my grandmother in mortal danger. I had left the potion and needle out where it was easy to find. I had left the grave disturbed and, worst of all, I had told the scarred man my name. My *name!* How could I be so stupid? And now Grandma -

I couldn't bear to finish the thought. It was too horrible. What could I do? How could we prove her innocence without just putting me – and the witch - in gaol with her?

As I sat there, the horror washing over me, I got to the point where if I really thought a confession would help, I would have done it, but all I could see coming out of that would be more people in the gaol. And Dad and Richard could be dragged into it too, then there'd be no way of helping Grandma at all. Not that I could think of anything I could do to help her anyway.

My thoughts just kept going round and round in circles. The bottom line was there was no way out of this horrible situation whichever way I looked at it.

When Dad and Richard came home from Thompson's they were both wet through and cold. I hadn't realised it was raining. Dad put a few vegetables onto the table, along with bags of oats and rye flour, then he sat on the bed next to Mum and Catherine while I cooked the evening meal.

Dad and Richard sat and ate their tea in silence while I banked up the fire to warm the room and dry their clothes, then Richard went out to chop wood for the fire. While he was outside, I tried to speak to my father.

"Dad?"

Silence.

"Dad? *Please?*"

He sat staring into the fire, unmoving. When Richard came back in with a pile of wood in his arms, my father turned to him.

"You'll need to go to Thompson's on your own tomorrow, Richard. I'll have to see if I can borrow Edward's boat again an' go down to Hawbury. Your Gran'ma will need some food, an' a blanket, an' I'll have to pay the gaoler extra for what she's had in the meantime."

Richard nodded, but he looked shocked.

I stared, open-mouthed. I hadn't realised that Grandma wouldn't be able to eat unless we provided the food. Or that we had to pay for her imprisonment. I must have made a sound as Dad's eyes flickered across me, but before I could speak he took his hat and cloak and left the cottage, a cold wind blowing into the room as he closed the door behind him.

After I'd managed to feed Catherine a little soup, she went straight back to sleep, then I tried to persuade Mum to drink some but I couldn't rouse her. She was feverish, and seemed not to know who I was. I bathed her face and neck and arms to try to bring down her fever, and her face blurred as I looked at her lying there, the tears running down my cheeks. The sheer powerlessness of the situation made me angry, and I scrubbed the tears away roughly with my sleeve.

I turned and saw my brother watching me. We looked at one another for a few moments, then he spoke to me for the first time in days.

"So. Where did you go, Eppie? Mum was nearly hysterical an' shoutin' at Gran'ma when we found you'd left in the night, but neither of them would say where you'd gone."

Before I could answer, he went on, "Though I suspect Dad had a pretty good idea because he suddenly stopped askin' an' stared at Gran'ma, an' just said *"You didn't?"* An' when she just looked right back at him without sayin' a word, he swore at her an' shouted that she'd signed your Death Warrant."

He looked at me, waiting.

I swallowed. I didn't know where to start. Or how much it was safe to tell him. For his own sake.

"Gran'ma sent me to see – someone – to get stronger herbs than she knows about. That's all it was, Richard," I pleaded, stung by the expression on his face. "Herbs, an' honey, an' – an' mushrooms an' bread mould, all mixed up together."

"But why the needle? An' what about the *grave?* Did you – take – you know, *remains* - from the grave?"

I shook my head.

"No. It was just earth. *Honest.*"

I could see he didn't believe me.

"It *was*. Just *earth*. I don't know why the wi– the *woman* I went to see thought it might help, but -"

I looked down at Catherine and Mum. "I didn't know what else I could do. Gran'ma thought the – the old woman might know of a cure," I finished, lamely.

He looked at me.

"You were goin' to say 'witch'."

"No. No, I was goin' to say 'woman'."

My brother stared at me for a long time. I knew he knew I was lying.

"Who was it?" he asked, quietly.

"I can't tell you."

His eyes hardened, and my brother turned away to the fire. He didn't look at me or speak to me again all night. As I carried on bathing Mum's face to try to cool her fever, I tried not to let my burning eyes give way to tears again, but I was shaking, even though I knew that Richard's blaming me was more than justified. After I'd got enough control over myself, I got up to sort out some food for Grandma.

After I'd finished, I rolled her cloak and blanket together as tightly as I could and stuffed them into the bottom of the bag with the food. I would wrap up some of the smoked fish for her too in the morning.

Dad came home long after Richard and I had blown out the candle and gone to bed. He was unsteady on his feet, and I knew he had been to the Inn. After sitting staring into the fire for some considerable time, he lay on the bed beside my mother and sister. I don't think he got to sleep for a long time.

In the morning, Richard set off for Thompson's just before dawn as usual, while Dad sat brooding by the fire until it was daylight.

Once it was light enough outside, Dad picked up the bag I'd packed for Grandma without a word, pausing only to kiss Mum's forehead and Catherine's before he left. I went to the gate and watched him heading towards the river, so I knew he must have borrowed a boat at least. That way he should be able to get to Hawbury and back before night-fall with no trouble, as long as the river was fair. It wasn't raining but the sky was heavy with clouds, and the wind was very cold.

Late in the night Mum had become very restless, moaning and disturbed, but when I got up to see to her, Dad had glared at me and I saw he was trying to persuade her to take some water from a cup. I watched from my blanket as he tended to her, persisting long after it was obvious she wouldn't take it, unable to co-operate in her delirium. He cooled her burning skin with a damp cloth and then he lay down again, cradling her in his arms.

After Dad had left for Hawbury, I tended to Mum as best as I could, but it was hopeless. She was sicker than ever, and the swellings on her neck were grotesque and black. She writhed and moaned, her flushed and bruised skin covered with a sheen of sweat, and there were small open wounds beginning to appear on her skin, glistening and bloody and round like coins.

Catherine lay still beside her. My sister slept pretty much all the time, but her swellings were smaller, the bruises fading. Sometimes she would wake enough to take a little water or soup but she stared at me strangely each time, as though unsure where she was or who I was, before she would fall back into a deep sleep. Mum's moaning and constant restlessness didn't seem to disturb her at all.

I realised I couldn't leave the goat for another day without being milked, so once I'd done what I could for Mum and Catherine for the time being, I took two jugs down to the meadow, one for fresh water, the other for the goat's milk. The goat was in a bad mood as she was obviously uncomfortable, so it was really hard work, but I managed eventually. I was relieved that I didn't see anyone else on the meadow and hurried back home.

I left the jugs under the bench by the door and went into the cottage. The first thing I saw was my mother on the floor.

"*Mum!*" I screamed, and ran over to her.

She was gasping and holding her belly, then she stiffened and groaned for a really long time before she seemed to almost collapse completely. I tried to lift her back onto the bed but I couldn't manage it, and then the next moment she stiffened again, her hands holding her swollen belly, and she groaned and groaned before collapsing back to the floor.

Then she seemed to come to herself for a few moments, more aware than she had been for days. She looked into my eyes, her hand on my arm.

"*The baby!*" she said. "Get your Gran'ma, Eppie."

Then she was groaning again, her eyes rolling up into her head as she struggled.

"Gran'ma isn't – Gran'ma can't come yet. What shall I do?" I asked her. "Mum? *Mum?*"

But she couldn't answer. She had collapsed back down again, and was moaning incoherently. I stood there, not knowing what to do.

How could she have the baby when she was so ill? She was too poorly. And surely it was too early?

I barely remembered Catherine being born, but then Mum had Grandma with her – and Mum hadn't been ill. I groaned aloud, wishing Grandma was here. She would know what to do. I knew I needed help.

I leaned over her, sweeping her hair away from her face.

"I'll go an' get help, Mum. I'll be as quick as I can."

I turned and ran out of the cottage and down the lane to the village. I was nearly hysterical by the time I reached the Parson's house and was hammering on the kitchen door. Ellen opened the door looking alarmed, and then shot back with a cry.

"You shouldn't be here, Eppie!"

"Mum's havin' the baby – an' she's ill. She needs help!"

Ellen shook her head.

"I can't, Eppie. The Mistress wouldn't allow it. Not after your Gran'ma -. An' especially if your Mum's ill too. We might catch the Plague!"

My face crumpled as I began to cry.

"*Please!*" I mouthed, "*please!*"

She shook her head again.

"I'm sorry."

Then she shut the door.

I stood on the step staring at the door and close to screaming. I got control of myself and whirled round and ran back to the lane, then stood looking at all the houses in the village, struggling to know where to turn for help. Ellen had been my best bet.

I started running towards the far end of the village, to see if Alice was home. I knew they often took Job's fish to Hawbury on market days so I might just be wasting time. I hammered on the door of their little cottage and then flung it open, but the room was empty. I groaned and reeled away, trying to think of who else I could try. Perhaps Mary Fordham at the mill would help. She was a sour and miserable woman, and never seemed particularly friendly to us, but I had to get help from somewhere.

I started running, but before I got even half way down the lane, I stopped dead. An overwhelming feeling rushed over me and I knew I needed to get back. I could feel the seconds ticking away and knew I shouldn't have left Mum. She needed me with her. Then I heard quick footsteps behind me and turned to see Adam running towards me.

"What's happened, Eppie?"

It felt so good to see a friendly face but I didn't see what he could do. I told him about Mum being ill and the baby coming.

"And Ellen won't come?"

I shook my head. "Then I tried Alice, but she isn't home."

Adam was shaking his head, confirming my fear.

"They're at Hawbury Market."

He hesitated a moment, then leaned forward and whispered.

"That – that potion my father took from your grandmother. If – if I could get some of it back for you, would that help?"

I stared at him and swallowed. "It might help her with her illness, but the baby - ?"

He nodded. "Go back to your mother, Eppie, I'll see what I can do but I may not be able to help. Do you want me to send up to Thompson's for your father?"

"He's not there." I looked Adam in the eye. "He's at Hawbury. Takin' food to my Gran'ma."

Adam's expression was unreadable.

"Go home, Eppie. I'll send help if I can." And with that, he was gone.

I ran back home as fast as I could, but as soon as I entered the room, I could tell something had happened. It was too quiet. Mum was just where I'd left her, slumped on the floor next to the bed. And she held a tiny body in her arms. Neither of them were moving. With my heart dropping like a stone, I bent over my mother. As soon as I saw her face I knew.

"*No!*" I screamed, "*No!*"

A while later, there was a tentative knock at the door, breaking the silence. I couldn't be bothered to answer. I just carried on sitting on the bed. After my first hysterical screaming and choking, dry sobs, I'd managed to lift Mum off the floor and back onto the bed, the baby still in her arms. I'd checked them both, time and time again, but I'd known it was too late for either of them as soon as I saw them. So I'd cleaned up as best I could and sat there, staring at their peaceful forms as they lay next to Catherine.

My sister hadn't moved a muscle in all that time, despite the noise I must have been making earlier, but her chest was at least still rising and falling. A few moments after the knock, the latch lifted and Adam's voice whispered into the room.

"I'm sorry, Eppie. I tried to find the potion but my father has it locked away somewhere. Mother won't let Ellen come, and didn't want me to come here either, but I'll run down to fetch -"

He stopped as I turned towards him, shaking my head, and his expression changed as he looked at my face.

"It's too late." I said, and turned away from him.

I didn't hear him leave, but when I turned back a few minutes later, Adam had gone. He had latched the door very quietly. I don't know how long I sat there, but it was nearly dusk by the time I stirred, realising that Richard would be home soon, if not my father, and the fire was almost out.

I stoked up the fire and hung the pot of colourless soup on the hook. Then I went and sat on the bed again, unable to stay away. I sat there for an endless time. I stroked my mother's hand and smoothed her hair, and kissed the baby's cold cheek, pulling the blanket closer around him. Poor, tiny little thing.

After staring at their still forms for what seemed like an age, I pulled the blanket up and lowered it gently, covering their faces. I was startled when something stirred beside me and a small voice spoke.

"Mummy?"

Louder, panicky. "*Mummy?*"

I leaned over Catherine. Her eyes shone brightly up at me, and she smiled.

"Eppie!" she said, then louder, "*Eppie!*"

I lifted my little sister onto my lap. She put her arms around my neck and squeezed. I started really crying then, weeping and wailing out loud as the sobs shook me. Catherine giggled and squeezed me tighter. Did she think I was laughing? I couldn't speak for several minutes so I just let the tears come.

I felt Catherine wriggling herself out of my arms, though she continued to sit on my lap, but I kept my head bent, crying and crying, putting my face in my hands. After a long while my sobbing calmed, and I looked up to see Catherine staring at me, her finger in her mouth.

"Don't cry, Eppie," she said. Then she looked confused. "*Eppie!*" she almost shouted, and looked round the room. "*Where's Mummy?*"

I pulled her back into my arms.

"Mummy's sleeping, Catherine," I said, speaking into her soft neck. Then I shook my head at myself. That's not fair.

"Mummy's dead." I said.

Catherine struggled out of my arms, leaning back so she could see my face.

"*Where's Mummy?*" she shouted.

"She – she's dead, Catherine." I said. "She was poorly too, an' she died."

Catherine stared at my lips.

"WHERE'S MUMMY?!" she shouted again, glaring at me crossly.

I stared back at her, exasperated.

"Mummy's dead, Catherine. Do you remember what that means? Like when Master Fordham at the mill died last year? An' when Edward Cowper's dog died in the winter? After he was very poorly. An' Master Cowper buried the dog in the meadow. Do you remember?"

Catherine looked furious and she pulled at my lips, digging her fingernails into the flesh.

"*Stop it!*" she shouted angrily. "*Tell me! Where's Mummy?!*"

I pulled her fingers away from my face and started to speak to her again, telling her not to hurt me like that, but she stared at my lips again. She began to cry.

"*Tell me!*" she sobbed, "*tell me. Where's Mummy?!*"

I froze and stared at my sister in sudden horror.

"Catherine," I said, "*Catherine*. Look at me. Can you hear me? Can you hear my voice?"

She carried on staring at my lips, then looked at my eyes, then back at my lips.

"Why won't you tell me?" she whispered, her eyes full of tears. "Don't like this game."

I stared at my sister. Then I pulled her into my arms and began to cry again, but she pushed me away, folding her arms and glaring at me. I kissed my finger and pressed it to her mouth, then I turned Catherine around on my lap and pulled the blanket back so she could see Mum lying on the bed.

"Mummy!" she shouted happily, and tried to climb onto Mum, but I held her tightly.

"*Let go!*" she shouted, and wriggled out of my grasp.

She climbed onto the bed beside Mum and leaned forward to touch her face.

"Mummy! Mummy? *Wake up!* Time to get up, Mummy. *Oh!*"

She stopped. "*A baby!*"

She gently touched her baby brother's face, then turned to look at me, frowning.

"Is baby dead?" she asked, then repeated it louder, shouting, as she looked earnestly up into my face.

I nodded, my lip trembling.

Catherine looked back at the baby, and at Mum. She touched the baby's face again. Then she touched Mum's face. Then she began to cry, and let me hold her as she wept.

9

A Baptism

I knew as soon as I saw him that Parson Burnett was going to make the worst day of my life even worse, if that were possible. His tall, black-clad figure stepped uninvited into our cottage without a word to my father, who was sitting staring into the fire, and he strode over to the bed without even taking off his hat. He stood there, looking down at my mother and baby brother silently.

I looked up at the Parson's face. His expression was impassive, but it almost looked like it wore a kind of quiet satisfaction and I shuddered. He finally broke the silence as he began to say a prayer over their bodies.

"Merciful God," he intoned, "forgive the corrupted nature of every man. As a bad tree bears bad fruit, these two sinners before you are of their own nature inclined to evil, and therefore, as with every person born into this world, deserveth of God's wrath and damnation - "

My father's voice cut across him.

"No." he said. "You can take yourself an' your God out of my house."

The Parson turned his head towards my father, sitting as still as a statue facing the fire, and I could see the tension in Dad's shoulders.

"I *beg* your pardon?" Parson Burnett said quietly, his silken voice carrying iron-clad menace.

"I think you heard me, Parson," my father replied.

He stood and turned, facing Parson Burnett down. Even though they were at opposite sides of the small room, I felt that they were almost nose to nose as an atmosphere of hatred filled the room.

"You killed my wife an' baby son, as surely as if you'd put your white hands around their throats," my father snarled, "an' I want you out of my house."

The Parson stared at my father silently, his pale eyes flickering in the firelight.

"I'll leave if you wish," he said smoothly, "but your child will not be buried in my churchyard if it is not Baptised."

Dad clenched his jaw. He saw he had no choice. After several long moments glaring at the Parson, he nodded stiffly, giving his consent.

Parson Burnett smiled condescendingly.

"Do you have any water?" he asked, turning to me, and I shuddered under his gaze.

I picked up the water jug and held it out towards him.

He didn't move to take it, and I stretched out my arm to hold the jug closer to him, but he stared at me coldly.

"Don't you have a bowl?" he asked.

Flushing, I realised what he needed and shakily splashed some of the water into a clean bowl and passed it to him. He took the bowl and blessed the water, then turned back to the bed.

"You must kneel," he said, his back to us.

Dad and I glanced across the room at one another, then knelt down on the floor where we stood. I bowed my head. There was a long silence.

"Does the child have a name?" asked the mocking voice.

"Tom," Dad choked, and I heard him swallow. "Thomas Creswell."

"Thomas Creswell, I baptise thee in the Name of the Father, and of the Son, and of the Holy Ghost. Amen," Parson Burnett intoned quickly.

He then sped through the rest of the brief litany so fast I only realised he had finished when I looked up to see why he had stopped speaking, and found his tall figure towering silently over me. I shuddered, remembering the terrified expression on my grandmother's face when he had come for her.

"Get up, Eppie," Dad said quietly.

I got to my feet, flushing again. My father was already standing.

"I will overlook your earlier blasphemy, Creswell," Parson Burnett said, still looking down at me while he spoke to my father, "as I am assuming your grief has turned your mind temporarily. But you need to be very careful what you say. I am not averse to arranging for Dissenters to languish in Hawbury gaol. False accusations made against Ministers of the Church – or anyone else, for that matter" he said silkily, "will lead you to the same place."

The Parson turned to look at my father but remained standing right next to me, the folds of his cloak brushing against my arm bringing goose-bumps pricking up on my skin.

"Your wife's association with witches has led to her death, and I suggest you tread very carefully, Creswell, if you don't plan on any more of your family joining your wife's mother at Hawbury." He licked his lips. "Or, indeed, joining her in Hell."

I saw Dad clench his fists, his lips white. When he spoke, his voice was hoarse with cold fury.

"Hephzibah Smalley is no witch. You have no proof that she's done anythin' other than use herbs to try to heal the sick, an' you know full well that she's a God-fearin' woman, as Martha is. Was," he corrected himself, shakily. He glared at the Parson bitterly.

"As for me, it's people like you that drive religion out of a man, with your hypocrisy an' lies. *God* knows what's in my heart. I'm no Dissenter, but I don't need your biased readin' of the Bible over the bodies of my wife an' child when you're responsible for them both lyin' there. An innocent woman is in Hawbury gaol instead of bein' here to help her sick daughter, an' that's at *your* door, Parson."

He paused. "An' we both know why *that* is."

Parson Burnett's eyes flickered dangerously. He stared at my father without blinking for a long time. Dad didn't flinch but glared steadily back.

"I hope, for the sake of the rest of your family, that Hephzibah Smalley goes to her death with her lips sealed, Creswell," the Parson's smooth voice said quietly.

It was said with such a lack of inflection that you would have thought he was just mentioning that it was cold out. Without another word, Parson Burnett opened the door and let himself out, the latch clicking softly into place behind him.

I looked at my father. He was staring into the empty space the Parson had vacated. He was trembling with anger. As I walked towards him, his eyes came back into focus and he turned to look at me.

"Eppie."

He looked at me silently for a few moments, then he sat back down but pulled me down to sit beside him while he calmed his anger.

"How was Gran'ma?" I asked, after a while.

Dad smiled, ruefully.

"In fine form," he said.

He looked me in the eyes.

"She told me off. She could see how angry I was, an' knew I'd be takin' it out on you. As though you had any choice but to go, once she'd asked you to. I'm sorry, Eppie," he went on, shaking his head while his hand pressed mine.

"It's alright," I whispered, my bottom lip trembling, "you were right. It *is* my fault. I should have -"

"*Don't you dare!*" he hissed, his hand suddenly a crushing weight. "None of this is your fault. An' especially not – not -"

He couldn't finish but stared at the silent bed, his lips white. He struggled with himself a moment, then he went on.

"It's not your fault your Gran'ma wasn't here to help your mum. An' even if she had been here, she might not have been able to –. Even without the baby comin' early, with your mum bein' so poorly, she might still have -"

He couldn't say it. He cleared his throat.

"Most people die of the Plague once they get it, Eppie. You know that. *All* of the tailor's family is dead apart from Ellen, an' more folk besides."

Mary Ann, I thought, but my own pain was too raw to feel the loss of my friend too.

"That Catherine survived is nothin' short of a miracle," Dad went on. "We have a lot to thank your Gran'ma for, on that front at the very least, because she knew who we needed to go to for help. I–I might not agree with it, but it's saved Catherine, an' it might have saved your mum too, if we'd been able to keep that potion for longer. There are precious few folk left who know the secrets of the herbs an' plants. People like the bloody Parson have seen to that with their superstitious nonsense."

I said nothing, afraid I might tell him what really happened at the witch's house. Or at least what had seemed to happen. I couldn't decide if it had really happened or if it had been a dream, forged out of the heady incense and my own exhaustion.

He misunderstood my look of guilt.

"It's *not* your fault, or your Gran'ma's for that matter, what happened next. They were lookin' for any excuse with your Gran'ma, an' had been for years. All that rubbish about the crow," he said, shaking his head in disgust.

I ignored that bit. "But why were they lookin' for an excuse?"

"I don't know," he admitted, "your Gran'ma won't tell me. I only know some of it, an' that they'll use what happened to – never mind. I don't think that's what it's really about. That's just their excuse, I reckon, because I know there's *somethin'* between her an' the Sylvestres, which goes back to before you were born. Before your mum was born, even, back to when your Gran'ma was a girl. You saw Burnett's expression when I made out I knew all about it?"

I nodded, but I was confused.

"But if it's to do with the Sylvestre family," I asked, bewildered, "what's it got to do with Parson Burnett?"

"Burnett was appointed as Parson to Witherstone by the new Squire, not long after the Restoration of the King, so he's the Squire's man. As soon as a King was back on the throne, Sylvestre drove the previous Parson out an' put Burnett in his place. The man he drove out was Matthew Cowper."

"Matthew Cowper? That was the name the – the old woman in the wild wood mentioned –"

"Don't tell me where she is!" Dad warned. "You must tell me nothin' that can be forced out of me, Eppie. If they find out where you got the potion from that'll be the end of any chance of gettin' your Gran'ma out of prison, an' it'd be the end of you too. They'd charge *you* with witchcraft as well. Not to mention – the old woman you went to see, an' there'd be no chance for you or your Gran'ma then."

He went on quickly.

"Matthew was Edward Cowper's brother. He was a Radical Preacher – with more liberal views of God an' religion than Burnett. Matthew didn't believe we're all sinful from the moment we're born, for one thing, an' he used to preach that all men are equal in the eyes of God – includin' the King. That the King isn't Divine, but a man just like the rest of us. He said the earth was given to all of us in equal measure, not just to the rich so they can treat the rest of us like slaves. You can probably guess he was good friends with your Grandad," Dad smiled.

"Anyway, after the Civil Wars were finally over, Matthew Cowper became the Parson of Witherstone durin' the Parliament years. The Parson we used to have before Cowper was turfed out – an' that was Burnett's own father, who was appointed by the *old* Squire. Burnett's father was even worse than his son, if that's possible. He was an evil old bastard."

I started with shock. My father rarely swore.

"When the old Parson Burnett was forced out durin' the Parliament, Matthew Cowper became our Parson. He was a good man, like his brother is. The Sylvestres didn't like it but they were keeping their heads down durin' Cromwell's time, with the old Squire an' the new havin' been up for the old King."

He sighed.

"But Matthew Cowper was driven out by the Sylvestres as soon as the new King came to the throne. Old Parson Burnett had died by this time, so the Squire put Burnett's son in his place as the new Parson. So we've had nowt but change at the church in Witherstone, each of them with their own agenda it seems to me, but this Burnett is the Squire's man, through an' through, same as his father was. Who do you think pays his wages?"

I struggled with all this for a minute, my head muddled. I tried to pick out the essentials.

"So... Parson Burnett is paid his livin' by the Squire, an' the Squire doesn't like Gran'ma? But it wasn't the same Squire, when Gran'ma was young, was it?"

"No. The Squire now is the younger son of the old Squire. The old Squire was wounded in the Wars, at Powick Bridge, an' he – he died at home some weeks later."

I met Dad's eyes for a moment, but neither of us mentioned Hannah Pendal. Dad went on.

"The old Squire's death meant that the younger brother Henry became Squire because the eldest son, William, was killed - at Edgehill I think it was, within days of his father's death. The eldest son was a Parliamentarian, fightin' against his own brother an' father."

Dad smiled at my confused expression.

"The easiest way to think about it, Eppie, is that the old an' the new Squires an' both Burnetts supported the King, an' what you might call the *official* religious view which has the King an' the landowners at the top of the pile, on God's right hand, with the rest of us doin' what we're told underneath - an' pretty much starvin' half the time. But William Sylvestre was against the King, an' had similar views to Matthew Cowper – an' your Grandad - so I'd like to think that if William Sylvestre hadn't died in the Wars an' had become Squire instead of his brother, he'd have kept Matthew Cowper on as Parson rather than brought a Burnett back to Witherstone, an' then things might have gone differently for your Gran'ma."

He sighed. "But who knows. He'd probably have been just the same as the rest of the Sylvestre family in the end."

Dad was gloomy for a moment.

"Anyway," he sighed, "the fact is that the new Squire seems to have carried on his family's antipathy towards your Gran'ma."

"But Grandad said William Sylvestre was missing. How do they know he was dead?"

Dad shrugged. "There were a lot just never came home. Your Gran'ma's dad an' brother were both killed at Naseby. They found her brother, but her dad's body was never found. There were mass graves, Eppie, with bodies just piled in. It was a grim time."

He stared into space for a moment, then smiled sadly.

"That was how me an' your mum became close, though," he said. "It was your Grandad Creswell who found Gran'ma's brother an' brought his body home. Even though they were fightin' on opposite sides. He'd known Joseph Smalley well, y'see, an' he did what he could to help your Gran'ma through a difficult time. Her mother had – well, she'd lost her mother already. So with her dad an' brother dead, all she had left was your mum, who was still a little girl then."

Poor Grandma. Her father and brother both killed in the Wars, and her mother already dead. No wonder she found it hard to talk about her family. I felt proud of her strength of character, and proud of my Grandad for bringing back her brother's body and for looking out for her even though their families had effectively been enemies in the fighting.

Dad's eyes filled with tears suddenly, and he looked towards the silent bed.

"That's what the Wars did," he said, his voice breaking, "split families an' friendships. An' what good did it do us all in the end? Us poor folk are right back where we started, at the whim of those who can treat us as they like, an' then leave us to die."

He almost sounded like Grandad Creswell then. We sat for a while, holding on to each other. Eventually Dad wiped his sleeve over his face and sighed.

"I don't know what it was really all about with the Sylvestres. Your Gran'ma remains tight-lipped on that score. I don't think she even told your mum, though I'm pretty sure your Grandad knows more than he lets on. But I do know that the new Squire, Sir Henry, was *livid* when your mum married me, so his antipathy to your Gran'ma extended to her daughter, it seems. Matthew Cowper had already been forced out and *this* Burnett was the village Parson by then. *He* refused to marry us, so we had to go to Hawbury in the end."

He snorted. "It's funny that the new Squire named his own son William, though, but I guess he was namin' him after his father rather than his dead brother because there can't have been much love lost between those two."

At that moment, the latch lifted and my heart jumped, but it was only Richard and Catherine. Dad had sent them down to fetch the goat up from the meadow earlier as he thought we might be in for some bad weather, and she was soon to kid.

Catherine was still pale but she ran over to Dad and leaped up onto his lap. She buried her face in his shirt and squeezed her arms around his neck. His eyes filled and his lips trembled as he hugged my sister.

"That took a fair while, Richard," Dad commented after clearing his throat, but I was glad that my brother hadn't been here to witness the scene between Dad and Parson Burnett. I think he would have really lost it.

He came to warm his hands by the fire.

"It took us a while to catch her," he said tonelessly.

He looked ashen. He hadn't said much since he'd come home from Thompson's earlier. Once he'd taken in the scene on our parents' bed he had sat on the other bed, leaning against the wall and staring at the silent forms across the room until Dad had come home from Hawbury. That had been the worst moment. Seeing my father's face as realisation had hit him. He had held my mother and cradled the baby and wept and wept.

Then he had turned and looked at us, me by the fire with Catherine on my lap and Richard still propped, unmoving, on the other bed. Once he had enough control of himself to speak, he had sent Richard and Catherine to fetch the goat up from the meadow.

Then he had got up from beside my mother and sat by the fire, staring into the crackling flames while I poured him a drink of mead. It was at that moment that Parson Burnett had stepped through the door.

That night I put Catherine to bed in Grandma's place, then laid down beside her and stroked her hair while she fell asleep, cuddling her rag-doll tightly. Raggedy-Ann. Mum had made it for her, and she and Grandma had laughed and shared a look when Catherine had named the doll, thinking of the old woman in the woods perhaps.

I was worried about my sister. She didn't seem to be able to hear anything at all. When she spoke to us she shouted, as though she couldn't even hear her own voice. We had to show her the answers to her questions, trying to explain with gestures, but she was as quick-witted as ever so she seemed to understand quite fast. I hoped it was a temporary thing.

I watched my sister sleeping for a long time, grateful that at least she had survived the Plague, and I cried silently over my mother. I would never be able to talk to her or feel her arms around me ever again. And I knew it was my fault, no matter what Dad said.

I woke with a start. It was already morning, and bitterly cold. My heart felt heavy and yet empty, as though the centre of my world had vanished and everything that was left felt lost, searching for something that could never be found.

I had intended to stay up all night, keeping vigil by Mum's body with Dad and Richard, but I must have fallen asleep beside Catherine. I got up to find that Dad had already built up the fire and made porridge. Richard was sitting sullenly by the fire, leaning against the wall and kicking his shoes against the stool, staring into nothing.

Dad looked up and smiled at me, but the smile didn't reach his eyes. He looked tired, and years older, and unutterably sad. He served the porridge into four bowls and I woke Catherine, who complained as I carried her to the table and sat her on the bench.

I went to the door to fetch the milk in and gasped as I saw the yard. There was snow on the ground and more falling. It was a shock after the warmer weather we had been having for the past few weeks, even though it had got a lot colder over the last couple of days.

I could see two sets of footprints crossing over one another to the gate and into the lane and back again. One set looked like my father's. The other must be Richard's. They must have got up very early this morning.

The goat bleated at me from where she was tethered in the shelter between the hen house and the hedge. She would have to wait. I got the jug from under the bench and took it inside. There wasn't much snow in the jug as the bench had sheltered it from the worst, but the milk had a thin layer of ice on top.

"You were right about the weather, Dad," I said, as I broke the ice with a spoon.

"It's a late snow, but it is still April, after all. I thought it was comin'." He paused then went on quietly. "Job Allen should still have been able to do what he needs to, as I don't think the ground is frozen deep."

I slopped milk on the table instead of into Catherine's porridge, realising at once what Job had to do for this morning. I looked over to my parents' bed, the tears coming thick and fast, and set the jug down, unable to see the table clearly. Dad's hand pressed my shoulder to make me sit on the bench and he put a spoon and bowl before me, but I couldn't eat.

Once my eyes cleared I could see that he hadn't much appetite either, and he scraped the uneaten contents of his own bowl back into the pot. I waited until he had gone outside to fetch more wood in to dry before I emptied my porridge back into the pot too.

Richard hadn't touched his either. He continued to sit there, leaning against the wall and kicking his feet. But he wasn't staring into space anymore. He was looking at me. Glaring might be a better word. I glared right back but he didn't move a muscle.

"What?" I asked defensively, but he just carried on glaring, and the accusation in his eyes was no less bitter for knowing that it was justified.

I turned away and left my brother's untouched bowl on the table, lifting Catherine from the bench – she had finished her own porridge – and dressing her by the fire. When Dad had stacked the damp wood in the corner of the room, he took the porridge pot off the hook and set it on the side of the hearth, then banked up the fire and laid a few peat turfs over to keep it burning slowly while we were out.

He turned to me.

"You'd best say your goodbyes."

A weight in my chest so heavy I felt I shouldn't even be able to walk, I picked Catherine up and went to sit beside my mother and baby brother on my parents' bed. Dad had already wrapped a blanket around them both, but had left their faces uncovered.

Catherine stared at them quietly for a few minutes but she didn't want to touch them today. I couldn't tear my eyes away from them. Looking at their still faces was terrible, but also something I wanted to be able to do forever.

There was a quiet knock at the door.

"Richard," Dad said.

I looked across the room at my brother. He shook his head sullenly, looking down at his feet.

"You won't get another chance, son."

Richard didn't move.

Dad opened the door, and invited Job and his brother Daniel into the cottage. They took off their hats and greeted us quietly, then walked towards the bed where I sat with

Catherine, next to Mum and our baby brother. With a shaking hand, I pulled the blanket across their faces and got up, carrying Catherine away from the bed.

With great respect and gentleness, Job and Daniel helped Dad carry the still bundle outside the cottage and through the yard to the lane. There they laid them gently onto a cart, and we put on our cloaks and followed behind as Job clicked the horse quietly forward, walking us down the snowy lane to the church.

Carrying Catherine on my hip, I walked beside my father, who held his hat in his hands. His hair grew whiter and whiter with the falling snow as we walked. I looked at my brother, walking behind us with his hat by his side, but he refused to meet my eyes. He trudged slowly forwards, staring at the tracks the cart made in the snow.

10

The Graveyard

As we reached the lychgate, Job brought the horse to a halt and the procession was repeated, this time with their burden carried through the graveyard to a snow-traced mound of earth in the west corner, where they carefully lowered it into the grave.

There were few mourners, but those who were there were welcomed. Job's wife Alice, her cloak wrapped warmly around her, put her hand on my father's arm briefly and greeted me with real sympathy, squeezing my hand and kissing Catherine's solemn cheek. Richard didn't respond to her, but she looked at him sympathetically before turning back to her husband, slipping her arm through his as they walked round and took their places at the graveside with Daniel, on the opposite side to Dad.

My father had never looked more alone than at that moment. Edward Cowper was standing at the head of the grave, his hat in his hands and his already silver hair dusted with snow. For a moment I thought he was going to lead the burial service, and felt both surprised and glad. But then I saw a black-cloaked figure gliding through the graveyard towards us, a broad-brimmed hat set firmly against the falling snow and a Bible dark in bone-white hands.

I watched Parson Burnett approach, and felt such hatred I was trembling. Catherine wriggled out of my arms and dropped to the ground beside me, walking us both forwards so she could take Dad's hand and look up into his bowed face. I saw Richard step into line on Dad's other side, my brother's eyelashes glinting with tiny flakes of snow.

Parson Burnett made no apology for his lateness, but he glared at Edward Cowper who smiled pleasantly and moved sideways to take his place opposite my father. Parson Burnett's smooth but carrying voice began to speak over the open grave.

I am the resurrection and the life, saith the Lord: he that believeth in me, though he were dead, yet shall he live.

I heard whispered voices behind me, and turned to see two cloaked figures making their way quickly between the gravestones. As they came towards us, I saw that one of them was Ellen. I didn't recognise her companion at first, but as they drew to a halt a long way back from where we were standing at the grave, I recognised Mary Fordham, who runs the bakehouse and mill.

Ellen met my eyes and glanced away nervously, then she looked back at me and smiled apologetically. I turned away without responding, anger rising in my chest, and looked down into the grave, the folds of the blanket already traced with snow. I tried to listen to the almost imperceptible sound of the snowflakes falling on my shoulders and onto the ground at my feet rather than have to listen to Parson Burnett's words, trying to blank out his silken voice.

We brought nothing into this world, and it is certain we can carry nothing out. The Lord gave, and the Lord hath taken away; blessed be the name of the Lord.

The snow sighed as it landed on my cloak, and I stared at the flakes, tracing the tiny laced patterns of each delicate shape as it clung to its fellows, watching as they slowly melted into the wool.

"This snow is *unnatural*," came a whisper behind me, barely louder than the breath of the snowflakes landing on my shoulder. Ellen and Mistress Fordham must have moved closer. I was surprised that the Parson didn't pause in mid-flow to shush them.

I said, I will take heed to my ways: that I offend not in my tongue.

"It is indeed, Mary," I recognised Ellen's whispered reply. "It makes a God-fearin' person's blood run cold. But then, *it's no wonder*."

I thought for a moment that she was referring to the terrible things that had happened to us – Mum's death, and Grandma's imprisonment on false charges of witchcraft – but then I heard her continue.

"I always *knew* there was somethin' about that family. Hephzibah Smalley especially. She was always a strange one. Secretive. Up to somethin', you can be sure - which is hardly surprisin', all things considered. Bad blood will out."

"Yes, I've always felt it too, Ellen. Maybe poor Martha is a victim of her mother's sin in more ways than one -"

Mary's whispers carried on but I couldn't make out what she said next. My blood was boiling and the Parson's voice had risen in tone, almost strident now, and it eclipsed the other sounds around me.

I will keep my mouth as it were with a bridle: while the ungodly is in my sight.

I turned my head to look behind me, my teeth clenched in fury. I was shocked to see that Ellen and Mary were still standing exactly where they were when they had first arrived in the graveyard, way back behind us. Ellen was staring at me. She knew I'd heard her and she looked frightened. She nudged Mary who turned her head and met my eyes. She stopped whispering at once.

I saw the almost imperceptible movement of Ellen's lips. Her tiny whisper came across the gravestones to me.

"*She can hear us!*"

I glared at both women. They looked terrified. Ellen crossed herself and I saw Mary make a sign with her hand, warding off the Evil Eye. My anger melted suddenly as, amazed, I felt laughter rising in my chest. It was unexpected and I felt the hysteria struggling to be free.

I held my tongue, and spake nothing: I kept silence, yea, even from good words; but it was pain and grief to me.

I knew it was a foolish thing to do as soon as I did it, but I couldn't help myself. It felt good. I smiled, slowly and deliberately, at both women, my face mocking their fear. They froze as though turned to stone, and Ellen's jaw dropped open. Slowly, I turned back to face the grave. My smile vanished as I found Parson Burnett's pale eyes fixed on my own.

Lord, let me know mine end, and the number of my days: that I may be certified how long I have to live, he said.

I heard a roaring in my ears, and it was all I could do to remain standing next to my father as the ground seemed to tilt and sway beneath me. I steadied myself and stared rigidly into the grave, afraid to look up, knowing that Parson Burnett's eyes were still upon me.

In the midst of life we are in death.

I daren't look up again until the service was over. Keeping my eyes down, I moved only to take a handful of earth from the mound beside us to cast onto my mother's body when it was time. The irony of that handful of earth was not lost on me.

It hath pleased Almighty God in his great mercy to take unto himself the soul of our dear sister here departed, we therefore commit her body to the ground; earth to earth, ashes to ashes, dust to dust.

Catherine held up her arms to me, and I swung her up onto my hip and leaned her over the grave so she could cast in her own handful of earth.

We give thee hearty thanks, for that it hath pleased thee to deliver this our sister out of the miseries of this sinful world.

I raised my eyes then, and looked at Parson Burnett. His face was smooth and untroubled as he looked back at me, his voice carrying across the icy churchyard. I looked back at those pale eyes and swore, right there and then, over my mother's grave, that I would do whatever it took to clear my grandmother's name.

Amen.

After the funeral we walked back through the village. Dad knew I was all for heading home behind the churchyard and across the meadow as soon as we left Job and Daniel filling in the grave, but he held my arm tightly, steering me through the snowy graveyard and into the lane. He reminded me that we needed to be careful to conform else Parson Burnett would have more 'evidence' he could use against us, and that could be a risk to all of us, as well as Grandma.

I couldn't help looking up at the huge lime tree on the village green opposite the church as we passed, its branches traced with snow. The tree that Ellen told me Hannah Pendal had been hung from. I shuddered, sick to my stomach.

It was difficult to ignore the stares and whispers as we passed our neighbours' houses. I could see Ellen standing with Mary Fordham at the gate to the Parson's house, but I pretended I hadn't seen them as we walked by. What probably hurt the most was seeing those I'd always considered to be my friends just staring at us as we passed – Emma Wright, Jane Thorpe and her brother Jacob – friends I'd played with on many summer evenings, now with cold and unfriendly expressions and shared whispers.

Witch, I heard. *Witch*.

I was so grateful for our true friends, Edward Cowper and Alice Allen, carrying her baby in her arms beneath her cloak, walking back home with us. Job and Daniel would be following on in a short while, once their work in the graveyard was done, to share a mug of beer and some bread and oatcakes with us.

Yet even though their presence walking through the village had been a great help, it was somehow a strange relief once they left us and we could be alone with our grief. It had stopped snowing and the sun was sparkling on the white blanket covering everything, and a blackbird was singing in the tree at our gate.

The village seemed far away in the distance as I watched the figures of our friends walking back through the snow to their homes. It felt as though life was continuing for everyone else in the world whereas for us life had stopped.

I got on with collecting the eggs and milking the goat, nonetheless. I felt bad for the poor goat, her milking time was becoming very erratic. A good handful of oats helped her to behave for me, but I had to work hard not to remember the scene which had been waiting for me the last time I walked back into the cottage after milking her. I focused on the sunlight glinting on the snow, and saw the blackbirds scraping beneath the hedge, looking for food for their young. I scattered more oats on the snow for the birds where the goat couldn't reach.

When we sat down to our midday meal, Dad said he wasn't surprised that Grandad Creswell hadn't turned up yet, with all the snow.

"Make sure there's enough left in the pot, Eppie, for when he does get here. He'll be in need of a good warmin' soup after he's walked through all that snow. I sent a message for him early this mornin'. It's a good seven miles or more down from Moors Farm but your Grandad is a good walker, even now. Mind you, he wouldn't have minded missin' Burnett's service this mornin'." Dad's voice was grim. "But I know he'll want to pay his respects to your Mum, an' offer us what comfort he can."

We were quiet at that, except Catherine, who was already busy with her soup.

I was keen to see Grandad and hoped he would be able to come. I hoped his master at Moors Farm was a fair man, as Grandad would miss nearly two days work while he walked down to us and then back up there again tomorrow morning - if he was able to stay until then. I hoped so. I wanted to get the chance to ask him what we could do to help Grandma, especially as he might know *something* of whatever it was between her and what he called 'Privilege'.

I was beginning to realise that Grandad must have specifically meant both of their dealings with the Sylvestre family, as that seemed to have 'cost' both himself and Grandma in separate ways. And for Grandma, whatever it was could now cost her her life.

After we'd eaten, only Catherine managing all of hers, Richard went out without a word to any of us. Dad sat by the fire with Catherine on his knee, talking to her and trying to work out if she was able to hear anything at all. I watched them for a while, and then I joined him to see if I could help.

I crept up behind my sister while she was watching Dad's mouth talking to her, and I said "*Catherine!*" behind her head. She didn't notice anything. Dad carefully kept his eyes on her face so she wouldn't realise there was something going on behind her, and turn and see me. I said her name increasingly loudly, but there was no reaction from her at all. I clapped my hands together. I shouted "*Boo!*" I squeaked like a mouse. I banged the stool on the floor. She stopped suddenly and looked at the floor beneath Dad's feet. I did it again and she stared harder, then felt her tummy and giggled.

I realised she had felt the vibration the stool had made on the floor through Dad's legs. My eyes met my father's. We both knew. Catherine couldn't hear anything at all.

As soon as Dad's eyes shifted to mine, my sister swung her head round and saw me right behind her. She laughed and held her arms out for me. I picked her up and swung her round and hugged her. She put up with this for a moment but then wriggled free, wanting Dad again.

I sat her back on his knee and we talked to her and asked her questions with pointing and gestures, and when she answered correctly, we clapped and nodded. I tried to show her that she didn't need to shout so loud by pressing my fingers to her lips and whispering in her ear. She felt my breath tickling and giggled, but she picked it up very quickly and was answering us in quiet whispers by the time Richard came back.

My brother came in carrying a long branch. He sat on the bench by the fire, resting one end of the branch on the floor and trimming off the bark with his axe, then he split it right down the centre, all along its length, making two long pieces. He shaved the splinters off the inside of the split lengths, working the flat inner surfaces until they were smooth. The three of us sat quietly, watching him work.

He chopped the end off one of the pieces to make it shorter than the other, and shaved the cut ends to make them smooth. I realised my brother was very skilled with his hands, working with precision. I think Dad knew what he was doing long before I did. It was only when Richard chopped sections out of both lengths of wood, then slotted them together to make a cross, that it dawned on me. He was making a grave marker.

Richard put the bark and shavings near the fire for kindling, then turned and spoke to me for the first time in ages.

"Where's the sheet of paper with the Letters on, Eppie?"

I got the paper down from the shelf and Richard unrolled it, looking at the symbols that Adam had drawn for me.

"Which one was 'M' for 'Martha'? he asked.

I hesitated for a moment while I remembered.

"That one," I said, pointing, then I watched as he cut the shape into the smooth surface with his knife. Soon a beautifully carved 'M' was etched deeply into the wood.

"'C' for 'Creswell'?"

I pointed to it, and marvelled as he carved the letter into shape.

"Is it oak, Richard?" Dad asked quietly.

Richard nodded, then he blew the last shavings out of the letters and looked up at Dad, grinning suddenly.

"I got it from Witherstone Hall Woods."

We grinned back at him. It felt like a tiny victory, taking something that was forbidden to us.

"It's beautiful," I said.

Richard didn't answer. He cut two short pegs from one of the finer branches he'd trimmed off earlier, and hammered them into the join of the cross using the back of his axe, then bound a strong leather cord round the join too.

Once he'd finished, he leaned the cross against the wall and we all marvelled at it. I could tell that Richard was the most impressed of us all, and he briefly raised his eyebrow mockingly when he saw I'd caught his expression, but then his eyes hardened and he turned away from me. I tried not to let it bother me but my heart felt it all the same.

We put on our cloaks and headed back down to the churchyard, Richard carrying his handiwork across his shoulder and swinging his axe by his side. Snow was still on the ground, although it had stopped falling, but it was easy enough to hammer the cross into the ground at the head of the grave as the earth was still soft from having been dug. We stood there looking at the cross for a long time. When we walked back home there were a few people around, but it was much easier than it had been that morning. I think Richard's beautiful cross had given us all something. I felt we all held our heads up, quelling most of the whispers before they'd even got started.

I heard the goat bleating before we'd even got in the gate. We found that she wasn't alone. Her spindly-legged kid, its coat still damp, was nuzzling for her milk. Catherine was enthralled, and she tried to hug the kid even though the goat was butting at her crossly. I held the goat by the horns so she couldn't do Catherine any damage and let my sister have free reign with the kid while it fed. Dad took the opportunity to check it over.

"It's a girl," he said, with satisfaction, "so we'll have two milkers by next spring. You'll be able to sell some of the milk, Eppie, an' make extra cheeses."

We persuaded Catherine to leave the kid to feed from its mother in peace, Dad and Richard taking her inside, but I stayed for a while watching the goats. As I sat there, I noticed something sticking out of the snow where the blackbirds had scraped for the oats I'd scattered earlier. It was a stem of bluebells. They were Mum's favourite flower, because they meant summer was coming.

I looked at the bluebells in the snow. Then I picked them and breathed in their delicate fragrance, and took them into the cottage, putting them in a small pot on the table. After looking at them for a moment, I picked up the pot and turned to Dad.

"I'm just goin' back down to the graveyard for a while," I said, and he smiled gently at the bluebells, understanding immediately.

Most people had stopped work for the day, and the glimpses of sound which came to me from the cottages as I passed were like knives in my heart. I could hear families sitting down for their meal, or talking and laughing round the fire, and I felt that all of that was lost to us now. We would never be a complete family again, even if we did manage to clear Grandma's name and get her home.

I sighed, knowing despair wasn't far away. I couldn't see how, but knew we had to do something to try to free my grandmother. I even wondered if the witch might be able to do something. More realistically, I was sure Grandad would be able to help, and I felt desperate for him to come, though it was getting so late now I was worried he might not have been able to come today, and I needed to ask him what we could do – and possibly more importantly, what he might know.

The graveyard was silent. I pressed the small pot into the ground at the foot of the cross, and stayed crouched down at the head of the grave, looking at the flowers and the beautiful letters Richard had carved and thinking about Mum and my baby brother lying beneath my feet. At least they would have each other for all eternity, I thought, as I wept. But I would never see my mother again. Not in this life, anyway.

I don't know how long I crouched there, but eventually realised it was getting late, the bluebells fading to grey in the lengthening shadows. I shivered, then suddenly felt a prickling on the back of my neck that was nothing to do with the cold. I felt as though someone was watching me. I looked round but could see no-one in the graveyard.

Straightening up, my ankles stiff with squatting down for so long, I turned round completely and was shocked to see a crow sitting on the churchyard wall behind me. His black feathers were vivid against the snow, even though he was beneath the shadowy branches of a tree which leaned over from the other side of the wall, and fear leapt into my chest.

I wasn't frightened of Master Nalgah, of course, but I was terrified of being seen with him. I looked around the graveyard, conscious that my dark clothes would be conspicuous against the snow, then I slipped over the wall and crouched beneath the crow, who cawed quietly and pecked my hand. I daren't set off towards home in case he flew across to me. Perhaps if I could find an insect for him he would fly away. I poked around in the crumbling mortar until I found a small beetle. Picking it up between my finger and thumb, I held it out for the crow. He pecked and the insect was gone. The beady eye regarded me, then suddenly his head swivelled and he looked over my shoulder. I spun round, heart lurching, and saw what Master Nalgah had seen. There was movement on the river.

A boat was making its way towards the bank. Instead of mooring alongside the majority of the boats, it was heading for the far corner of the meadow by the coppice wood, and I pressed myself into the shadow between the tree and the wall, terrified of being seen.

The figure in the boat shipped the oars and jumped onto the bank, dropping a bag to the ground before pulling the boat up onto the grass just as the sun began slipping below the horizon. I was surprised when, instead of walking across the meadow and past me towards the village, the shadowy figure looked around before picking up the bag and walking quietly into the coppice wood, heading towards the stream and Hall Farm Woods.

Instead of feeling relieved that the man was heading away from me, I felt sudden, overwhelming fury. I shot out of my hiding place without another thought and ran across the snow towards the spot where he had disappeared. In that moment of madness, I didn't care whether anyone saw me. I didn't care what his business with Hall Farm was. I had recognised him. It was the scarred man.

11

Homeless

I shot into the trees barely moments after he had disappeared, following his footprints through the snow. I ran through the trees and across the stepping stones after him, skidding for a moment as I adjusted to the unexpected change of direction the footprints had taken. Instead of heading straight on towards Hall Farm, he had turned sharp right. Then I saw him, to my right and just ahead of me, walking quickly through the trees towards Witherstone Hall Woods.

As I launched myself towards him, he was already turning to face me, having heard my feet pounding after him. I flew at his face but he was quick and strong, grabbing my flailing hands and pinning them to my sides. I didn't realise I had started shrieking at him until he squeezed both of my wrists into one of his hands and clamped his other hand across my face, crushing my nose and bruising my lips against my teeth as he squeezed my jaw closed. He pulled me into his iron grip, and within seconds I was panicking that I would suffocate.

I struggled against him but it was hopeless. I almost collapsed to the ground, hardly able to breathe. He yanked me up to face him and stared at me, bewildered. He could see the panic in my eyes and shifted his hand a little, freeing my nose but keeping my jaw tightly closed. I sucked air into my lungs so fast my nostrils almost clamped themselves shut.

Master Nalgah, I thought, my eyes looking around wildly, remembering how he'd helped me to escape from this same strong grip only days before. The man kept darting looks through the trees around us as though worried about the same thing I was hoping for. My panicking began to ease as I was no longer suffocating, and the man watched me carefully.

"*What the Hell's wrong with you?*" he hissed, when he thought I was calm enough to listen.

I glared at him. That he had to *ask!* The fury returned to my eyes and every muscle in my body. He could see it and tightened his grip on my jaw and wrists. After a few more moments I sagged again, knowing it was hopeless. But then he looked at me just as helplessly. He knew that he had to keep hold of me otherwise I'd turn into a raging Fury again. So I continued to glare at him and he continued to stare at me, his eyes puzzled and his mouth a grim line.

"*If* I let go of that loud mouth of yours," he said finally, "will you promise to keep it quiet, an' *talk* to me instead of shriekin'?"

Grudgingly, I nodded. The man had a warning look in his eyes as he slowly released the pressure on my face and jaw. Once he let go of my face, I could feel the blood throbbing into the bruises and I grimaced with pain. He actually looked apologetic, but I still glared at him.

"Well," he said, relaxing a little. "Perhaps I could also let go of your wrists, if you promise you won't try to gouge my eyes out again, young Mistress?"

I nodded, and as he released my wrists, I rubbed them to ease the pain as I looked at him. He was more tanned and weathered than he'd appeared in the moonlight, but his scar was just as vivid, cleaving down his face and into his beard. His hair was a dull brown, heavily streaked with grey. He looked as though he must be older than my father, but not as old as Grandad.

Suddenly his eyes widened as he caught sight of something behind me. He grabbed my arms and whirled me round to face back the way I'd come, holding me in front of him with one hand and raising his other to protect his face.

As I spun round I saw the black crow arrowing towards us through the dusk. My heart sank. I'd been wishing for him just moments earlier, but now I was free of the man's grip I realised that Master Nalgah would only put me in greater danger. It would be all too easy to use the crow coming to me once again as evidence for Parson Burnett to claim that I too was a witch.

Master Nalgah landed on my shoulder, his claws gripping me through my cloak. I felt the man move away at my back as he tried to get some distance between himself and the crow. I turned back to him, my face defiant.

"Well," I said angrily, "here's more evidence for you. You'll be able to tell Parson Burnett he can throw *me* into Hawbury gaol alongside my Gran'ma now."

The man's eyes narrowed. "What do you mean?"

"*You know exactly what I mean!*" I hissed at him, my voice rising.

His hands tensed as though he was thinking of clamping my jaw shut again, despite the proximity of Master Nalgah, whose claws tightened on my shoulder. I forced myself to speak more quietly, but the anger still burned through my voice.

"You *told* them about me takin' the – the earth from the graveyard," I said, and had to swallow the screaming rage rising suddenly in my chest. "An' now my Gran'ma's in gaol, charged with witchcraft, an' – an' my mum - "

I couldn't finish, my fury in danger of collapsing into sobs of grief.

He stared at me, shaking his head.

"It wasn't me," he said. "*I swear!*" he insisted, seeing the fury in my eyes again as I fought against the tears.

"Look," he went on, "I don't know what your, er, business was in the graveyard, or up in the woods for that matter – though I had my doubts about the goat story at the time - but I swear I've told no-one. It's none of *my* business. I haven't spoken to anyone in Witherstone at all. Actually," he gave a brief laugh, "that's a lie. I've spoken to *you*."

I stared at him, suddenly realising something blindingly obvious. If he'd told anyone what he had seen, especially in the graveyard, then Parson Burnett would have been looking for *me* not Grandma. Someone else must have seen her collecting herbs and talking to Master Nalgah, and Parson Burnett had found the disturbed grave and either assumed she had been the one to disturb it – or had been given the perfect excuse to use it against her. After all, being seen collecting herbs wasn't enough on its own. And as for Master Nalgah. Well, the witch's crow would be just as happy greeting my grandmother as he was coming to me. He must know her too, of course.

The man looked at me while the thoughts were churning round in my head.

"I was actually afraid *you'd* have told someone about *us*," he said, once my eyes were focused back on him again.

"Me an' my friend are, er, keen to keep ourselves to ourselves, an' would rather it wasn't known that we were here."

He looked at me questioningly.

I shook my head. "No," I said, "I haven't told anyone I've seen you."

"Look," he said, "could we move deeper into the trees? I'd rather stay out of sight, an' with the noise you were makin' earlier..."

He raised his hands in surrender quickly, to try to dispel any fears I may still have that he would harm me.

I nodded, knowing he meant me no harm otherwise he wouldn't have let me go when he had me trapped. He picked up his bag, which must have fallen to the ground during our struggle, and I followed him into the darkening woods. I found Master Nalgah's presence on my shoulder very reassuring.

Once the man was satisfied that we were more hidden from the meadow, he stopped and turned, leaning against a tree and folding his arms.

"Well... Eppie, isn't it?" he began.

I nodded.

"Eppie Creswell," I said, deciding that I must be able to trust him after all.

"Well, Eppie Creswell, it seems to me we both have secrets which we need the other to keep. I swear I mean

Witherstone

you no harm. I'm sorry I frightened you, especially when I saw you in the churchyard, an' I hope I didn't hurt you then - or this time?" he asked.

I shook my head, even though the bruises were still throbbing painfully. He looked doubtfully at my jaw.

"Well, I'm sorry if I did hurt you, either time. I suppose I was shocked when I saw you in the graveyard the other night, but I'm an open-minded man, an' what you were doin' there is your own business."

He paused for a moment. "I think *I* was actually frightened of *you*, especially as you'd managed to be in the same place as we were two nights runnin', an' as I said we're keen to stay out of sight. I thought that you must have been spyin' on us for – someone – but I guess if you had, they'd have been up in the woods lookin' for us after you'd seen us there, but there's been no-one, so I suppose I can trust you?"

I nodded again. "I won't tell anyone." Then I smiled bitterly. "Not that there'd be anyone I *could* tell."

"Are you alone, then? You don't have to tell me, of course."

"No, I'm not alone. There's still my dad an' brother an' little sister at home, but – but – now my Gran'ma's in Hawbury gaol, an' most of the village are happy gossipin' about us, though we still have some good friends."

He nodded. "I know what that's like."

I felt my temper flaring up again.

"How?" I asked angrily. "Has your Gran'ma been sent to gaol accused of witchcraft, an' has your mum an' baby brother died because of it?"

He held his hands up, warning me to keep my voice down.

"I'm sorry," I said. "I-I'm so *angry*."

"An' it sounds like you have every right to be. I'm not surprised you attacked me, if you thought I'd brought *that* down on your family. I'm truly sorry to hear about your trouble, especially about your mum an' baby brother. I just mean I know what it's like to be – the subject of gossip, an' pushed out by your neighbours," he sighed.

"Is that why you're hidin' up in the woods?"

"Not exactly. We'd been livin' a long way from here but had to leave some years back, due to, er, unforeseen circumstances. Well, as we're bein' honest with one another…"

His expression shifted into bemusement.

"Durin' the Parliament we were livin' in a village in the south-east, more than a hundred miles from here, with a few like-minded friends. But after they put a King back on the throne, we were driven out. We've been wanderin' ever since, lookin' for somewhere to settle, managin' to live in places for a year or two but then movin' on, always movin' on it seems," he smiled ruefully.

"We're only passin' through here on our way further north, thinkin' that maybe settlin' in Yorkshire or Lancashire might put enough distance between us an' the King's men. My friend wanted to come to Witherstone on our way, to visit the grave of his wife an' baby son. Sorry," he said, as he saw how close this remark brought me to my own grief.

So they had been looking for a particular grave in the churchyard. I felt sympathy for his friend. There's more than one mother lying with her baby son in Witherstone graveyard then.

"So that's us, anyway," he said, shrugging, "livin' like outlaws these days. We've had to lie especially low for a few days, with me thinkin' you might be spyin' on us," he grinned, "so we were gettin' rather hungry. We trap what we can, of course, but I had to, er, 'borrow' a boat to get us some food from Hawbury. A bit risky in daylight but we need to eat. But we'll be movin' on soon. There's nothin' for us here."

We were both quiet for a moment, and I realised that it would soon be fully dark.

"I need to be gettin' home. My Grandad might be there by now."

"Of course," he said, and I could see his teeth gleaming as he smiled and leaned forward, his hand pale in the shadows. "I'm Robert, by the way, Robert Newstead of Norfolk. Pleased to have met you, Eppie Creswell of Witherstone."

He pronounced it like Wether*stun*. We shook hands, Robert making sure he still kept a respectful distance from Master Nalgah. I smiled. As I turned to leave he spoke again.

"If you need a friend over the next few days, Eppie, we'll be up near the waterfall 'til we leave. I hope your Gran'ma is home with you soon," he said, but I could hear in his voice that it was a hope made without conviction.

"Thanks," I said, and he nodded.

I left him then, and walked back towards the meadow. I looked back once, expecting him to have disappeared into the shadows, but he was still standing in the same place, watching me leave. When I reached the edge of the trees I stroked Master Nalgah and then shrugged my shoulders, urging the bird to fly off.

"*Go on.*"

The crow took off at once, flying up behind me into the woods. I made sure he was out of sight before I ran across the meadow along the riverbank edge. It was becoming second nature, making myself as invisible as I could. The woods at my back were dark and silent but somehow I knew that Robert Newstead was watching me safely home.

Dad looked relieved to see me when I opened the door, but then he frowned and came over to me, looking at my face. He tensed angrily.

"What happened? *Who did this to you?*"

I saw Richard look up sharply. He was sitting next to Catherine who was fast asleep on the bed, her small face looking cosy in the blankets.

"N-no one. It's nothin'," I said, wondering how bad the bruising was. "I–I tripped in the churchyard an' caught my face on somethin' as I fell," I improvised quickly. "Have I got a bruise?"

Dad raised his eyebrows. "*A* bruise? More like a whole patch of bruises, all along your jaw here," he said, touching my face gently.

He looked me in the eyes, his face deadly serious.

"If someone did this to you, Eppie, you must tell me."

I shook my head, meeting his gaze.

"Honest, Dad, it's nothin'."

I changed the subject, looking round the room. "Hasn't Grandad come?"

"No," Dad sighed, turning back towards the room. "The snow must be much worse up on the moors, to have kept him away. Or the yeoman at the Farm might not have let him come, of course. Unless your Grandad didn't get the message, but Adam -"

There was a knock on the door and Adam Burnett let himself into the cottage.

I was confused for a moment, then I realised that Dad must have meant that Adam was the messenger he had sent up to Moors Farm that morning. It occurred to me then that I hadn't seen Adam in the village at all that day, but I'd been avoiding the eyes staring at us from all corners anyway.

I realised all of these things in a moment, as I stared at what Adam was holding in his hands. Dad and Richard were staring too. Adam was holding a cloak, wound into a bundle. Grandad Creswell's cloak. I looked at Dad's face. It was ashen.

Wordlessly, Adam put Grandad's cloak down on the table, unwrapping its folds. Inside was Grandad's weathered hat, his canvas bag, and his father's old Bible. We all stared at Grandad's things and at Adam without saying anything. Adam cleared his throat. His face and hands were red and blue with cold, and he was shivering despite his thick cloak.

"I-I'm sorry," he said. "The Plague has taken nearly all of them up at Moors Farm."

He looked at Dad, then at Richard and myself, then back at my father. The long seconds stretched out and no-one said a word. Adam turned to leave.

"No. Stay Adam," Dad said quietly. "Warm yourself by the fire an' have some hot soup. You're perishin' cold, walkin' all that way an' back in this snow."

He made Adam take off his hat and cloak, and sit by the fire with a bowl of soup. The soup I'd been saving for Grandad. It was all that seemed to come into my mind. I felt strangely distant, numbed by the news. I couldn't take it in. He couldn't be dead too. Not Grandad Creswell.

While Adam ate, Dad asked him for more details. When had Grandad died? How many others had been taken? Were others still suffering with the disease?

"I hope you haven't put yourself at risk, Adam. I'm indebted to you, for offerin' to go an' tell my father about Martha, an' the last thing I would want is for you to be gettin' ill yourself."

Adam shook his head.

"I don't think I was at risk," he replied, swallowing the last mouthful of his soup before he went on.

"Master Creswell was the last, and he died nearly a week back, they said. The Plague had already taken all the yeoman's family – wife and four children – and two of the labourers. There's just the yeoman, his young nephew and an old man left now."

He looked at Dad. "The old man fetched Master Creswell's things for me to bring back to you. He shook out the cloak, bag and hat outside before he gave them to me, to make sure the bad vapours were dispelled into the air. I'd set off home a good mile or two when I heard the young lad shouting after me to come back. I could just hear him. He was way back behind me, wading through the snow, which is much deeper up on the moors than it is down here and he was only a little lad. He was waving something in his hand. When I finally got back to him, he gave me Master Creswell's Bible. They'd forgotten all about it at first as I don't think he looked at it much."

Adam smiled wryly. Grandad's outspoken views on religion were well known in the village, but we didn't want to embarrass Adam by pointing out that another reason Grandad may not have looked at his father's Bible much was that he couldn't read.

Richard opened his mouth to say something, Adam's feelings clearly not in the forefront of his mind, but Dad raised his finger to silence him. Adam noticed the gesture and frowned, then he looked up at me and a deep flush suddenly reddened his face. I think he had remembered our conversation about reading and I looked down, embarrassed for him.

"But the old man remembered about the Bible after I'd left, anyway," Adam went on quietly, trying to ignore his own mortification, "and he sent the lad out after me."

He paused and I looked up again to find Adam frowning slightly, his eyes on my jaw and cheek, and realised the bruises must be very obvious, even in the poor light cast by the fire. I looked away quickly. I didn't want Adam asking questions about the bruises either.

Adam cleared his throat.

"The yeoman at Moors Farm said to tell you how grateful he was to Master Creswell for helping to look after his children after their mother died. She had been the first. Then all the children died, one after the other, and two of the labourers, then Master Creswell succumbed."

I saw Dad glance at myself, Catherine and Richard then, and knew he was counting his blessings.

"They buried him at Dunham, as it's the nearest village to Moors Farm, of course," Adam went on, "and the yeoman was sorry he hadn't been able to send Master Creswell's mortal remains home to be buried beside his wife in Witherstone churchyard. But he said that if there was ever anything he could do for Master Creswell's family, you're to let him know."

"Thank you, Adam," Dad said. "We're indebted to you for your kindness in goin' up there for us, an' for bringin' my father's things home."

It must have been Adam's footprints in the snow of the yard this morning, alongside my father's. I said my thanks too, but Richard avoided Adam's eyes and said nothing. I think my brother casts all Burnetts in the same light.

Adam left us then, and we sat in silence by the fire while Catherine slept on, each of us lost in our own thoughts.

The next morning was a working day as usual, so Dad got ready to go to Thompson's. He couldn't afford to stay idle at home. Richard was clearly feeling his grief over Mum badly this morning, so Dad told him to stay in bed for a while and come to the farm when he felt more like he could, and set out alone as the sun was rising over the horizon.

We couldn't afford for Richard to take the whole day off, of course. We were already well down on what money we should have had coming in over the past couple of weeks, with days lost through Thompson sending Dad and

Richard home, and with Dad going to Hawbury, and having to give money to the gaoler, and then staying at home yesterday meant even less wages of course. Although Job and Daniel had refused to let us pay them for digging Mum's grave.

We'd taken no laundry in since Catherine had become ill either, and I didn't know how I would manage it now, with just my sister to help me. Mind you, I wasn't going to accept laundry from the Parson's house any more, no matter how poor we were, so that probably only left Edward Cowper – especially as the other odd baskets we usually got would probably not be forthcoming from our suspicious and gossiping neighbours. Thinking about it, I had no idea whether Edward Cowper would still want us to be doing his laundry either. But I did know there was no way I would ever agree to work in the Parson's kitchen again. That we wouldn't be needing as much food on the table now I just couldn't bear to think about.

So when Dad walked back through the door just over an hour later, leaving the door wide open, both Richard and I stared at him in shock. Dad's face was white. Whether with rage or distress was impossible to say. Then he told us.

Master Thompson and both of his sons had died, and Mistress Thompson had taken her surviving children to live with her brother in Hawbury. The Squire had bought the farm from her, which means the Sylvestre family now own Thompson's Farm. The new farm manager told Dad that he has been instructed not to employ a Creswell.

"He said he was sorry about it," Dad finished grimly, "but that his hands are tied. He's employed by the Squire an' has to run the farm as the Squire tells him."

I stared at Dad who was now sitting slumped over the table with his head in his hands, and felt a wave of despair and then white, blinding anger. *What had we ever done to them, that they could treat us like this?*

"Who's the new manager?" demanded Richard, looking as furious as I felt.

Dad shrugged. "New man from Hawbury," he replied. "Never set eyes on him before. An' he doesn't know me either, but he's dead set against me nonetheless."

Then, as I recovered enough to take a step towards him, Dad spoke again, his voice so bleak it sent a shiver down my spine.

"An' we'll have to leave the cottage, too, of course," he said.

My hands flew to my face in shock. *Of course. The cottage belongs to Thompson's Farm and is tied to the job. We would have to leave.*

Then I realised with another jolt that Dad and Richard would have no work anywhere in Witherstone. The only other farm in the village was the Hall Farm, and that was the Sylvestre family's, of course. Farm labouring was Dad's livelihood, and his only realistic means of earning a wage. We would have to leave Witherstone altogether.

I stood stock still, my eyes wide with dread as I looked from Dad to Richard and then to Catherine, obliviously poking sticks into the dying embers of the fire. We were homeless.

I sat down next to Dad.

"Did the – the new man say when we have to leave?" I asked, my voice a whisper.

"Tomorrow. He's bringin' other labourers in from Hawbury. We have to be out by tomorrow night."

Dad turned and looked at us with an expression of pure despair, then he swung back to the table and stared at the worn surface unseeingly, his shoulders slumped in defeat and his voice a flat monotone.

"I don't know where we'll go. We need to find somewhere quickly, at least to tide us over while we sort out what we'll do in the long run."

He fell silent then, staring in front of him, and Catherine turned and saw the sombre faces in the room. Large-eyed, she climbed up onto my knee and stared at us all in silence, twisting my plait in her fingers.

Richard got up and walked to the table. He picked up Grandad's hat and ran his fingers along the brim. After a moment, he set the hat firmly on his own head and walked out of the cottage. I heard the latch of the gate click shut behind him.

I carried on sitting next to Dad. I didn't know what to do. I'd never seen him look so defeated. After a while, Catherine left my knee and went out into the yard, coming back in a few minutes later with an egg in each hand.

"Got the eggs, Eppie!" she smiled at me.

I smiled back at my sister and hugged her, then put the eggs in the pot to boil while Catherine went back outside to watch the goats. Dad just went on sitting at the table, lost in his own thoughts. Richard returned over an hour later, grinning fiercely. He sat at the table opposite Dad, Grandad's faded brown hat still on his head.

"I've got a job at Thompson's Farm," he said. "I start tomorrow afternoon." Then he laughed out loud at Dad's look of incredulity. "I told the new man my name was Richard Cowper."

"That's brilliant, Richard!" I said, my voice rushing out in relief. My brother's eyes didn't move from Dad's face.

Instead of staring into nothing, Dad was looking at Richard now.

"But where will we live?" Dad asked after a moment. "We can't stay in the cottage because someone in the village would be bound to tell him we're not Cowpers."

"That's the *really* brilliant part. He asked me if I knew someone who could cook an' clean at the farmhouse, as he's a widower. An' you know that cottage at the far side of the farm, overlookin' the river towards Hawbury?"

Dad nodded.

"Well," Richard went on, "I asked the new man – his name's John Freeman by the way – if I could move my family in there, as my sister is a fine cook an' could easily come over to keep the farmhouse in good order for him, for a fair wage. *You* start tomorrow afternoon too, Eppie."

He looked at me briefly. It was difficult to read the expression in his eyes, but I smiled at him nonetheless. He really *was* brilliant. The cottage he was talking about was nearly four miles from the village, at the far side of Thompson's farm, but not too far to walk from there to keep house for the new manager. And surely far enough outside Witherstone to keep prying eyes from the village realising that we Creswells were still on Sylvestre land? For a while at least.

We both looked at Dad.

Gradually, his face was taking on a look of quiet determination and banishing that awful, empty look of despair he'd had since he came back from Thompson's. He said nothing for a moment, but then he looked at Richard and Grandad's hat on his head and nodded.

"It might well work," he said, "for the time bein', anyway. While I see what else we can do. But I won't be able to come with you. The new man knows who *I* am well enough."

My face must have fallen because Dad reached up and tweaked my chin, just as Mum used to do, and I felt both pleasure and pain in that simple gesture.

"Don't you worry, Eppie. I've got an idea. My father's name was held in esteem at Moors Farm," he said, quietly. "So I'll go an' see if his son's name might be greeted with equal respect. Adam Burnett seemed to think so."

"But it's miles away."

"I know, Eppie, but we have no choice."

Then my father stood up from the table, the feet of the stool scraping on the dirt floor, and lifted Grandad Creswell's hat off Richard's head and set it firmly on his own. Richard picked up Grandad's cloak and passed it to him. Dad took the old grey cloak and slung it over his shoulders, fastening the tarnished metal buckle across his chest and turned to my brother.

"Ask Job if you can borrow his cart to move everythin' up to the other cottage in the mornin', Richard," he said. "You'll have to tell Job what we're doin, but he's a good friend. He won't give us away. If I'm not back before tomorrow night, then you know Moors Farm has taken me on. I'll do my best to make sure I come home – come to the other cottage, I mean – on Sunday if I can, but I can't promise. If I do make it, I'll come through the woods from the Hawbury road side so the new man doesn't see me from the farmhouse."

He hesitated.

"If you're found out, an' have to leave there before you can let me know, take Catherine an' what you can to Job's, Eppie. An' Richard, you help your sister then come up to Moors Farm to tell me. You know where it is, on the road to Dunham. If that happens, we'll have to see whether we can all stay up there. They may not want all of us, an' your Grandad always said it's a hard livin' up there, but we may end up with no choice."

He paused before he went on quietly.

"An' somehow, in all of this, I need to go an' see your Gran'ma. Take her more food an' pay the gaoler, an' – an' tell her about your mum."

My heart lurched. Of course. Grandma still didn't know. She must be worried sick about all of us. How on earth was Dad going to be able to tell her about Mum? My eyes glanced involuntarily at the empty bed.

"Don't worry, Dad," Richard said, his expression stony, "I'll take care of Eppie an' Catherine, an' go to Hawbury gaol to tell Gran'ma."

Dad shook his head.

"No, you won't. I'm not havin' you or your sisters anywhere near that place. I'll go myself on Sunday, if I'm able to come to Thompson's that is, as I can go on to Hawbury from there. But I might not be able to come this Sunday. I just don't know. Of course, Moors Farm might not want me anyway, but from what Adam has told us, I think there's a good chance."

I tried not to look bothered about the thought of Dad being so far away for days or weeks at a time, but I couldn't have hidden my real feelings very well because he laid his hand on my arm.

"We'll still be together, Eppie – still be a family, even if we have to spend time apart. The Creswells won't be broken," he said firmly, sounding just like Grandad.

He stood in thought for a moment, then he tugged at something round his neck and lifted a leather cord out from inside his shirt. There was something swinging on the cord, glinting in the sunlight coming in through the open door. I realised at once what it was.

Dad lifted the cord over his head and came across to me, putting it over my head and placing Mum's wedding ring into the palm of my hand and folding my fingers over it. He must have taken it from her finger and hung it around his neck the night he kept vigil at her side, while I lay sleeping next to Catherine.

"But –" I protested.

"No, Eppie, she'd have wanted you to have it."

Dad squeezed my hand gently, then he turned towards my brother.

"Take care of Eppie an' Catherine, Richard. I'll be back when I can."

Then he strode from the cottage and was gone. I stared at the empty doorway for a long time, still holding my mother's ring in my hand. Then I tucked the thin band inside my bodice and felt it hard and cold over my heart. I knew I should feel that all hope might not be lost after all, but I couldn't.

Witherstone

That evening, Richard fetched Job's cart up from the village and left it outside our gate. I tried not to think about the cart's last load as we piled our household goods onto it.

As well as our meagre furniture and kitchen things, we packed as much of our firewood and peat turfs onto the cart as we could, stacking it between the legs of the upturned table. We got all but the heaviest branches on there, and tucked the axes well into the pile so we wouldn't lose them off the cart on the way. Richard managed to heave the old bench from the yard onto the pile too. Grandad had made that bench, a long time ago, so we didn't want to leave it behind. It was dark by the time we finished.

All the while we were clearing the cottage, Richard only spoke to me when he needed to. I knew he still blamed me for what had happened, and no matter how much I agreed with him, it still hurt that he was so cold towards me. He sat by the fire all night instead of coming to bed, although he was slumped against the wall fast asleep by the morning.

When I'd tucked Catherine up in bed for her last night in our home, I sat and looked around our tiny cottage for a long time. My whole life was here. Had been here. I'd been born in this room. As was Richard before me, and later Catherine, of course. It was the only home we had known and it had been, I realised now, mostly a happy one. But now. Now there were fewer of us, and we were scattered to the four winds, just as Grandad used to say.

We let the fire die down overnight, and by morning there were just cold ashes on the hearth. I packed our remaining things onto the cart, including our blankets and personal belongings we hadn't wanted to leave out overnight, such as Dad's hat and cloak and Grandad's family Bible, while Richard went down to fetch Job's horse.

While he was gone, I tied two baskets together to transport the last two hens. They watched me from the gaps in their temporary prison with head-bobbing interest as I loaded them onto the cart. I'd already packed that morning's eggs, along with the last of our food. Finally, I tied the goat to the back, her spindly-legged kid sticking to her as closely as her shadow with Catherine happily stroking its soft ears.

Richard got back with the horse and was harnessing it to the cart, when suddenly I heard someone running up the lane behind us. It was Adam.

"What's happened, Eppie? Why are you leaving?"

I took a step towards him but Richard butted in before I could speak.

"That's none of your business, Burnett."

Adam flushed with anger.

"I wasn't talking to you."

"An' you can stay away from my sister," said Richard, turning his back on Adam.

"We're goin' -" I began, but Richard pushed me to one side hissing, "Shut up! You can't tell *him*!"

"He's my friend."

"He's a Burnett! He's no friend to us. You're to stay away from him."

"You can't tell me who to talk to!"

"Yes I can. Dad told me to take care of everythin', an' I'm the eldest so it's up to me who you can speak to."

I tried to push round him but he grabbed my arm and yanked me back, and I whirled round and hit my brother hard. "*Let go of me!*"

"Adam. Home. Now." A smooth voice behind us.

We all turned then. Parson Burnett was standing a few feet behind Adam. No-one had heard him coming. Adam ignored his father and turned to face me, his cheeks suddenly pale.

"Eppie?"

I looked at him but knew I couldn't tell him now, not with his father standing right there.

"'Bye, Adam," I said, and watched the hurt expression come into his eyes.

He turned away and marched past his father towards the village. Parson Burnett's pale eyes flickered over Richard, Catherine and me, and our loaded cart, then he turned and followed his son down the lane, his black cloak billowing out behind him just as I had seen it doing once before.

Richard glared at me, then he lifted Catherine onto the horse's back and she sat there clutching its mane and looking excited. My brother turned away without a word and clicked the horse forward, and we set off up the lane towards Thompson's Farm, Catherine crying out, "Look Eppie! Look at me!"

I smiled up at my sister's bright eyes, glinting almost green in the sunlight, as I walked beside the horse with one hand on her leg to make sure she was secure, but my hand was trembling. I looked back towards the village, but Adam and Parson Burnett had already gone. I felt like I'd betrayed my only remaining friend.

213

Witherstone

I turned back to Catherine. I was glad she was seeing this move as an adventure. I'd tried to explain the day before that we had to move to another cottage, but I think it was only as we loaded the cart with all of our things that she began to understand what I meant. I hoped she would settle in the new place – and that we'd be able to stay there long enough for her to settle.

As we passed the Hawbury turn-off and approached the curve of the lane round towards Thompson's, I thought I heard music coming from the village. I turned. Far back down the road, the families from Weavers Cottages were running away from us towards the centre of the village. The sound of fiddles was clear on the air now and I suddenly realised that it was the first day of May. May Day. I felt a lump in my throat.

The first of May was a special holiday. Most labourers had at least part of the day off so they could enjoy the festivities, watching the crowning of the May Queen and playing music and singing and dancing. This year the Creswells would not be a part of it. Instead, we were leaving our home - and so much more - behind us. Especially in Witherstone graveyard. And Dad was miles away and we didn't know for sure when we would see him again, while Grandma was in prison awaiting trial for witchcraft. If she was found guilty, she would die.

And it was my birthday. Today I turned fourteen. The next moment, we rounded the curve in the lane, and Witherstone and its music was lost behind us.

12

Changes

Most of the snow had gone, apart from a few thin patches in the shade. After we'd walked for a while, Richard said we should keep going right past the farmhouse, arriving at the cottage from the back way in case someone from the village happens to be at the farmhouse and sees us. His voice was curt as he spoke, and he avoided looking at me.

I didn't reply. I was still furious with him for stopping me from talking to Adam while I'd had the chance – before Parson Burnett had appeared and made it impossible.

As we came to the track to the farmhouse, we both looked across nervously as we carried on past, but could see no-one around. The lane climbed steadily on, curving round in a long arc as it wound through the trees, giving occasional glimpses of the river below.

"You'd better tell Master Freeman that your name's Mary or somethin'," Richard said, his voice carrying a slight tone of accusation. "There's only one Eppie in Witherstone, an' usin' Hephzibah would even worse for givin' us away."

My stomach turned over. *Of course.* To pull this off I'd have to lose my name as well as my father and my home. Pretending to be called Cowper instead of Creswell was one thing, but having to pretend my name was Mary or something was worse. It felt like everything I was, everything that made me *me*, was disappearing.

I still didn't answer but brooded miserably, the steady pace of the horse's hooves giving a rhythm to the names coming into my head.

Ma-ry, Ma-ry, Ma-ry-Ann, Ma-ry-Ann, Ann-ie. Annie. That would do. I didn't want to choose 'Mary' because Richard had suggested it. Ann was my middle name anyway, as it had been Mary Ann's, so at least it would be easy enough for me to remember. And with it being the old woman's name, whose potion had saved Catherine's life, that would give me some satisfaction that I was getting one up over our enemies somehow.

"Annie," I said, sullenly.

"Well, Annie Cowper, say hello to your new home," Richard said quietly as we turned the last curve of the track.

I wished he'd looked at me then, so that I could have made up with him, but he was looking straight ahead as the cottage came into view. I sighed and looked away from my brother towards the cottage.

I hadn't been up here for years. The whole place looked pretty neglected. It was the same kind of crook-framed cottage as ours, except this one had a stone built chimney, and tiny panes of glass in the window instead of oiled linen. The roof was thatched with oat straw, as ours had been, but it was full of green grass and holes and there were gaps in the daub on the outer walls, so it looked like there were plenty of places for the wind and rain to get in. But at least it was a roof over our heads.

The cottage was surrounded by scrubby hazel and hawthorn, so that might give us some protection from the wind, and there was a tumbledown old shed too, which hopefully held a privy. Or it soon would do. There was no yard as such, so we would have to bring the hens into the cottage at night to protect them from foxes. We used to do that when I was younger, but when Catherine was born Dad had built a hen coop in the yard. Behind the cottage, the hill sloped steeply down to the river, and it was thick with grasses, so the goats would be fine there.

I helped Catherine down while Richard shoved the door open with effort, and we followed him inside.

"I'll have to fix the door - an' the roof," Richard said, as we found a small snowdrift against the back wall.

Catherine went back outside and I checked the fireplace. There was an iron grate and a couple of hooks inside the chimney, so keeping ourselves warm and fed should be easy enough, if nothing else. I was surprised when I turned away from the fire. There was a rickety old ladder leading up to a small sleeping platform in the roof space. The platform extended nearly half way across the room, and Richard climbed up and said it seemed sound enough to hold us all, although there was a dusting of snow on there too so he'd have to take a look at the roof as soon as he had some free time.

"We'll have to sleep on the floor 'til I can get the roof fixed. It'll give us some shelter under there if it rains before I can get it done. We'll need to get some straw to sleep on though, if Master Freeman will let us have some in advance of our wages."

I went outside to start unloading the cart. I let the goat loose on the grassy slope with the kid nudging her for milk, then left Catherine watching them while I helped Richard unload everything. It didn't take long.

I got the fire going, though it took me a frustratingly long time to start it from scratch, even with Grandma's tinderbox, and I was mad with myself for not thinking about that at home – at our old home – because I could have lit the match cord before we had let the fire go out during the night. I got it going in the end, thankfully, and was pleased to see more than half the smoke heading straight up the chimney.

"I'll have to try an' get some straw to fix the roof on Sunday, an' I'll sort the walls out as soon as I can, but I think the roof is the worst," Richard said, then went on quietly. "It's not so bad, Eppie, is it?"

I turned to my brother, grateful that he was talking to me like he cared how I was feeling.

"No, it was a really good idea, Richard, an' a whole lot better than havin' nowhere. I just hope Dad can come back on Sunday."

But Richard turned away before I'd even finished speaking, and as I looked at his retreating back I wished he had spoken to me for longer. I missed my brother.

The morning was almost over by this time, and we had to get back across to the farmhouse by early afternoon. It was quite a way, and we didn't want to be late so I went to fetch Catherine. Before we left, Richard led Job's horse onto the slope to graze while I covered the fire with peat turfs. We released the hens into the cottage and scattered a handful of our remaining oats out for them. They would make sure our bed for the night was insect-free at least.

Richard heaved the door shut and we set off, eating a piece of bread each for our midday meal as we walked. My stomach was churning nervously, getting worse and worse the nearer we got, and by the time we were walking up to the farmhouse, I was almost trembling. For one thing, I was afraid I would look guilty. Grandma *always* knew when I was lying. But I was also terrified that someone from the village would be there, someone who knew us.

And then there was Catherine.

On the way I tried to explain to her that she must always whisper to us, and *never* shout, but I'm not sure whether she understood or not. Only time would tell. One loud "Eppie!" from Catherine and our charade would be over almost before it had begun.

The back door was already open, and I could see a figure inside sitting at the kitchen table. The man turned his head to look at us as we approached. We stopped at the door, Catherine holding my hand but half-hiding behind my skirts and peering out at him.

The man carried on sitting there, and I could see his meal in front of him. He regarded us all for quite a few minutes while he went on chewing his food, saying not a word. I began to feel really awkward, standing there at his door and watching him eating, so I kept looking away across the yard, watching the hens scratching in the dirt or gazing over towards the cows in the field, but his silent stare was hard to ignore and my eyes kept coming back to the man in the kitchen.

After finishing off a thick slice of black pudding, he looked at my brother and finally spoke.

"You've got here earlier than I would have expected. Have you moved into the cottage?"

Richard nodded. "Yes, Sir."

"And this is my new housekeeper, I presume?"

Master Freeman turned his eyes towards me. His face was smooth and expressionless. There was something about his inexpressive manner which reminded me of Parson Burnett, and I swallowed.

"Yes Sir. This is Annie, my sister," Richard answered, without so much as a stumble. "An' this is our younger sister too," he went on, nodding at Catherine. "She's a good girl, an' won't be in anybody's way."

The man looked at us standing together on the step, including Catherine, who was staring solemnly back at him, then he drained his mug abruptly and stood up. He picked his hat up off the table and strode towards us, and we moved out of the way quickly and stared after him as he swept past us and into the yard. When he reached the gate, he turned to look at Richard.

After a moment Richard realised that Master Freeman was waiting for him and shot forwards, murmuring "'Bye Eppie – *Annie*, I mean," and walked quickly across the yard.

I watched them go into the field behind the house, heading towards the old barn. Then I turned and looked into the kitchen.

"Well," I said to Catherine, her large eyes peering up at me, "I guess we'd better get on."

The farm kitchen was bigger than our old cottage and without the clutter of beds. It was smaller than the Parson's kitchen, although it still had a large fireplace and a bread oven. There was also an iron spit and several hooks, and a lot of cooking pots. The fire was lit, although the kitchen didn't look as though it had been used for cooking for several days. The remains of Master Freeman's meal was a poor affair of what looked like stale bread and a rather grey-looking cold pie. The black pudding must have been the best bit as that had all gone. It didn't look like he was used to cooking for himself, or maybe he just hadn't had the time, with taking over the running of a new farm with few if any labourers.

I got Catherine sweeping the floor while I cleaned out the cold bread oven and heaped the largest hot logs from the fire inside it, and closed the door, then built up the fire again in the grate. There was a well in the yard, and the water was clear and fresh when I drew up the bucket, so that would save me having to go down to the river for water. Then I looked to see what I could cook for Master Freeman.

There was rye and wheat flour, barley, oats and fine oatmeal, and a jug of fresh milk and several eggs, plus butter, salt, sugar and raisins, as well as cinnamon and cloves and other pungent spices, salted mutton, smoked fish, and several thick sausages. A larder fit for the King, Isaac would have said. I suddenly wondered how the old pedlar was, and hoped he had escaped the Plague outbreak. I knew he would miss taking a meal with us when he next passed through Witherstone.

There was also a large basket of vegetables, including what I recognised as artichoke roots. I'd cooked these in the Burnett's kitchen, and had tasted them, liking their earthy flavour, but my family had never eaten them. I think Ellen had said they came all the way from Jerusalem, on the other side of the world, but when I'd told Mum she had laughed and said she bet they came all the way from Hawbury, which is like being on the other side of the world as far as Ellen was concerned. With a jolt I brought my mind back from raw memories, pressing my mother's ring into my heart.

I made bread dough and left it to rise near the heat of the fire, then made a mutton and vegetable stew, a herb dumpling, and several pasties with some of the meat and vegetables from the pot. Once the bread oven was hot enough, I scraped the red-hot embers to one side and put the loaf in, praying it would cook properly in the middle as Ellen had always been responsible for the bread at the Parson's house. Finally, I made a batch of raisin and cinnamon griddle cakes. I was making the best food I could, keen to make a good impression with Master Freeman so he'd want to keep us on.

When the pasties were cooked, I looked across the yard and the field outside. There was no sign of anyone, so I quickly went back in and gave Catherine the smallest pasty I had made, and kept watch out the back while she ate it. When she'd finished, I gave her a cinnamon scone, and then left her sitting by the fire with a drink of milk and went outside again.

I looked over to where Richard and the new manager had disappeared earlier, but still couldn't see anyone around. They could be anywhere on the farm. I wasn't sure whether I was supposed to be cleaning the rest of the house or not. There were obviously several rooms, and no bed in the kitchen, so Master Freeman must sleep in one of them. I decided that I ought to have a quick look around the rest of the house to see if anything obvious needed doing. I didn't want him to think I was a poor housekeeper.

The kitchen led onto a long passageway leading to the front door, a small leaded window to one side letting in a dim light. It was similar to the passageway at the Parson's house. The first room had a long dining table with several high-backed chairs, and a plain fireplace with a pock-marked glass mirror in an old frame hanging over it. The room didn't look as though it had been used for a while.

After a quick look over my shoulder, I walked over to the mirror and studied the face which looked back at me. I saw a serious-faced girl with thin cheeks and dark circles under her eyes. She had yellowing bruises on her cheek and jaw, and dark brown hair either side of her face beneath her linen cap, and eyes so dark in the shadowed room they looked almost black. She looked back at me without blinking.

I practiced a smile. The girl smiled back thinly, but her eyes remained serious as she continued to stare back at me. I turned away from the mirror and walked back into the passage, past the staircase to another door. This must be the parlour, although I'd never been in the parlour at the Parson's house so I was only guessing. I lifted the latch and opened the door. There were two plain oak settles with worn upholstered seats arranged facing one another in front of a panelled chimney breast. This room had been used recently as there were footprints scuffing across the dusty floor. I closed the door and turned to the stairs.

The staircase was narrow and crooked, rising up into the shadows. I climbed nervously, worried about whether I was supposed to be there, each step creaking beneath my tread. At the top of the stairs two doors faced one other across a gloomy corridor. The first latch *clacked* as it lifted, loud in the narrow passageway, and the door creaked away from me, revealing a dim room with a large wooden bed which had been slept in, the blankets thrown back untidily and there was a chamber pot on the floor. But by now I felt so jumpy with nerves, scared that I wasn't even supposed to be up here, that instead of making the bed and taking the pot outside to empty, I pulled the door closed quickly, then fled down the creaking stairs and along the dark passageway to the kitchen.

There I found Catherine helping herself to the raisin cakes, with another one already gone from the platter, and I was angrier with her than I'd ever been in her life. By the time I'd finished raging at her, my little sister was crying loudly, even though she hadn't been able to hear a word I said, of course, but my angry face and gripping fingers must have been bad enough. Then I dropped her arms in horror and ran to the door, cursing myself.

Idiot! Master Freeman hadn't actually been here to see Catherine taking the cakes, and yet I could have told him all about it myself with my shouting. I was also sure I'd been shouting her name. I could see no-one around, but it was the final straw for my already nervous state.

By the time Master Freeman returned an hour or so later, Catherine was still sulking by the fire, and I was so ridden with anxiety that we'd been found out and would be forced to leave that I jumped as he walked into the kitchen. If he noticed my guilty start he didn't say a word, but threw his hat on the table and sat down.

"You can be off home now, as it's May Day," he said, without turning to look at me stirring the stew over the fire, "but I'd like you here as early as your brother tomorrow. As well as cooking me an early breakfast, I'd like you to sweep out the rest of the rooms. Can you manage laundry?" he asked, turning to face me.

I nodded but avoided meeting his eyes by concentrating on stirring the stew. I was terrified he'd be able to read my guilty expression.

"Well, there's some washing to do, and I've a couple of shirts could do with mending too, if you're able?"

I nodded again and brought him a large bowl of the stew, still avoiding his eyes all the while.

"You don't say much, you Cowpers, do you?" he said, and I could see him looking from me to Catherine, then he turned back to the table and began to eat the stew.

I grabbed our cloaks and my sister's hand and we headed back to the new cottage, where I was surprised to see a lot of smoke coming out of the chimney. Catherine forgot about her sulking and shot off to see the goats as soon as we got near enough, but I peered in at the window.

It was dark inside the tiny room, apart from the glow of bright flames in the iron grate, so I couldn't see if anyone was there. I pushed the door open and found Richard sitting on the bench by the fire. It was a strange moment as it was almost like coming home. Like nothing had changed.

"I've had quite a busy afternoon," he said, and jerked his head up towards the roof.

I followed his hint and saw that the holes in the roof had been mended with fresh straw.

"But how?" I asked, amazed. "Did Master Freeman let you come an' mend the roof instead of workin' on the farm?"

"Not only that, it was *his* idea. He helped me fix it, too, workin' alongside me as if we were both labourers. He said that after I'd first asked him if we could move in here, he'd come over to take a look at the place an' found that the roof wasn't sound, so he decided it would be my first job. An' he helped me fix the door an' the walls too."

I realised then that the door had been much easier to open than when we'd arrived that morning, and I looked at the walls. Patches of riverbed clay were showing dark where it had been used to fill the gaps in the daub, the criss-cross lines of straw pale against it. The larger holes outside had been filled too, and Richard followed me, keen to show off his handiwork.

"They need limin' of course, but they'll have to dry out first. When we left you an' Catherine at the farmhouse, Master Freeman took me across to the barn an' told me to pick up as many sheaves of straw as I could carry, takin' as large a bundle himself, an' got me to follow him across the farm without a word of where we were goin' or anythin'."

He grinned.

"As we got nearer to this place, I was hopin' I might get the chance to ask if we could have a bit of straw to sleep on an' fix the holes in the roof, but he brought me right to the door anyway, an' said we'd be fixin' this place up as the first job."

Richard looked at me for a moment, his grin vanishing and his face serious.

"He seems like a good man, Eppie, so if we can just keep him from findin' out who we really are, we'll be alright here. Shame that he knows who Dad is, though, but as it is..." he trailed off. "Anyway," he said, changing the subject, "how did you get on at the farmhouse?"

I hesitated, not wanting to spoil my brother's good mood by telling him that I'd looked round the farmhouse without permission and nearly blown it by losing my temper with Catherine, so as we walked back inside I only told him what I'd been doing in the kitchen. Talking about the food I'd cooked for Master Freeman made my stomach groan. Richard smiled at that, then he nodded towards the corner of the room behind me. A sack leaning against the wall was full of bags of oats and rye flour, vegetables, a parcel of salted pork, and even raisins and sugar.

"Is all this for us?"

He nodded.

"How long will it take us to earn *this* lot?" I asked.

Richard laughed out loud then, an almost hysterical edge to his voice.

"Master Freeman said this is to cover our wages 'til the end of next week, as he needs to wait 'til then before he has any money to pay us *'properly'*."

"'Til the end of *next week?*" I exclaimed. "This is nearly as much food as we could earn in a month!"

Later that night Catherine was curled up asleep in a deep bed of straw on the platform, her face flushed from the amount of food she had insisted on eating before she went to bed.

I sat by the fire with my brother, both of us painfully full of food even though there was still half a pot of rich stew left for tomorrow night. I'd also baked pasties for our midday meals tomorrow too, and even some raisin griddle cakes.

Richard had taken Job's horse and cart back while I'd got on with cooking, and we had both been feeling our losses more sharply since he'd got back. Witherstone had been enjoying the May Day evening, the village full of singing and dancing and laughter. A full stomach wasn't enough to fill the emptiness we felt inside us.

"We're not the only ones, though, Eppie," he reminded me. "An' Mistress Thompson lost her husband an' two of her sons, an' *she's* lost her home too."

"I know," I sighed. "But you need to try an' call me Annie all the time, Richard, to make sure we don't slip up. Perhaps we should try an' call Catherine somethin' else too? Though I'm not sure I'll remember to do it."

"I wouldn't remember, either. It's bad enough tryin' to remember to call you Annie. Perhaps we shouldn't use her name at all – it's not like she can hear us, anyway, so *she* won't mind."

Knowing my sister, I thought she *would* mind, but it made sense so I didn't say anything. For a moment I nearly told Richard about my outburst at the farmhouse, when I'd found Catherine eating the cakes, but I bit my lip. He would be furious with me for letting her steal the cakes *and* for shouting at her, putting us at risk with my temper as I could have easily revealed who we were. The anger my brother had shown towards me since I'd got back from the witch seemed forgotten for the moment, so I didn't want to spoil his mood. He had even remembered it was my birthday, bringing home a small bunch of bluebells. They were a painful reminder, too, but I didn't mention that as I put the small pot in the centre of the table.

The next morning we were at the farmhouse by dawn, keen to keep Master Freeman happy. I cooked eggs for his breakfast, and then he asked me to cook extra, telling Richard to sit down and share them with him and telling me to cook some for myself and "the little 'un" as he called Catherine.

"Oh, we couldn't do that, Sir," I said in surprise and confusion.

"Don't be ridiculous," he replied. "You all look half-starved, and there's far too much food in the house for me alone. You cooked enough yesterday to keep me going for a week, so I won't be able to eat all the eggs as well. The other men won't be coming until the weekend, and the eggs won't keep. And I'd prefer 'Master Freeman', not 'Sir'."

I did as he asked, all the time trying to find the words to thank him for fixing the cottage up for us, and providing all that food. I decided I'd thank him while we were eating, so I sat Catherine at the table with her eggs and sat opposite her. Catherine looked at me wide-eyed, looking nervously from me to Master Freeman and back again, but not touching the eggs.

I could feel my cheeks reddening as I realised my scolding of the day before was the reason for this. I leaned forward and smiled encouragingly, telling her to eat up and gesturing to the eggs, showing her that I was eating mine.

"Is the child simple?" Master Freeman asked. I flushed more deeply, this time with anger.

"*No, she's not!* She just can't hear, that's all. She was ill an' nearly died. She got better but she's deaf now - she's not *simple!*" I finished, then felt my stomach drop like a stone as I realised with horror that I'd been really rude.

Richard's face was livid. I tried to back-track, speaking more politely.

"What I meant -"

Master Freeman stopped me, holding his hands up defensively, and I was reminded then of the scarred man – Robert Newstead – rather than Parson Burnett. I was mortified by my outburst.

The rest of the meal was eaten in silence, Master Freeman's expression stony. I ate quickly, cheeks burning, then got up from the table and went to get the wash barrel from the shed, determined to get to work and put the memory of my rudeness to the back of Master Freeman's mind. We couldn't afford for me to ruin everything now.

Master Freeman and Richard were leaving as I brought the half-barrel into the kitchen, my brother glaring at me as he walked past, and my heart sank. I wished I could take the words back. I knew Richard would blame me for this forever.

I got Catherine sweeping the dusty floors in the dining room and parlour while I hung a large pot over the fire, filling it with water from the well and adding soapwort and the cool ashes from the hearth tied up in a muslin bag. Once the water was hot, I poured it into the wash tub and gave the linen a good bashing and then left it to soak while I washed the breakfast things. After the linen had been soaking a while, I scrubbed it and then wrung it out, then put the blankets into the barrel with a pot full of fresh lye, and left them to soak while I checked on Catherine.

She had made good inroads into the dust but the floor needed washing too, so I poured some of the soapy water into a bucket and gave Catherine a cloth to wipe down the floors while I started cooking Master Freeman's evening meal, making sure there were still pasties left from the day before for him to eat if he came back for some food at midday.

After I'd wrung out the heavy blankets as best I could, I dragged the heavy barrel outside and emptied it onto the yard, then filled the barrel with clean water from the well. I squeezed and pounded the soap out of the linen and the blankets, then wrung them out and hung them outside to dry.

There was a warm breeze so the linen should dry in a couple of hours. The blankets would take much longer, the water still running out of those as they were too thick and heavy for me to wring out properly by myself.

By the time the laundry was all hanging out in the yard, and the pie I'd made for Master Freeman's evening meal was ready to go in the oven, I was helping Catherine to finish cleaning the parlour. I heard heavy footsteps coming down the passageway from the kitchen and I straightened and stood politely, taking Catherine's hand and looking down at the ground as Ellen had with Mistress Burnett as Master Freeman came into the parlour.

"Well, this is looking much better," his voice said, after a slightly awkward few moments of silence.

"Thank you, Sir," I said.

"Master Freeman."

"Master Freeman," I repeated, then I looked up and carried on speaking before I could put myself off with worrying about saying the right thing.

"I-I want to thank you, Sir – Master Freeman – for fixin' the roof, an' for the food you brought. I'm sorry for my rudeness this mornin'," I went on, although I could feel my chin jutting into the air defiantly despite my attempts to be contrite. "It's just that my sister means a lot to me, an' we thought she was goin' to die so we're glad it's only her hearin' that suffered."

He held up his hands as he had that morning, but this time he was smiling.

"I'm not surprised you were so cross, then, *and* I apologise to your sister."

He turned towards Catherine, who was staring up at him with her solemn eyes, and he smiled at her too and politely bowed his head. He was rewarded with a shy smile which lit up her entire face.

He turned to face me abruptly, and I was taken aback by his expression as he looked almost angry, despite Catherine returning his smile.

"As for the food," he said, his face tense and his eyes hard, "it needs eating, and I need a work-force that can stay on its feet long enough to put in a good day's work. Can you clean the bedchambers this afternoon?"

"Y-yes, of-of course, Sir – Master Freeman," I stammered, made nervous again by his suddenly abrupt manner.

He nodded and turned on his heel, and I listened to him striding back down to the kitchen. When we went back down the passage ourselves a few minutes later, the room was empty and one of the pasties had gone too.

I sat outside on the wall of the well with Catherine while we ate our own pies we'd brought with us that morning, then we got straight on with cleaning the rest of the rooms. We tidied and swept and scrubbed both bedchambers, then went back to the kitchen to put the pie in the oven and put the kitchen in order.

Later, when I was taking the pie out, I heard Catherine laughing outside where I'd sent her to play for a while, and she came running in the door with Master Freeman close behind her. He was laughing too, and it made me smile to see Catherine happy, but I couldn't help wondering at Master Freeman. I couldn't make him out. His face was inexpressive most of the time, so you didn't know what he was thinking, but then he would suddenly be smiling one minute and angry the next.

Catherine came over to me as she usually did, but she didn't hide behind my skirts this time. I quickly gave her a drink of water so she wouldn't have to ask me for anything. I was constantly dreading that she would say "Eppie" out loud.

Master Freeman poured himself a mug of beer then sat down at the table, and said we could get off home now, and that he wouldn't be expecting us to come tomorrow as it was Sunday.

"Oh!" I said. "But I haven't cooked extra food for you for tomorrow."

He laughed, waving his hand towards the pie and the other food around the room. "I have plenty here, Annie. Come back on Monday."

I thanked him and, before we left, I folded his dry shirts to take back to the cottage, determined to spend Sunday mending them as neatly as I could, although I knew my sewing skills were nothing to Grandma's. I felt a sudden rush of guilt. I hadn't thought about the terrible situation my grandmother was in very much over the past few days.

It was always *there*, of course, like a lead weight in my stomach to add to the deeper pain of Mum's death, but I hadn't been trying to work out how we could prove Grandma's innocence and get her out of the gaol. I'd been putting so much hope on Grandad Creswell being able to help us that now I didn't know who else we could turn to. But we had to do *something*.

As we got back to the cottage, I felt an echo of something like happiness – of course, Dad might be able to come home to us tonight.

But by the time midnight came, we'd waited up so long I'd finished mending all of Master Freeman's linen, and Richard and I were both in a gloomy mood.

"Well, he might be settin' off early in the mornin' instead," my brother said, but I knew he was sure that Dad must have had to stay up at Moors Farm instead of coming to us, and we were quiet as we went to bed that night.

13

Hawbury Gaol

Richard was up and pacing outside the cottage by dawn, and I was preparing food for Grandma just in case Dad did manage to come. After I'd finished packing enough food to keep her going for two weeks or more, Richard came back into the cottage.

"No sign of him. I'm goin' to Hawbury myself, to take the food to Gran'ma," he said, picking up the bag.

"What? *You can't!* Dad said we weren't to go – he doesn't want us to go to the gaol. We have to wait for him."

"But Dad's not here, an' Gran'ma needs to eat."

"I know she does, but -"

"I'm *goin'!*" he said, and turned and walked out of the cottage.

"Well, then I'm comin' with you!" I shouted after him. He came right back in again.

"Oh no you're not!" he said, outraged.

"I need to see Gran'ma too," I said, trying to keep the pleading note out of my voice. I didn't see why it should be up to him. "We need to tell her about - about Mum, an' we need to ask her what we can do to get her out of there."

"What can *we* do? We'll have to leave that to Dad."

"Dad's not here." I said, and folded my arms, ready for a fight.

My brother stared at me, exasperated.

"You're too young," he said finally.

"So are you."

"I'm fifteen."

"Well I'm fourteen now, an' anyway, neither of us are adults."

"But what about Catherine?"

"She's nearly five," I said sarcastically, deliberately ignoring his real meaning.

"I know *that*," he said crossly, "I mean, where will she go, if you come?"

"She'll have to come with us. What difference does it make? They're not goin' to *arrest* her."

As I said that, I had a horrible feeling of vertigo. What if they arrested all of us?

But why on earth would they? I argued with myself. *We haven't done anything.* Well, *I* have, but they don't know that. Unless - unless they've forced Grandma to tell them what really happened. *But she wouldn't ever betray me.* Yet, what if she was tortured into telling them the truth? I felt sick just thinking about it. I tried to reason against my fears, knowing that Grandma would do anything to protect us – that's why she had hidden me and put herself in my place. But I was terrified of ending up in gaol with her.

I didn't let on to Richard, though, I just stared him out while he stood there trying to think of another reason why I couldn't go with him. I knew I had to go. I don't know why I hadn't realised it before. I *had* to see my grandmother. Not just because I wanted to see her, but because I needed to ask *her* what we could do to get her out of there. Who else could I ask?

Finally, Richard sighed.

"Come on, then. We've got to walk to Witherstone first, though, to borrow a boat."

I got Catherine and myself ready quickly, then we set off to Witherstone. It didn't take us as long to walk back to the village as it had seemed to take us to get to Thompson's cottage on the morning we'd left. As we arrived at the track to the river meadow, just before we would have come to our old home, Richard sent me and Catherine to wait on the riverbank while he went into the village to see if he could borrow either Edward Cowper's boat or Job's. After a while, Catherine pointed across the meadow towards the back of the churchyard.

"Richard's coming!" she said, and I saw he was cutting through alongside the churchyard wall, near where I saw Master Nalgah when I was at Mum's grave and had chased across the meadow after the scarred man.

I wondered if Robert Newstead and his friend were still up in the woods, or if they had continued on their journey now, heading up to Yorkshire or Lancashire in search of a new home. I shivered. I hoped we wouldn't have to go as far as that if Master Freeman discovered our charade and sent us packing.

I lifted Catherine and the bag into Edward Cowper's boat and climbed in, sitting her on my knee in the stern as Richard got in after us. He pushed us away from the bank and slipped the oars into the rowlocks, then pulled us round into the mainstream, and we headed back towards Thompson's Farm.

Richard rowed expertly, although the flow of the river would take us down fast enough anyway. It was on the way back upriver from Hawbury that Richard would have to work hard, rowing against the current. Within a surprisingly short while we could see the hill leading to Thompson's rising alongside the riverbank, then the chimneys of the farmhouse, and a little later, I saw our goat grazing near the trees at the top of the hill, her kid curled up in the grass a few feet away.

Catherine saw them too and shouted, and the animals raised their heads sharply and looked at us, then the kid bounded over to its mother and butted her for milk and my sister laughed. Seconds later, we swept round the curve and they were gone.

The river was pretty quiet all the way down to Hawbury, and as the smoking chimneys of the town came into view, Richard pulled us nearer to the bank in readiness. We could see a number of rowing boats moored there, and my brother pulled us in alongside them and jumped onto the bank, holding the boat steady while I lifted Catherine out and climbed ashore myself. Richard secured the mooring rope, and we turned to walk into the town.

The quayside was lined with small fisherman's cottages, and there was a wide road leading up into the centre of the town. I took Catherine's hand. We soon reached the market square, which was quite busy despite there being no market on a Sunday. The people of Hawbury were at their doors or strolling across the square, chatting to one another and passing the time of day.

As we reached the centre of the square, we slowed to a halt, and I realised that neither myself nor Richard knew where the gaol was. We didn't come to Hawbury often, and only when it was market day, so we'd never been anywhere else in the town other than the market square.

I looked at Richard and he looked at me, and he rolled his eyes humourlessly before turning to a man walking past us.

"Excuse me, Sir, could you tell us how to get to the gaol?"

"That's easy, son," the man said. "Pick my pocket an' I'll haul you up there meself!" and the man roared with laughter, as though it was the funniest joke in the world.

Richard flushed deeply with anger and embarrassment, the same sensations flaming in my own cheeks. I was acutely aware of other faces turning to look at us in response to the man's loud voice. Richard turned away angrily, but the man called him back and my brother glared at him, waiting.

"Now then, young man, no need to take offence. You'll find the gaol at the top of the hill there, y'see? Go up past the Anchor Inn, an' you'll come to the gaol soon enough. It's a grey stone castle, you can't miss it. Just make sure they remember to let you out again!"

Richard pulled me across the square without a word of thanks to the man, leaving him laughing at his own wit again as we walked quickly towards the inn the man had pointed out. As we passed the Anchor and entered the narrow lane, I knew Richard was as relieved as I was to be escaping the interested stares of the townsfolk in the square, but at the same time, I was feeling more and more anxious about seeing Grandma, knowing we would have to tell her about Mum and the baby.

As soon as we got to the top of the lane we could see the man had been right. You couldn't mistake the gaol for anything else. Its grey stone walls spread out massively on either side of the studded oak doors, and it had narrow windows high up in the walls with iron bars set deeply into the stone.

We crossed the street and Richard knocked on the door. His knuckles made barely a sound against the heavy wood but a small panel swung inwards just above my head. I stepped back and looked up at a man's face demanding to know what we wanted.

"We've come to see Mistress Smalley," Richard said, and the large face peered down at us.

"*More* visitors for Smalley? Well, well, the witch *is* popular. I wonder what conjurin' she does, to have so many visitors, half of 'em lookin' like the Devil himself," he mocked. "I'll have to have a little chat with her, an' see if she'll tell me."

"Can we come in or not?" I demanded, my voice both seething and scared at the same time.

For once, Richard didn't give me one of his angry looks for losing my temper but glared at the gaoler himself. The man smirked at us, his voice still mocking as he answered.

"Impatient to get into gaol, aren't we? But whether you'll be so keen once this door closes behind you is another matter."

The locks turned noisily and one of the huge doors swung inwards. As we stepped through the door was closed and bolted behind us. It took a few seconds for my eyes to adjust to the gloom, Catherine's hand hanging on to mine tightly. Richard was in front of me, glaring at the gaoler swinging a huge ring of keys around in his hand. He smirked at us, then led the way. We went along a dark corridor and through an archway to a winding stone staircase twisting down into the shadows.

Catherine asked Richard to carry her, and she clung to his neck as we walked down the steep staircase, turning round and round on ourselves as we descended into the gloom. We finally emerged onto a dark passage with a couple of windows high up in the wall casting a dim light along the passage. We followed the gaoler along the passage until he stopped at one of the doors and unlocked it, then he moved to one side to allow us to pass him into a blank of darkness which made me shudder before I'd even crossed the threshold. We stepped through and the gaoler closed the door behind us, and the key turned in the lock.

The first thing to hit me wasn't the dark, it was the smell. It was rank in there, stale sweat and urine and worse. The second was Grandma's voice, coming out of the shadows.

"Hephzibah Creswell! What in God's name do you think you're doin'?

I saw her then, getting to her feet in the shadows, and I rushed over and threw my arms around her and found I was sobbing. She hugged me tightly until I was over the worst, then she held me away from her and glared at me.

"Well?" she demanded.

"We br-brought you some f-food," I said, trying to get a hold of myself.

I was shocked at the overwhelming feelings which had burst out of me as soon as I had seen her. I hadn't realised how much I was locking everything away until that moment.

Richard looked like he wanted to cry himself but I knew *he* would manage to hold it back. Catherine was leaning out of his arms towards Grandma, and Grandma suddenly became aware of this, releasing me and sweeping Catherine into her arms.

"Hello, my angel!" she said, looking directly into my sister's beaming face as she said it, almost as if she knew that Catherine couldn't hear her.

"Are you comin' home, Gran'ma?"

Grandma shook her head, keeping her eyes on Catherine's.

"No, honey, not yet."

My sister's face creased up and she started crying even louder than I had been.

It was emotional chaos for a while as Grandma tried to calm Catherine, and then I tried, even while still trying to keep my own tears in check. Richard stood back from us all and let us get on with it. He looked up at the dim light seeping in through the tiny high window most of the time, his lips a thin line.

Even after we'd calmed Catherine down, she carried on clinging to Grandma as though her life depended on it, pressing her cheek against Grandma's chest, tear-tracks on her face.

Grandma sat down on her cloak in the corner of the room with difficulty, Catherine making it more complicated than it needed to be of course, but I could see that Grandma's hip was really paining her. As Richard and I sat down next to her, I realised there was someone else in the room. A girl was sitting a few feet away from us in the shadows, leaning against the wall, but she had turned her back to give us some privacy.

Grandma looked pale and thin, even in the dim light of the gaol, and there were dark circles under her eyes, but the worst thing was that she looked like – well, like a *witch*. Her hair was dirty and tangled with bits of straw sticking out of it, and her face and clothes were grimy. You could see she was trying to keep herself neat and tidy, but you could also see that it was impossible in there. The room was filthy.

Grandma's cloak and blanket were on a thin spread of dirty straw, an empty water jug nearby. There was a bucket with a cloth thrown over it in the furthest corner, and apart from another feeble scattering of straw which the girl was sitting on, there was nothing else in the room except the dirt-smeared walls and floor. Grandma's eyes watched me taking all this in and she nodded grimly.

"You shouldn't have come, Hephzibah," she said, and I was annoyed then that she still seemed to be telling *me* off for coming, when Richard was quite obviously here as well, and he was older than me.

I opened my mouth to tell her that but she cut me off.

"You know *why* you shouldn't have come, an' all," she said, her dark eyes glittering. "It's the last place any of you should be, but especially you, Hephzibah."

It was Richard's turn to look annoyed then, and Grandma laughed quietly.

"I don't know. You Creswells. You're always so keen to be doin' what you know you shouldn't, it seems to me. But then I suppose I'm no better for all that, so what chance do you have," she smiled, "full of Creswell an' Smalley blood as you are."

"That's not *all* they're full of, from what I hear," laughed a voice from the other side of the door, and Grandma froze.

"*Bastard*," she spat with fury, visibly shaking with anger, and I was shocked at such a word coming from her.

Richard leaped to his feet and hammered on the door with both fists.

"How dare you listen in on us! You wait 'til I get out there!"

"Careful now, boy, else you won't be gettin' out here at all," the mocking voice replied. "Attacking the King's gaoler carries a heavy sentence."

"I haven't attacked you – *yet!*"

"Ah, well, who are they gonna believe, d'you think? A respectable man, such as meself, the King's loyal servant, or the Devil's Spawn of a Witch?"

"*Richard*," hissed Grandma, "*get back over here!*"

With a final thump of the door, Richard came away, but he was too wound up to sit down again so he paced around the room instead. Grandma leaned towards me and whispered as quietly as she could.

"It was good of you both to bring the food, but you're not to come here again, do you hear?"

I looked at her in exasperation for a moment, but then I nodded. I could see there was no point in arguing. Apart from anything else, I didn't know how long we would have with her and there were more important things we needed to talk about. I took a deep breath, but Grandma got in first.

"Your Dad makes sure I get what I need, Hephzibah. You know he came this mornin', not long before yourselves?"

"*What?*" I said, my breath whooshing out in shock. "We didn't know! We thought he'd been held up at Moors Farm..." I faltered, looking at her with realisation.

She nodded, her lip trembling and her eyes welling with tears.

"I know," she said, "your Dad told me. My poor girl -"

I was Grandma's turn to cry then, and I realised that her eyes had already been red from crying when we arrived.

I put my arms around my grandmother and we cried together. After a long while, I let go of her and looked up. Richard was leaning his head against the wall, his face turned away from us, and I knew he was crying too. I felt that Mum's death would weigh down my heart forever. But the last thing she would have wanted was her own mother in gaol on charges of witchcraft.

"I wanted to see you anyway, Gran'ma, to ask you what we can do to get you out of here. To prove your innocence.'

She shook her head.

"There's nothin' you can do, Hephzibah," she said, and leaned forwards to whisper so quietly I could barely hear her myself, "without gettin' yourself in trouble, anyway. An' that would just lead to you bein' in here *with* me. It wouldn't get me out. It's a miracle Catherine survived the Plague, an' perhaps God's price was her hearin', or perhaps it's somethin' worse. Either way, tryin' to save your sister was the right thing to do, an' it's best *I'm* in here an' not you. It was my idea to send you to – to the old woman, after all. I've managed to keep myself an' my family safe for a good many years now, but I always knew it was just a matter of time."

She sighed heavily.

"It's bad luck bein' seen with Master Nalgah as that's given them the excuse they've been lookin' for all these years. All I can do now is stand up at the trial an' deny the charges brought against me, an' trust in the Lord."

The idea that there was a price to be paid for Catherine's life, and that it might be Grandma's life in some kind of macabre exchange - or that we could just sit around and wait for everything to turn out alright in the end - was absurd. I looked at my grandmother with her filthy clothes and wild hair and knew she'd be condemned as soon as anyone saw her.

"But what if I go an' see Parson Burnett -"

"Absolutely *not*."

"Well, obviously I'd rather not. I don't trust him Gran'ma, he looks at me like he's hopin' I'll slip up -"

"*Exactly*. You must stay out of it."

"But what exactly *is* 'it'?"

Grandma shook her head warningly. I ignored her.

"Dad said he thinks it's somethin' that happened when you were a girl, somethin' to do with the old Squire, an' I remember Grandad sayin' -"

"*No*," she hissed. "Your Dad means well but he knows nothin', an' nothin' I can say or do will ever change the – the situation between me an' the Sylvestres."

I tried again. "But what did the gaoler mean? Was that to do with the Sylvestre family too?"

Grandma sighed. "You just won't let it go, will you?"

"No, I won't."

"It's complicated, Hephzibah, an' it all stems from somethin' I can't change. If I tell you anythin' about it, your life will be in danger, *an'* your brother's an' sister's lives too."

She looked at me and knew that everything she was saying was creating more questions in my mind and no answers, and sighed.

"I've sworn to keep quiet, to protect my family, an' that's what I'm goin' to carry on doin', no matter what it costs me."

"But -"

"But *nothin'*. I've already lost my daughter, an' a baby grandson, an' if I lose you three as well there'd be no point in anythin'."

"But *Grandad* knew," I managed to get in, before she could stop me again.

She shook her head.

"Your Grandad Creswell only knew the *consequences* of other folk knowin', those consequences bein' the murder of my own grandmother."

I gasped and saw that Richard was shocked too, having moved close enough to hear that last bit.

"It's my grandmother that the gaoler was alludin' to – her blood bein' in your veins too, of course – an' you'll find out why *that's* a problem for all of us soon enough. But the real secret stays a secret, forever. For your own safety."

We both waited for her to carry on, but she had set her mouth firmly and sat back, and I knew we had got everything we were going to get.

Witherstone

"You need to be off now," she said, struggling to get up with Catherine still clinging on to her. "An' you're not to come back here again, d'you hear? *Any* of you."

I nodded, resigned.

"Your Dad gave the gaoler enough money to keep me in food an' water for a few weeks, an' I don't need to start usin' that money for a while with all the food you've brought me too. I'll be sharin' it, mind you," she went on, nodding towards the girl behind me, "as not everyone is as fortunate with family as me."

The girl turned her head and smiled shyly. She looked about my age. I was glad they had each other in that dark and filthy hell-hole. It would be unbearable to be locked up in there alone.

We persuaded Catherine to transfer her grip from Grandma to me with difficulty, and as I was leaning over, Mum's ring swung out of my bodice on the cord, glinting in the gloomy cell. Grandma caught her breath and reached out to hold the ring in trembling fingers for a moment, then she held it back towards me.

"Make sure you keep it safe, Hephzibah," she said. "It's a symbol of what we've all lost now, an' you need to take good care of it."

I nodded and slipped the ring back over my heart. Grandma gave me a quick, fierce hug before she whispered, "You must keep your head down, Hephzibah, an' stay out of it, d'you hear? They'll be lookin' for any excuse to throw you children in here as well."

I nodded again, and she smiled grimly before turning to my brother.

"Now, Richard, *you* must stay away too, an' make sure your sister behaves herself."

She meant me rather than Catherine, of course, and I scowled at Richard's nod. When the gaoler opened the door, his mocking expression infuriated me, but Grandma gave me a warning look and pushed me towards the door.

Richard avoided meeting the man's gaze as we came out into the passage, and we looked back at Grandma's face disappearing into the gloom as the door closed. Catherine started crying again.

"*Gran'ma! Gran'ma!*"

Her wailing echoed all around us, seeming to close us in. When we reached the entrance to the gaol, she was still sobbing, and the gaoler made a big deal of looking for the right key to let us out. I could see Richard getting more and more angry. By the time the man was slowly turning the key in the lock, I could see my brother was about to explode so I tried to deflect a showdown by engaging the man in conversation, to make sure my brother went out first.

"Erm, when will we need to come back with more money an' food?"

"*You* can come back any time, darlin'," he replied, running his finger down my cheek.

My skin turned to ice and I pulled away at the same moment Richard lunged towards him, and I pushed my brother out into the street to keep him from getting hurt, or worse, thrown into gaol too. We could hear the man's laughter even after the door had closed behind us, and Richard kicked the door then turned and stormed ahead of me back towards the market square. I put the still-sobbing Catherine down and took her hand as we ran after him.

By the time we came to the square, I'd managed to catch up with my brother but he was glaring straight ahead, still absolutely furious.

"Richard – it doesn't matter."

"Yes it does!" he stormed. "What did you speak to him for? He's a – a complete *bastard!* You're so *stupid* sometimes!"

I didn't answer. It wasn't fair. I'd been trying to stop him from getting into trouble. We walked the rest of the way back to the river in silence, Richard's expression still livid as he marched along. *Well, two could play at that game*, I thought, setting my lips into a thin line, but unfortunately my intention of being just as pig-headedly silent was spoiled by Catherine asking me why Grandma wasn't coming with us.

I looked down at my sister's teary face and wondered how on earth I could explain.

"Gran'ma has to stay there," I said, pointed back the way we had come, "to – to work," I tried, miming rolling my sleeves up and kneading dough.

That didn't work so I mimed sweeping the floor. She seemed to get that one, but then she frowned again.

"But it's so *dirty*," she said, and I nodded.

"Yes, that's why Gran'ma has to stay. To clean up," I went on, sweeping my invisible broom again.

Catherine seemed slightly more satisfied at that explanation, but I could see she was still unhappy about leaving Grandma behind. But then, she wasn't the only one.

As we came out by the river, Catherine suddenly pulled out of my hand and shot forwards.

"Daddy!" she shouted, "*Daddy!*" and threw herself into the surprised arms of the man standing next to Edward Cowper's boat.

"Catherine!" Dad exclaimed.

I felt such a rush of emotion, seeing Dad, that I broke into a run myself. He didn't look very pleased though, and I stopped short of throwing my arms around him as Catherine had done. I stood in front of him instead and sighed, knowing we were going to get another telling off, and I was right.

By the time Dad had finished being angry with us for going to Hawbury gaol, against his specific instructions, we were already nearly half way back upriver to Thompson's. Dad had waved Richard into the back of the boat with me and Catherine, much to my brother's annoyance, and we squashed ourselves into the stern as Dad took the oars and rowed us back to the farm, his strong arms making good progress despite going against the flow of the river and half his energy being spent telling us off.

He got a lift on a cart from Dunham to Hawbury the night before, and after visiting Grandma this morning, went down to the river hoping to persuade a boatman to take him upriver to Thompson's to see us. When he saw Edward Cowper's boat he waited, expecting Edward to turn up at some point of course, rather than us. When we reached the riverbank below the new cottage, we got out and Dad pulled the boat up onto the bank.

"Samuel Clayton, my master at Moors Farm, said I can stay 'til tomorrow," he said, "so I'll take the boat back to

Witherstone in the mornin' an' call in on Edward an' Job, then walk up to Moors Farm from there."

He saw my expression and smiled, putting his hand on my shoulder and we walked up the hill to the new cottage together.

We had an evening so reminiscent of our old times at home that it was painful. Being together again showed us all the more how much we'd lost, and how much more we may yet lose if we couldn't prove Grandma innocent of the charges against her.

I watched my brother listening to Dad as he talked about Moors Farm, and it sounded a much harder life compared to down here in the valley, despite Dad trying to make light of it. Catherine snuggled on Dad's knee, looking up at his face while he was talking.

We were just ordinary folk, what was left of us, so what on earth did the Sylvestre family have against us? What was it that had marked Gran'ma out as the object of their wrath? And that she daren't tell us for fear it would seal our doom too?

14

Friends and Enemies

Before he left the next morning, Dad warned us he was unlikely to be able to come back from Moors Farm more than once or twice a month. It was too far to do the journey there and back in one day, especially with the extra miles from Witherstone to the new cottage added on. He'd have to try to earn an extra day off as often as he could to make it worthwhile coming.

He set off upriver towards Witherstone, his face looking back at us on the hill as he rowed until he was out of sight. We went to the farmhouse straight after.

The next few days were busy at the farm. The other labourers had arrived and were living in our old cottage in Witherstone, and my heart turned over at the thought of strangers living in what still felt like our home.

Master Freeman asked me to cook extra food for the midday and evening meals as the new labourers would be eating at the farmhouse with him. I managed, with Catherine helping, and she helped me with scrubbing the pots afterwards too. One afternoon I was making bread and Catherine was playing out in the sunshine. She hadn't been out there for long when I heard a sound ringing through the yard I'd been dreading since we first arrived to work for Master Freeman.

"Eppie! Eppie! Come quick! It's Old Isaac!"

I shot outside and ran towards my sister, frantically waving my finger in front of my lips to stop her shouting my name, but she was running away from me towards the figure coming in the gate, still calling, *"Eppie! It's Old Isaac!"*

"Well, Bless me! Catherine an' Eppie Creswell!" the old pedlar called out, his delighted voice carrying across the yard.

"What on earth are you two doin' 'ere? Are you workin' with your Dad an' Richard now? A Creswell family job-lot?" he laughed.

Isaac held his arms out for Catherine to run into as he smiled towards me, but then his face registered my panic and his smile disappeared. I was shaking my head as I ran, reaching him in a moment and grabbing his arm, gasping, "No Isaac! It's Cowper - *Annie Cowper!*" but it was too late.

Master Freeman was walking towards us across the yard, Richard a few paces behind him, his face white. I knew they had heard everything.

I dropped my arms to my sides and turned to face the music. Master Freeman was looking directly at me as he crossed the yard, then his eyes shifted to Isaac as he held out his hand.

"John Freeman of Hawbury," he said. "I'm the new manager here. Master Thompson's widow sold the farm to Sir Henry Sylvestre, and he took me on to run the place. And you are...?"

"Isaac, Sir. Isaac Bailey. Pedlar," said the old man, his voice trembling and his face turning ashen as he removed his hat and shook Master Freeman's hand.

Isaac's eyes flickered back to me as he licked his lips. I could see he'd caught the whole situation at once. He knew all about the Sylvestre ban on employing Creswells, of course.

"I–I call this way on my route between Hawbury an' Witherstone, if you're ever wantin' new cloth or pans or tonics or knives sharpenin' or shoes mendin'."

Isaac was speaking so quickly to try to take back the words he knew should never have left his lips that he was almost babbling.

"Well, come in, Master Bailey, and take a mug of beer with me," said John Freeman, and he turned and walked right past me and across the yard to the kitchen.

Isaac looked at us, his face stricken, then he picked up his bag and followed Master Freeman, Catherine trotting along behind them and calling out to Isaac to wait for her. I turned to Richard.

"What do we do?" I whispered hoarsely.

My brother shrugged and snorted, his eyes cold as he looked at me.

"What can we do? He'll undoubtedly want an explanation an' then he'll turf us out."

He looked up at the sky. "It's gettin' too late to be walkin' up to Moors Farm today. We'll have to hear him out, I suppose. Let him blast us for our lies. Then I'll take you an' Catherine to Job's, an' I'll walk up to Moors Farm tomorrow to tell Dad what's happened, an' see if we can go up there after all – although from what Dad said on

Sunday, I'm not sure it'll be possible, so God knows what we'll do."

He looked back at me.

"You should have kept Catherine with you," he said flatly, then turned away and walked towards the farmhouse.

I glared at his back. I knew he was right, but it didn't help. I should have kept Catherine close to me all the time. *Of course* Isaac or someone else who knew us was bound to call at the farm sooner or later. I felt sick. Our days here had seemed a sanctuary, and now we would have to leave. Worse, we would feel the force of Master Freeman's anger first. I hated being caught out lying, especially to someone who had been so good to us.

Stomach churning, I followed Richard across the yard and into the kitchen. Catherine was sitting on Isaac's knee, her arm round his neck, smiling happily and showing him that she was still wearing the ribbon he had given her around her tiny wrist.

"Look, Isaac! My red ribbon."

The old man smiled down at my sister but he didn't look at all like his usual relaxed self. He sat stiffly on the chair, his cloak and doublet still on and his hat still clutched tightly in his hand. It didn't look as though he'd touched the mug of beer on the table in front of him.

Master Freeman was sitting in his usual chair, his beer in his hand and his eyes turning away from Catherine and Isaac to watch Richard and then me as we came into the kitchen and stood awkwardly just inside the door. It reminded me of when we'd first arrived barely a week ago, standing uncomfortably in the doorway while he finished his meal and regarded us silently. Except this time Richard stood ahead of me a little, preparing to take the brunt of Master Freeman's anger.

"Well," said John Freeman, after several long moments in which no-one said anything. "I don't need my shoes mending, nor any new cloth at present. It might be an idea to look over the knives and see if any need sharpening. Perhaps you could do that, *Annie*," he said with emphasis.

This is it, I thought, and braced myself for the onslaught.

It never came. He sat there looking at me, his face expressionless. After several long moments he spoke again.

"Get the knives for Master Bailey, please Annie."

He said it more gently this time, without emphasis, and when I looked at him, frowning, trying to interpret his meaning, he nodded at me then drained his mug and stood up.

"Perhaps Master Bailey might like to take one of your loaves with him, too, when he's finished with the knives," he said, putting a couple of coins on the table in front of Isaac before turning to my brother.

"I'll be in the top field with the new men, Richard, when you've finished talking with Master Bailey."

And we watched in amazement as he headed out the door and strode across the yard without another word.

After a few moments, Richard sagged down into a chair, blowing out his breath with released tension, and then he shook his head, bewildered.

"He *must* have heard. I heard *everythin'!* Catherine shoutin' "Eppie!" as loud as humanly possible. Isaac sayin' "Catherine an' Eppie *Creswell*". Even you tellin' Isaac to call you Annie Cowper instead, Eppie."

I stared at Richard, realising I was shaking my head in disbelief as well.

"But why? Why isn't he saying anythin'?"

"I don't know. But it looks like we might have a reprieve of execution. Unless he's savin' it until Isaac's gone, of course," Richard went on, suddenly glum again.

Then he realised what else he'd said and swallowed.

"You won't know about – about Gran'ma, then, Isaac? Or – or Mum?"

Isaac shook his head but I could see from his expression that he feared the worst. We told him then, about Mum and the baby, and about Grandma – though not about my part in going to the witch - and the old man was devastated. We told him about Grandad Creswell too, and Catherine's deafness. Richard couldn't stand to talk about it anymore and he stood up abruptly.

"I'll go out to the field, in case Master Freeman was just savin' his wrath until after Isaac has left. Then at least we'll know where we stand."

He went out, and Isaac talked to me while he sharpened Master Freeman's knives. He talked about Mum and Grandma mostly. He said that if he could do anything at all to help us, or help Grandma, we were to let him know. How he could possibly help, or how we could even contact him, I didn't ask, but it occurred to me that he might know something about the Sylvestre's mysterious hatred for my family.

"Isaac, do you know what the Squire - an' Parson Burnett - have got against Gran'ma? Why they're so keen to accuse her of witchcraft, even though she hasn't done anythin'? Or why the Sylvestre family won't allow us Creswells on their land?"

"Well, I would think the Sylvestres took against Hephzibah - your Gran'ma – because of what happened years ago, when the *old* Squire died, surely? With her own mother an' grandmother -"

He stopped sharpening suddenly, and looked at me.

"What has your Gran'ma told you?"

I shifted uncomfortably.

He nodded.

"Just as I thought. If your Gran'ma wanted you to know," he said, waggling the knife he was sharpening at me, "she'd have told you herself. But she won't, so you're fishin' around. Am I right?"

"Yes, but -"

"Well then, it's not my place to say anythin'," he interrupted firmly, going back to his sharpening. "I've a great deal of respect for Hephzibah Smalley, an' she'll have good reason for keepin' you in the dark. She's a good woman who's helped many a soul over the years, whatever other folk may say about her. She's always had a meal for me even when times have been hard, an' I'm not goin' against her wishes."

I sighed in frustration, my mind whirling with questions, but then he went on.

"But what the Sylvestre family have got against the Creswells is another story, an' I really don't know what that's about. I think it goes way back, to when your Grandad was a boy an' his father died, I reckon – back when your Grandad an' his mum had to leave the Hall Farm. I suppose she couldn't take on her husband's job, with two young 'uns to look after, an' the Squire would be wantin' another man in to manage the place. I wasn't much more than a lad meself then, mind you, but I remember callin' at the Hall Farm with my father, on our rounds, when your Grandad's family were still there."

He sighed and felt the edge of the knife with his thumb.

"It seems to me them Sylvestres fall out with folk too easily, an' why that should be, I don't know. Although, with your Gran'ma -"

He clammed up then, his expression making it clear the subject was closed, concentrating on whetting the knife on the grindstone. I sighed and watched the old pedlar while I thought about everything he'd said, and about what he was trying to keep back from me, with just the whispering of the blade in the silence.

When Isaac spoke again, I realised he'd finished and was packing his grindstone away.

"Now, take care of yourself an' your sister, Eppie," he said, and hugged us both goodbye.

"I'll be comin' back this way in a few weeks, so I'll come an' see if you're alright. I-I hope the new man doesn't throw you out because of my foolishness."

"But you weren't to know, Isaac."

"Even so. I'd never forgive meself if you three kids end up kicked out through my prattlin'."

He looked outside into the gathering dusk. There was no sign of Richard coming back yet, and I felt a jolt of nerves, wondering whether our apparent reprieve would hold true, or whether Master Freeman was just waiting until we were on our own before he had it out with us, and then threw us out.

Catherine cried when Isaac left, and held on to me tearfully all the while I finished the cooking. She was still clinging on to me when Master Freeman, Richard, and the other labourers crowded into the kitchen a while later.

Richard sat on a bench by the fire while the others ate their meal, his face sullen, and my heart sank. I saw Master Freeman looking at Catherine's tearful face while she clung to me as I cleared up the kitchen. I cleaned and scrubbed everything in sight, desperate to make him see that he needed us here, even though I knew it was pointless now. He had to do as his own master told him.

When I finished and fetched our cloaks, Richard shook his head at me, and I knew then that Master Freeman was waiting for the labourers to leave, just as Richard thought he would. I hoped that the long delay since Isaac had arrived might mean Master Freeman's anger would be less fierce, as he had at least had time to calm down.

Once the men had gone, Master Freeman told us to come to the table. I lifted Catherine onto my lap as we sat down and waited for his judgement upon us. He looked down at his hands, then back up at us, waiting silently.

"It's clear now, who you are, and I'm presuming that Tom Creswell – the man who came to see me about a job - is your father?"

Richard said nothing so I nodded.

"Yes, Master Freeman."

He sighed.

"I'm in a difficult position here, Annie – or Eppie, is it?"

I nodded, and he went on.

"Sir Henry Sylvestre took me on to manage this farm, and he made it clear from the start that I wasn't to employ a Creswell, and that your family had to leave the cottage in Witherstone. I don't know why that's his desire but he's my Master and it's my job to obey him."

He paused for a moment, then his voice was more gentle.

"I understand from what your father told me that you've lost your mother?"

Richard was still staring at the table sullenly, waiting, I knew, for the axe to fall.

"Yes," I said, then felt my lip trembling and had to recover myself for a moment before I could carry on. I wasn't going to cry in front of him.

"She – she was ill, the same illness our sister had, but she was havin' a baby too, an' they both died. But Catherine – Catherine somehow lived," I stumbled out, terrified he'd also found out about the potion and Grandma's arrest for witchcraft, and that his anger, when it finally came, would be about much more than our lying to him. That he, like the gaoler, would condemn us as the Devil's Spawn.

But a strange look passed over his face and I could swear there were tears in his eyes. He cleared his throat and looked back down at his hands.

"My own wife and daughter died a few months ago," he said, quietly, "and your sister -"

He stopped and looked at Catherine for a moment then back at me.

"For the sake of their memory, I'm going to pretend I never heard what the pedlar said. I don't know what quarrel the Squire has with your father and I don't want to know, but it doesn't seem right to me that his children should suffer for it. I'd like to think that if my wife and child had been left alone in the world, they'd have found friends enough to make sure they had a roof over their heads and food in their bellies. So we'll say no more about it. I only know you as Cowper. If it comes to light who you really are, I'll deny knowing anything and you're on your own."

"Oh!" I gasped, scarcely able to believe our good fortune. "Thank you, Master Freeman, thank you!"

Richard let out a shuddering sigh beside me, and Master Freeman smiled gently as he looked at us all, his eyes lingering on Catherine for a moment as she looked up at me with a frown, aware of the change on our faces but confused about what was going on. Then he waved his hand to dismiss us and Richard leaned forward to thank him quietly as we left, and I almost rushed us all out of the door before he could change his mind.

Despite our reprieve I lay awake for hours that night, unable to sleep. The wind had got up and was roaring through the trees and round the cottage, rattling the door and window endlessly, and moaning down the chimney like a lost soul. Wisps of air blew across my face and through my hair like the breath of a ghost.

I was exhausted by the strain of constantly living on my nerves, feeling afraid all the time – for Grandma, for all of us – and beneath it all the terrible emptiness of not having Mum to comfort me and make everything alright again.

The things Isaac had said kept churning round and round in my mind, mixing up with the sound of the wind and other voices. Something about when the old Squire had died. Grandma warning us to stay out of it. Ellen and Mary Fordham whispering in the graveyard. The old woman's voice croaking out of the gloom. Robert Newstead fearful in the shadows. A crow calling. Parson Burnett's smooth voice and pale eyes above an open grave.

I was back there again. In the graveyard.

I always knew there was somethin' about that family... this snow is unnatural... poor Martha is a victim of her mother's sin... She can hear us... it's somethin' from this grave... you can hear them long nails scratch-scratch-scratchin' at the door... the Circle is cast... let me know mine end, and the number of my days... you must stay out of it... the murder of my own grandmother... bad blood will out... you are hereby accused of Witchcraft... their own nature inclined to evil... you killed my wife and baby son... white hands around their throats... your wife's association with witches... goes to her death with her lips sealed...

And then I was running along a long passage which was never ending, stretching on into the gloom, and I couldn't find Catherine or Richard anywhere. Voices whispered along the passage behind me. *Bad blood will out... You are hereby accused of Witchcraft.* My feet pounded against the stone floor as I ran, but still I couldn't find them. I was alone. Until I turned and saw the figure emerging from the shadows behind me, white hands reaching for my throat, and the whispering voices turned to laughter.

I shot up in bed, gasping for breath. The wind was still rattling the door and window and moaning round the cottage. I climbed down off the platform, careful not to disturb Catherine and Richard, and sat by the fire, moving

Witherstone

the peat turfs to one side and putting logs on to get the flames blazing up. I was shivering but not with the cold. I knew. I felt I'd always known, deep down. Ever since I went to see the old woman in the wild wood.

Old Isaac knew. And Grandad had known. I was sure my Dad knew too. They knew it was to do with Grandma's own mother and grandmother, and somehow mixed up with the old Squire. Grandma said her grandmother was *murdered*. I remembered what Ellen had said about the old Squire – that he was killed by witchcraft. That the witch Hannah Pendal had killed him, and then she was hung and her body burnt in the village. Her daughter had been accused too but she disappeared from the gaol at Hawbury.

And I knew just where she'd disappeared to because I'd visited her there, and I thought about that dream-like afternoon, the coils of smoke stroking my cheek as Master Nalgah seemed to fill the room, the shimmering sword pointing down into the black cups.

The witch had admitted she was Hannah Pendal's daughter. I remembered her strange, sly smile when I asked her, and her black eyes glittering in the shadows. My skin prickled and I shivered, even though the fire was blazing up now, and I huddled over the flames. The old woman said she knew who I was because she'd known Grandma as a girl, and I knew with a strange certainty that this was because she was Grandma's mother. That she was, therefore, my great grandmother.

That was what the gaoler had meant. *Hannah Pendal's blood ran in my veins*. No wonder Grandma didn't want us to know. We were all in terrible danger.

Witherstone

Richard gave up asking me what was wrong the next morning. I refused to say anything at all, not trusting myself to keep the fear out of my voice, and we walked to the farmhouse in silence.

I was terrified by the images which kept coming into my mind. Of being hung as a witch. The rope creaking and tightening round my throat, my legs kicking helplessly. *And Grandma. Richard. Catherine.* I shuddered and tried to push it out of my mind, afraid I would be sick. I didn't see how we'd ever be able to prove Grandma's innocence. She was the daughter and granddaughter of condemned witches – witches accused of murdering the old Squire. No wonder the Sylvestre family were dead set against us. And if we try to save her, we risk being accused alongside her. *Bad blood will out.*

As we walked, I stared at the empty path unfolding before us, fighting against despair. *Let me know mine end, and the number of my days...* I remembered Parson Burnett's cold eyes piercing through me over my mother's grave, and I felt the anger rising. As we turned towards the farmhouse, I didn't know what I could do, but knew I couldn't just stand by and watch my grandmother die.

Later that day, Catherine was scrubbing the pots in the tub and I was baking, when I heard the sound of hooves approaching and then voices in the yard.

"John?" a man's voice boomed out. "John Freeman?"

I wiped my hands and was walking towards the open door when I heard Master Freeman's voice in reply, and the sound of his feet striding across the yard towards the visitors.

"I'm here, Sir Henry. This is an unexpected pleasure, Sir. I saw you riding over from the top field."

I shrank back from the doorway. *Sir Henry Sylvestre?*

"We've come to discuss the finances of the farm, John, and a number of changes I want to make."

I heard the sound of heavy feet thudding to the ground, and then they were all coming in the doorway before I'd had a chance to move.

Master Freeman came in first, and he turned his back to me and Catherine as he gestured his hand towards the door to the passageway.

"Please go through to the parlour, Sir Henry and Master William, and I'll send through some refreshments."

Both of the visitors strode down the passageway without a word and Master Freeman turned to me.

"Ale and pasties, *Annie*, and some of your fine cinnamon and raisin scones," then he followed his guests down to the parlour.

Hands trembling uncontrollably, I poured a jug of ale and took three mugs down off the shelf, piled several pasties and scones onto two large platters, then stood in the kitchen in sheer panic. How could I go in there?

I looked at Catherine, still scrubbing the pots slowly, daydreaming. There was no way I was taking my sister in that room.

I took a deep breath and picked up the ale and mugs and walked down the passage, my legs shaking so much I felt as though they would give way at any moment. I opened the door as quietly as I could and walked into the room, keeping my face so low I could barely see past the sides of my linen cap, only the legs of the three men standing in the centre of the room visible to me. Two of the men were wearing shiny leather boots, and the other a pair of muddied working boots.

"Just put them on the windowsill, Annie, then you may go. We'll help ourselves."

I bobbed a quick curtsy then turned my back on the room and put down the ale and mugs, then fairly hurtled down the passageway to the kitchen, coming back again with the pasties and scones and slipping back into the room and putting them next to the ale. The three men were seated on the two settles now, still talking, two sets of shining boots stretched out expansively.

"- calling it De Sylvestre Farm, now, of course," the Squire's voice was saying.

I didn't look up but kept my face averted and left again at once.

Back in the kitchen I was still shaking in blind panic. Should we just run for it? If the Squire realised who we were, one word from him and we could be arrested and thrown into gaol with Grandma. And then – and then –

It didn't bear thinking about. We couldn't just stay here to be swatted like flies. At that moment John Freeman came back into the room with an empty platter.

"More scones please, Annie. The Squire and Master William seem rather keen on them."

He frowned at my face while I piled more onto the platter, then he went back to the front parlour. I knew my expression must be one of blank terror. I tried to think straight.

Master Freeman was ensuring there was no need for me to go back to the parlour, and of course there was no reason at all why the Squire should even recognise me. I'd never even met him. Nor his companion. Master William, was it? The other visitor must be the Squire's son, named after his grandfather, the old Squire, rather than his uncle I bet, the elder brother who had died in the Wars fighting for Parliament.

The thought of the old Squire sent my panic reeling again, and I was still standing there in the middle of the kitchen, unable to decide the best thing to do, when footsteps were coming back down the passage. Footsteps belonging to more than one person. I caught Catherine's attention and held my finger to my lips in warning. She *must not* say anything incriminating now. She nodded, her fearful expression showing she'd read my mood at once.

"Annie? I need you to do something for me."

I turned towards Master Freeman, keeping Catherine half-hidden behind me and my face obscured by my cap as I looked down to the ground.

"Extra help is needed at Witherstone Hall for Master William's birthday celebrations, and the Squire has asked me to send you to the Hall kitchens. Your fine scones have persuaded him you're a cook worth having so I'll have to make do without you for a while. Sir Henry has promised I can have you back again afterwards," he said in a jokey voice, and I knew he was trying to reassure me.

But he didn't know what I now knew – that discovery wouldn't just cost us our home. It could cost us our lives. I daren't look up. The sheer terror in my eyes would be obvious. I gave a curtsy.

"Annie's a quiet girl, too, as you see. Sir Henry, shall we?"

I saw Master Freeman gesture towards the door, allowing his visitors to precede him into the yard. I didn't move as they headed out, talking about farm business, and I guessed that Master Freeman was taking them over the farm. As their voices faded, I crept to the door and peered out.

They were crossing the field towards the barn. Master Freeman was the tallest of the three and walked by Sir Sylvestre's side with quiet assurance, though he looked rather dull and faded by the side of the Squire and his son. The Squire was a large, well-fed man with thick waves of silver hair and a beard. He wore his green velvet cloak across one shoulder and his black hat was crisp and unweathered. His boots gleamed. His son was nearly as tall but leaner, his vibrant blue cloak billowing out behind him in such a way that he almost looked familiar.

As soon as they disappeared into the barn, I hurried Catherine upstairs through the darkening shadows, hoping the visitors were unlikely to go up there if they came back to the house. I was determined to keep my sister away from them.

We sat at the top of the stairs while I listened, and worried about Richard, out on the farm where he might be recognised. Catherine was tired and eventually fell asleep in my arms. My shoulders began to ache after a while, so I shuffled round and leaned against the wall while I listened and waited, and my stomach lurched with anxiety.

What was I going to do? If I go to Witherstone Hall to work in the kitchens, how could I keep my real identity secret? If I *don't* go, the Squire might start asking questions which might be even more likely to lead to our being found out, and get Master Freeman into trouble into the bargain.

I only knew I'd fallen asleep when a creak of the stairs woke me straight into my nightmare. The hall was dark and a figure was climbing slowly towards us, pale hands and face looming out of the shadows. I gasped in terror and clutched Catherine to my chest.

"It's alright, Annie – *Eppie*. It's me. John Freeman. The Squire and his son have long since gone. I hadn't even realised you were still here but then I saw Catherine's cloak by the fire. Come downstairs."

I carried Catherine down the stairs after him, arms trembling. As I reached the bottom step, he lifted my sister into his arms and carried her to the kitchen. He sat down and rested Catherine's head against his shoulder, pointing to another chair. I sat down.

"There's no need to be quite so terrified, you know," he said, frowning at my face. "What's the worst that can happen if the Squire discovers that the Creswells are still on his farm after all? You'd have to leave, I know, and being on the road is hard, but you might be able to go to your father, or find employment and a place to live somewhere else in Witherstone – or even Hawbury."

He smiled, trying to reassure me. "But if I can keep your identity secret, I will. You seem good kids – though your brother barely speaks and you have a temper on you!" he laughed quietly.

He frowned again as I failed to smile in response to his joking, and shook his head.

"I don't know. You act as though discovery would be the death of you. Come on, let's get this sister of yours home."

He stood up, hoisting Catherine across his chest.

"It's fine," said Richard from the doorway. "I'll take her."

"It's no trouble, Richard."

"I said I'll take her."

Richard lifted Catherine out of John Freeman's arms, then turned and walked outside. Master Freeman frowned at Richard's back and then shrugged and turned to me.

"You're to go to the Hall first thing tomorrow. Catherine can stay here if you like. Your brother can bring her over every morning, and she can either go out on the farm with him or stay at the house, just as she likes. She might be able to help me do some cooking, too. Or would you rather she came with you?"

I bit my lip. I certainly didn't want my sister at Witherstone Hall. I could ask Job and Alice if they would look after her while I was working at the Hall, but Parson Burnett might see her in the village. I shuddered.

"I–I'll talk to Richard about it tonight, but it might be best if she stays here. Thank you."

He smiled.

"You're welcome. And stop worrying. You look like the weight of the world is on your shoulders. The Sylvestres won't eat you."

The next morning, the walk to the farmhouse was gloomy, the sky overcast with rain which had been falling

Witherstone

since the night before. I felt thin and shivery, almost as though the rain was falling right through me.

Richard was really unhappy about me going to the Hall but didn't see how we could get out of it. Of course, he was only worried that if my real identity was discovered we'd have to leave the farm, and he thought I'd be bound to slip up. I couldn't tell him just how serious my going to Witherstone Hall really was, because then I'd have to tell him why – tell him that Grandma's own mother and grandmother had been condemned as witches and so all of us were in danger by virtue of our tainted blood. And that any hope we had of proving Grandma's innocence was now gone.

Now I knew why Grandma had kept the truth from us, and I was determined to protect Richard and Catherine. If we're all accused, it will be the end. How could we defend ourselves? Catherine especially. Her deafness might even be seen as a sign of witchcraft for all I knew. I shivered, and Richard scowled at me.

"I'll ask Master Freeman if I can take you to Witherstone in his boat."

"No, I'm fine to walk. You need to work, to keep Master Freeman happy."

He shrugged, still scowling, and we walked the rest of the way in silence. Richard had been really angry last night, and I knew he blamed me for all this. I wished I could think of some way to make everything all right again, but I felt so helpless – pulled along by things I could do nothing about.

When we arrived at the farmhouse, it turned out that John Freeman was going up to Witherstone Hall in his boat anyway, so he would take me. As I turned to say goodbye

Witherstone

to Richard in the wet yard, I suddenly felt tears threatening, but my brother's eyes looked distant. I pulled myself together. I wasn't going to cry in front of him or John Freeman, and if I cried Catherine would be upset.

I leaned down to my sister, and told her she must be a good girl. Her own mood changed then, and her eyes grew wider, tiny raindrops fringing her eyelashes.

"Where you goin, Eppie?"

"I have to go an' do some cookin'," I said, miming stirring pots and wiping a hot brow, "but I'll be back soon. *Back soon*," I said, exaggerating my lips, "*so be good for Richard an' Master Freeman*," pointing at them both.

I gave her a big hug and she let me squeeze her for a moment, but then she wriggled free and ran to Richard. He lifted her onto his shoulders and they watched me as I followed John Freeman down to the river, only Catherine waving every time I looked back at them.

I couldn't stop the tears mingling with the rain on my face as the boat pulled away, but waved at their blurry figures until they were out of sight, wiping my face with my free arm. I was relieved that John Freeman rowed all the way in silence, concentrating on managing the boat on the grey and churning water. When we reached the old familiar meadow with its rowing boats on the bank, the shadow of the church towering across the place where my mother and baby brother were buried, I vowed to sneak down to the grave at least once while I was in Witherstone.

As I watched John Freeman haul the boat up onto the bank, I heard a voice calling behind me.

"Eppie?"

I turned to find Adam hurrying across the wet grass.

"Adam!"

"Job told me you went to Thompson's – *oh!*" he said, and stopped dead with a look of horror as he saw John Freeman.

Adam looked back at me, his eyes wide. He had remembered what else Job had told him.

"Are you coming up to the Hall now, *Annie*?" John Freeman asked, his face bemused as he looked at Adam.

Adam stared back at him, his face still frozen in shock.

"Can I have a minute?" I asked.

"Of course. I'll walk on slowly so you can catch up."

Adam watched as John Freeman sauntered across the meadow, his hat pulled low against the rain, then he turned back to me with a sigh of relief.

"I thought he'd heard me," he whispered quietly. "I'm sorry, Eppie. I forgot Job said you weren't using your real names. I'm such an idiot!"

"He did hear you. Old Isaac has already given that one away, but Master Freeman's bein' very kind about it – only you mustn't tell anyone he knows who we are if we're found out or he'll get in trouble."

"Of course not. But why are you going up to the Hall? That's really not a good idea, Eppie."

His face was full of concern and I felt the tears coming back. *No crying*.

I replied abruptly. "I know it isn't, but I haven't any choice. I've been told to help out in the kitchens for Master William's birthday celebrations, so that's what I have to do."

Adam's expression changed at my tone, and his reply was more distant.

"You don't understand. I was trying to warn you. You'd be in danger."

"You mean because of Gran'ma? An' *her* gran'ma?"

His expression changed again and he stared at me, open-mouthed.

"You *know*? And you're *still* going there?"

I nodded. "Like I said, I haven't any choice. If I don't go they're even more likely to be askin' questions. If I keep my head down, they'll just see a kitchen maid an' nothin' else."

I hoped I sounded more confident than I felt. Adam shook his head. I didn't like the scared expression on his face, and the cold rain seeped into my pores.

"I hope you know what you're doing. I hadn't realised that you knew," he frowned. "I suspected *something* a few days ago, when Ellen was gossiping with Mistress Fordham, but I only worked out what it all meant yesterday when I overheard my father talking to my aunt."

I was confused.

"Your aunt?"

He nodded.

"Lady Sylvestre. She's my father's sister."

It was my turn to stare open-mouthed. "His *sister*?"

There was a quick whistle from across the meadow. John Freeman was at the corner, waiting. He jerked his head to hurry me.

"I have to go."

"But Eppie -"

I began to walk towards John Freeman, but felt Adam's hand on my arm and turned back to him.

"Eppie – if you ever need me, you know where I am."

Witherstone

He glanced over at his house and the hairs prickled up on the back of my neck. We were in full view of the small, dark windows.

I nodded and hurried across the meadow to John Freeman, but I barely paid him any attention as I followed him down the wood-lined avenue to Witherstone Hall. My mind was whirling. Lady Sylvestre is Parson Burnett's sister! I remembered the white face at the window, and Mary Ann's message fell into place.

She knows it was you, an' she's really angry.

I shuddered, more scared now than ever, and as Witherstone Hall came nearer, fear tightened my throat. John Freeman led me round the back. I knew the kitchen door well enough from my visits to Mary Ann, of course.

"I'll see you back at the Farm when they've finished with you in a few days," he said. "And remember what I said – don't look so worried. What's the worst that can happen?" and with that John Freeman turned away.

The rain began to fall more heavily as I knocked at the door. The girl who opened it a few moments later frowned, and then my heart plummeted as soon as she spoke.

"Have you come for Mary Ann? She's not here anymore."

"N-no. I've been asked to work in the kitchen for Master William's birthday."

"Oh!"

She turned away and called out behind her. "Sarah? Do you know anythin' about a new kitchen girl?"

A woman bustled over to the door, her sleeves rolled up and her face hot.

"Are you Master Freeman's girl?"

I nodded, swallowing.

"Well, don't just stand there, then," she almost shouted, her eyes bulging in her red face as she glared down at me. "Come in an' get started. I haven't got all day."

She turned away and the girl smirked as she held the door open wider, and I stepped over the threshold into Witherstone Hall.

15

Into the Belly of the Beast

The kitchen at Witherstone Hall was like a furnace, and I soon learned that Sarah, the cook in charge, ruled the servants under her with an iron hand. She didn't allow any of us a minute's rest. By the time I'd finished work that night I was exhausted. But not just from hard work. The day had also brought a frightening encounter, although even that was nothing compared to what came after.

Agnes, the girl who opened the door to me, was in charge of me for most of the day, and she obviously saw herself as second-in-command to Sarah and wouldn't even let me get a drink of water let alone something to eat.

"Sarah will have your guts for garters if you stop for a rest," she said, in a tone of smug satisfaction rather than friendly warning. "You can have a drink when you've finished for the day."

From the moment I arrived I was scrubbing floors, so I managed to sneak quick drinks of water whenever drawing water from the well, ignoring the cold spreading across my shoulders as the rain fell. I was only actually in the kitchen when either coming through with the bucket or heating water in the huge fireplace.

Whilst being in that overbearingly hot room under the baleful eye of the cook was unpleasant, I was more afraid of being in the parts of the house where I was more likely to run into the Squire or anyone else from the Sylvestre family. And now I knew that Lady Sylvestre was Parson Burnett's sister, I was more terrified of being seen than ever.

But the relative safety of the kitchen was not an option. My main task, as far as Sarah was concerned, wasn't cooking, but cleaning the Great Hall, a long, high room with dark oak timbers, stretching up from the grey stone floor and across the arched ceiling high above my head like the rib cage of a huge beast.

Agnes watched my every move for the first hour or so, but then she left me to it, although she would suddenly appear behind me without warning from time to time, trying to catch me slacking. I didn't give her the satisfaction but kept hard at work all day, although I didn't let scrubbing the floors stop me from keeping an eye out for the Sylvestre family. Being in the Great Hall made me feel very vulnerable.

At the top end of the room was a long oak table, black and gleaming, with ornate chairs and two strange figures of dull metal at either end, standing silently over me as I worked. Their faces were covered masks with slits for eyes, and each had a long sword as high as their chest, the point resting on the stone between their metal-clad feet. They reminded me of the pale stone knight lying in Witherstone church, marking the Sylvestre vault, his cool-cheeked wife beside him.

The Great Hall had a huge fireplace and chimney, a faded yellow shield with a battered emblem hanging on the chimney breast, and paintings in heavily-carved frames on the walls. Three plain tables ran along the wall towards the kitchen, with benches behind them, and I supposed that the Sylvestre family must sit at the top table and their guests at these tables. It was only later that these lower tables became much more significant than I had at first thought.

Despite the elaborate furniture and paintings in the room, the only things that took my eyes away from my work were the two huge windows facing one another at either end of the long table, chasing the shadows up into the dark-ribbed ceiling. One window looked out over the front of the Hall grounds and the tree-lined avenue leading up to the main door, and the other overlooked the kitchen garden at the back.

Each window was like a thousand jewels, even against the rain-washed sky, refracting the grey light coming through the glass into quicksilver, blue and green, ochre, and blood red. As the day wore on, the rain eased and the sun occasionally shone, intensifying the colours cast across the flagstones as I scrubbed, iridescent cobalt, emerald, gold, and ruby light glowed with the borrowed light of sky and sunlight streaming in through the glass.

As I worked my way through the Great Hall, the sun moved the vibrant splashes of colour across the floor until they faded into the dusk of the stone passage which ran past the entrance to the kitchen into the rest of Witherstone Hall.

The passage led past closed doors to a stairwell with a large wooden staircase leading to the bedchambers upstairs, and I hated every minute I had to spend scrubbing the stone flags in that dark passageway. Not because it reminded me of the most recent incarnation of my nightmare, but because I was terrified that any one of the Sylvestre family could come down the stairs or out of one of those rooms at any moment.

Which is exactly what happened.

I was taking a fresh pail of water along the passage to finish the final stretch of flagstones when one of the doors opened and a boy about Richard's age came out, closing the door behind him. Instead of walking past me, pressed against the wall with my face averted towards the floor, he stopped right in front of me.

"Aren't you Freeman's kitchen girl?"

I nodded.

"Yes, Sir."

"Look at me when I address you."

I felt the blood draining from my face as I raised my head and found myself looking at the Squire's son, Master William. He was taller than he had seemed next to John Freeman, taller even than my brother. His face was mocking as he looked at me speculatively.

"What's your name?"

"A-Annie," my voice whispered.

"Well, *A-Annie*," he whispered back, and my skin crawled as he stepped close enough for me to feel his breath on my hair. "I might want you to do some work for me when you've finished for the day -"

He broke off and stepped back in one swift movement as the door opened again and a woman swept into the passage. I turned my face away quickly and looked down at the floor, which tilted unsteadily.

"William?" the woman spoke sharply.

"Yes, Mother?" he said, his voice bored.

"I've told you about this before."

"Yes, Mother."

I heard him laughing under his breath as he turned and walked casually away from me down the passage.

"*You. Girl.*"

My heart stopped.

"*Get about your business.*"

I kept my face down and bobbed a curtsy as Lady Sylvestre swept after her son, but as she passed me the ground lurched again. The colour of her long velvet cloak stopped my breath as it brushed past me. It was a deep, blood red. Before she even reached the staircase, I turned and almost ran down the passage to the kitchen.

It was now early evening, and Sarah ordered me to help Agnes and the other kitchen girls take heaped platters of food into the Great Hall to lay on the Sylvestre's meal table. I was anxious to be out of there before the family came into the Hall to eat, and it was a huge relief when we had finally finished taking the last platters in and the family still hadn't entered the room.

But when I got back to the kitchen, I was given a bowl of stew and a piece of bread and told to take it into the Great Hall for my own meal. I tried to hide my horrified realisation but Agnes frowned as she caught my expression. I knew now what the other tables were for. The servants ate in the Great Hall with the Sylvestre family.

Keeping my eyes on the floor in front of my feet, I followed Agnes into the now busy Great Hall to one of the servant tables. I tried to keep my face hidden from the other servants as well as the top table, in case any of them were from the village and recognised me. I hadn't seen anyone from Witherstone since I'd arrived at the Hall but I didn't want to take any chances. As soon as we sat down, I picked up a spoon and began eating, anxious to be out of there as quickly as possible, but Agnes slapped my hand down.

"You have to *wait*," she hissed, outraged.

The next moment there was a scrape of benches and movement all around me as the servants along the tables all stood. Agnes hauled me to my feet as the Sylvestre family swept into the room from the passage. Sir Henry and Lady Sylvestre and their son passed us as they headed towards the top table.

I kept my face down and pressed as far back against the wall as I could, trying to hide behind Agnes but trying not to look like I was hiding, as the family took their seats. Once they were seated, Sir Henry nodded and all the servants sat down, and I waited to see when Agnes started eating before I dared touch my spoon again. Only when the family had loaded their platters and begun to eat did she pick up her spoon and start to eat her stew. I had little appetite but didn't want to draw any more attention to myself so I forced the food down.

It was the longest meal of my life, and all the while I was eating I was intensely aware of the presence of the Sylvestre family, cutting their meat with their knives then putting it to their mouths on long forks. It didn't take me long to finish the bowl of stew, even though my mouth was so dry it was difficult to swallow, so then I sat there, head down and desperate for the meal to finish and the servants be dismissed.

It was when the sun was setting, the light fading fast from the iridescent windows, that I finally realised what had been niggling at my mind since earlier that day but had been burned into the background by the fiery colours of the glass. I'd seen the pattern in the windows before.

All in a moment I realised it was also on the battered shield hanging over the fireplace, everything falling into place as the colours in the glass muted with the coming dusk. It was the figure of a snarling dragon, with arching wings and raised claws. The same crest I'd seen on the fork Isaac had in his pack just a few weeks ago.

That's why he'd looked troubled by it. He had realised where he'd seen it before and was worried that – what? Why had it bothered him?

A man I met on the road sold it to me, though the Lord knows who I'll sell it on to. He said he'd come across it durin' the Wars. There was a fair bit of thievery from some fine houses durin' them dark times, of course, but -

Isaac must have realised where it was from, and thought the man he bought it from had likely stolen it from Witherstone Hall, and that *he* might get the blame as it was now in his possession.

At last the Squire, Lady Sylvestre and Master William rose and left the Great Hall, and as soon as they had disappeared into the passage the servants all stood, most of them leaving to go about their business while Sarah supervised myself and Agnes and the other kitchen girls in clearing the tables. I spent until late that night scrubbing pots in the kitchen scullery until, exhausted, Agnes said I had finished for the day and could go to bed.

She gave me a thin blanket and a lumpy, straw-filled sack, then laid out her own bed in front of the huge kitchen fireplace next to the other girls, leaving me the draughty space by the archway into the passage and the Great Hall.

"You need to sleep there because it's your job to check on the fire in the Great Hall in the night. *Don't* let it go out."

The other girls sniggered, and they whispered together as Agnes settled beside them. I went through to the Great Hall straight away, hoping they would all be asleep by the time I got back. The fire was still burning well, but I stacked a few more thick logs on anyway to make sure it would stay in long enough for me to get some sleep before I had to check on it again.

When I went back through to the kitchen, the huddled forms by the fire were quiet, and I wrapped myself in my cloak and the blanket to try to protect myself against the cold air rushing through from the passage, then tried to get comfortable on the lumpy mattress. It was so unpleasant to lie on that I thought I'd be awake all night, but sheer exhaustion made my body forget how uncomfortable it was as I did fall asleep. Only to find myself trapped in my nightmare again.

Even though I knew I was dreaming I couldn't wake myself up. I was running down the stone passage in Witherstone Hall on silent feet, trying to find the way out. I needed to get back to Catherine and Richard but I couldn't find the kitchen doorway, or the Great Hall, and every door along the passage was locked. I know someone is behind me as I can hear their quiet steps on the flagstones, and I run faster, feeling the panic rising, and no matter how familiar it all is the terror is just the same. The shadows loom towards me and I hear a door closing quietly behind me as finally I turn, a scream already rising, to find a pair of white hands reaching for my throat from the folds of a cloak the colour of blood.

I woke up gasping, and there's an odd, ringing silence as though a sound – a scream, a whisper - has just died away. I lay there, heart racing and eyes staring into the dark, listening to the sounds of the other girls' quiet breathing.

After I'd calmed down, I knew I ought to check on the fire in the Great Hall, trying to persuade myself there was nothing to be scared of out in the passage as I felt its cold air at my back. I guess I'd dreamt of *that* passage because of my encounter with Lady Sylvestre and her son. A cloak the colour of blood trailed across the inside of my skull and I shivered.

I forced myself to sit up because I knew I'd be in real trouble if I let the fire go out, drawing attention I could well do without. I kept my cloak around me as I stole into the passage and the Great Hall. The fire was still burning well so I must have been asleep for less than an hour. Sighing, I piled several more logs on anyway, then, as I headed back into the passage, a door opened slightly, pale light from the room pointing onto the flagstones near where I stood, frozen to the spot.

"Not yet, Silas." I heard a voice whisper, and knew at once it was Lady Sylvestre. "We need to be sure."

A smooth voice answered, freezing my blood. Parson Burnett. I could barely make out his softly-spoken words, but I heard enough to chill me to the bone.

"*- rid of Hephzibah Smalley years ago, when you had the chance.*"

More whispers, more urgent this time, then, "- sure she has told no-one?"

Parson Burnett's whispered voice was suddenly closer.

"She swore that Creswell was bluffing when he claimed he knew."

"Well, even if she has told him, they can prove *nothing* now," Lady Sylvestre's voice hissed back. "I have seen to that."

I heard the sound of papers rustling, then the door closed suddenly, cutting off their whispers, and I was across the passage and at the door before I was even aware I'd moved, my ear pressing into the wood.

I could hear Parson Burnett's smooth whisper.

"- but that's a different problem. If Creswell finds out -"

A soft laugh.

"How can he? The old man is dead and his son is an illiterate labourer. If they knew, why would they keep quiet? The old man was only a child. His son marrying Hephzibah Smalley's brat is just a coincidence. They even let us send the boy away when they were starving. It's a pity he came back. No, they don't know, and there's no-one left to tell them. There's nothing for us to worry about there. But Hephzibah Smalley is another matter. She's far more dangerous…"

The whispers faded suddenly although I could hear they were still speaking. The floorboards creaked in the room and I realised they must be moving away from the door. I stood there, ear pressed to the wood and my muscles tensed to breaking point. I couldn't make out anything they were saying. I heard the sound of something closing – a cupboard or a chest? - then the floorboards creaked again.

"But you'll need to be careful, Elizabeth." Parson Burnett's soft whisper was suddenly right behind the door. "If she even suspects you'll go after her grandchildren anyway, she'll tell the world -"

"Shhh. What was that?"

My heart stopped as their whispers cut off abruptly, and I knew they were listening. Had I made a noise? Without breathing I backed away from the door, my mouth and eyes wide with terror, then I turned quickly and ran silently through the shadows to the kitchen. I was wrapped in the blanket and lying on the mattress as though fast asleep within seconds, my face huddled inside the blanket as I lay there, ears straining to hear anything at all in the passage.

After a few moments I heard a door open and close quietly, then two sets of footsteps were moving softly along the passage. They paused at the kitchen archway. I daren't breathe as I lay there, just a pace away from them.

The footsteps resumed, almost imperceptible as they moved through the Great Hall, then there was the sound of a bolt drawn back quietly and a rush of night air blew through the Hall and across my neck. The door closed and the bolt slid home, then quick, light footsteps came back alone, heading past the kitchen without pausing and along the passage, skirts whispering. I heard the stairs creak as Lady Sylvestre made her way upstairs.

I lay there cocooned in the blanket for an age, my mind numb and my stomach sick with dread. Had I really heard Lady Sylvestre and Parson Burnett plotting my grandmother's death? And my own, along with my brother and sister? No matter how I played and replayed their urgent whispers through my mind, I could come up with no other interpretation. I knew I had to get out of there. And that I had to get Richard and Catherine from Thompson's and away from Witherstone altogether.

I knew my grandmother was doomed, condemned to death before she's even had a trial. My chest tightened at the thought that we might have to abandon her to her fate. It was obvious that, whatever her secret was, there was no point in her keeping it as they were planning to come after us anyway. Presumably they'd told her we would be safe if she kept silent. What the other thing was – something about Creswell finding out about something? My father? – it was impossible to guess, but what I did know was devastating. Not only was Grandma in mortal danger, so were my brother and sister, and me.

Whatever Grandma knew that the Sylvestre family were willing to silence her – and us – forever, perhaps the same thing that had caused the death of her own grandmother Hannah Pendal so many years ago as Grandma suggested in the gaol, I knew I couldn't just abandon her. Somehow I needed to get a message to her, and then get Catherine and Richard and myself as far away from Witherstone as possible.

I made myself get up quietly, putting my shoes on in the dark, and crept across the kitchen to the back door and lifted the latch as silently as I could. The door wouldn't open. I tugged at it, then felt all over the back of the door in the shadows, but could find no draw bolt. It must be locked with a key. I realised there was only one way out. Through the main door in the Great Hall, the way someone – presumably Parson Burnett - had gone.

I crept back across the kitchen and stood at the archway into the passage for several long minutes, listening for any sounds in the house above the sick pounding of my own heart.

All was quiet so I crept into the passage, involuntarily glancing at the door behind which Lady Sylvestre and Parson Burnett had been whispering. As I turned to cross the Great Hall, it suddenly occurred to me that the papers I had heard rustling might hold some kind of evidence. What was it Lady Sylvestre had said? Something about having seen to it that we could *prove nothing now*? And then there had been the sound of papers shuffling together.

I hesitated, listening to the silent house, and then for the second time that night I found myself at the door to the room without having consciously decided to move.

Ear pressed to the wood, I listened for any sounds, then quietly lifted the latch and peered round the door. The fire was dying in the grate but it gave out enough light for me to see there was no-one in the room. It was a parlour, with two high-backed settles either side of the ornate fireplace and a long court cupboard against the back wall. There were heavy drapes across the wall opposite the door and I knew I'd better check that these were across the window rather than a bed.

I was half way across the room when I heard creaking above my head and froze. After a few moments the creaking stopped. Heart pounding as I listened to the silence, I made myself carry on across the room and opened the drapes a tiny crack and peered through. It was the window, the small leaded panes dark.

I let the drapes fall back and walked over to the cupboard and opened one of the doors. There was a tiny sound behind me and I stopped dead, every nerve on edge. It had sounded as though it had come from the window. Just a quiet click. I listened so hard that I nearly jumped out of my skin when a log collapsed lightly in the grate, then came a spatter of sounds against the window and I released a shaky breath. It was raining again.

I moved along the cupboard, opening each of the doors and rummaging quietly but unsuccessfully through the contents, finding only silver platters and ornate goblets, and the rain began to really beat against the glass. Then I found a large wooden box. Hands clumsy with nerves, I slid it out of the cupboard and tried to open it. It was locked. Frustrated and scared in equal measure, I shook the box gently and it sounded as though there were papers inside. I was sure this must be it. I felt around inside the cupboard for a key, but found nothing. It was then that the sound of the rain grew suddenly louder as someone opened the window behind the drapes and climbed into the room.

I was across the room and hiding behind the settle nearest to the door in a second. Pressing myself into the far corner where the shadows were the deepest, I listened as the intruder slipped in from behind the drapes, then footsteps came into the centre of the room and stopped. I could make out the sound of their quiet breathing and held my breath, afraid they would be able to hear me too.

The next moment, the door from the passage opened and a dark figure leapt past me at the intruder. There was a grunt and the sound of a struggle as the two bodies met in the middle of the room.

After a few seconds of violent struggling, there was a gasp and then a man's shocked whisper.

"*You! That's impossible!*"

A short, bitter laugh from another man.

"Well, it is me nonetheless, Henry."

There was the sound of someone brushing himself down.

"What do you want? You're not welcome here."

"Oh, don't worry, I'm not staying around to play happy families. I just want to know where my wife and son are buried, and then I'll be on my way."

Silence.

"Well?"

"What does it matter?"

Anger. "It matters to *me*. *Where are they?* I've checked the inscriptions on the family vault, and all the other gravestones inside the church, and I've been up and down the graveyard outside a thousand times but I can't find them."

"In a pauper's grave, unmarked, where they deserve to be."

"*How dare you!*"

There was a thump and the sound of a struggle in earnest, and the settle jolted and skidded closer to the wall, nearly crushing me where I was crouching behind it, terrified. The sound of fists hitting flesh was sickening.

"*Where are they?*" The furious voice demanded, and was answered with a strangled gasp.

"Where you'll never find them! There's nothing for you here, d'you hear me? Nothing!"

Suddenly a pale blur swept into the room and flew at the two men. There was an awful cry and then Lady Sylvestre's voice, hissing, to the sound of blows.

"There. Is. Nothing. For. You. Here."

A man groaned, and the sound turned my insides to water. Then he sighed heavily and fell to the floor, and was silent.

"We need to get him out of here, Henry."

"Check the passage. Someone may have heard."

A figure in a long white shift swept to the door and peered out into the passage, then she bent down and placed a darkly gleaming blade on the floor quietly before gliding silently out of the room. A moment later, I heard voices.

"No, one of the servants has been taken ill. Go back to bed, I have it in hand. *Now*, girl. I *said* I have it in hand."

A moment later, Lady Sylvestre came back into the room and picked up the knife.

"We'll have to think for a moment," she whispered. "The kitchen girls have woken up. We can't take him out through the Great Hall. Go and get William. He'll have to help us. We can lift the body out through the window, then take it and throw it into the river. With this rain, it'll be swept down miles past Hawbury with any luck. No-one will find him. *Go*," she hissed.

The Squire left the room quietly, and I listened to the sound of Lady Sylvestre's quick breathing. Then suddenly she swept from the room, closing the door behind her, and I heard the key turn in the lock then her light, quick step hurrying along the passage and up the stairs. Then came a soft groan and the sound of someone trying to get to his feet in the middle of the room.

Witherstone

"*Ah,*" he moaned again.

I heard him stagger to the window and lift himself back out, then the sound of his body landing heavily on the grass. I knew I couldn't stay where I was. The Sylvestres would find me as soon as they got back and started searching the room for their victim. I got out from behind the settle and ran to the window, and was over the sill in a second.

As I landed on the wet grass I could see the injured man weaving across the kitchen garden towards the wall, one arm held tightly to his side. The rain ran into my eyes as I stared at him. There was no way he was going to make it, and I didn't know what to do. All my senses were screaming at me to run, get out of there fast. I couldn't help him, I needed to save myself and get back to Richard and Catherine. But I knew I couldn't leave him.

I ran through the rain and grabbed his arm, intending to try and help support him as far as the wall, but he pulled away from me with a gasp.

"*No! You Devil!*"

"It's alright," I whispered urgently. "I'm tryin' to help you!"

He seemed to grasp at once that I really was trying to help, and he leaned on me heavily as I half-dragged him to the wall, then he started to haul himself up the slippery stone, and I held and pushed him as much as I could, looking back over my shoulder a thousand times to see if anyone was coming through the rain towards us. I scrambled up after him as soon as he swung his legs over the top. He half-fell down the other side, crashing to the ground in a heap, and he seemed to collapse into himself then, flopping down unresistingly as I slithered down after him and tried to help him to his feet.

"Oh, come *on!*" I groaned. "Before they come!"

He roused himself then, and staggered to his feet, leaning on me all the while, and I started pulling him through the dank woods, heading towards the stream and the crags. I figured his only chance would be to head away from the river for now as they might look for him there first, but I couldn't see him getting very far at all. When we reached the stream, fast and full with rain, I stopped, taking his weight as he leaned on my shoulder and I listened behind us for sounds of pursuit.

The rain was lashing down, filling the woods with sound and movement, but after listening hard, I was sure there was nothing behind us but the rain. I began to guide the injured man up through the woods, trying to encourage him to keep walking and hushing him when he groaned. All the while my ears were straining for any sound of pursuit. We'd been making our way alongside the stream for a while when the rain started to ease, and I heard the sound I'd been dreading. There was someone moving stealthily through the woods behind us, and gaining on us with every step.

I knew if I ran now, I had a chance of saving myself, and I also knew that the wounded man wouldn't be able to run in a million years. Even though his life depended on it. I couldn't just leave him to be butchered, so I pulled us both away from the stream and down into the thicker bushes, whispering urgently in his ear to be quiet. He seemed barely aware as we crouched there, and I prayed he wouldn't groan.

Our pursuer was coming closer, and I could see him now. He was alone as he crept towards us but I didn't see how I could overpower him on my own, and the thought of showing myself, even to attack him, was terrifying. Our only chance was to hope he passed us by and then we could somehow double back once he was out of earshot – and hope we didn't run into the rest of the Sylvestres lower down.

We might have to head down to the river after all, although the thought of trying to handle a boat on what I knew would be a churning torrent in this rain filled me with dread.

I peered through the leaves as the man drew closer, my eyes straining to see if it was Sir Henry or his son, Master William, but it was impossible to tell in the deep shadows of the woods as the dark, cloaked figure flitted in and out of my vision. As far as I could see though, he was on his own. They must have spread out to search.

I held my breath as he grew closer, his tread quiet but not quiet enough as I marked his steady progress towards where we crouched in the undergrowth. My heart pounded and I realised my fingers were digging into my companion's arm as our pursuer drew nearer, but I couldn't lessen the tension in my muscles. And then he was past us, and I couldn't believe our luck as I watched him move on through the trees. But then he stopped dead, and I knew he was listening.

I looked at the injured man's face in the dark shadows. His eyes were closed and I had no idea if he knew how close his enemy was. All I could do was pray he kept quiet, and I turned back to watch our pursuer. After several long minutes, the shadowy figure moved. He turned round and started walking slowly back, body tensed and listening as he approached us. He stopped again, just feet away in the shadows.

"*William?*" he whispered hoarsely. "*William?*"

My heart felt as though it would burst out of my chest in terror. It was Sir Henry, and his son must be close behind us.

My companion stirred suddenly, and began to stand up. I grabbed his arm to stop him but he pulled away and I fell back, the undergrowth crunching, and I saw the Squire's head snap round to face us. My heart juddered as the two men stared at one another.

The Squire whispered urgently, "William! *Thank God!*" then he was moving towards us at speed, and I knew that all was lost as he reached us and grabbed the wounded man.

Then he cried out, "*You're hurt!*"

"Stabbed," the man groaned. "Girl helped me."

Then he half-fell, and I jumped up as he collapsed, our pursuer keeping him from falling as he exclaimed at my sudden appearance.

"What the - ? *Good God!*" Our pursuer peered at me in the gloom. "*You* again!"

I stared at his face, straining under the weight of the injured man collapsing against him. It was Robert Newstead.

"*Oh!*" I gasped, trembling so much I could barely speak. "I-I thought this must be your friend! He was fightin' - with the Squire I think, askin' about his wife an' son's grave – but they stabbed him. L-Lady Sylvestre -"

Witherstone

It was Robert Newstead's turn to gasp. "We have to get him out of here quickly."

He whipped his neckerchief off and unbuttoned the wounded man's doublet, then tied the linen around his friend's body, pressing it tightly against the black shadow spreading across his pale shirt. Then he heaved the man up over his shoulder and turned and headed up towards the crags, moving quickly through the trees.

I followed him without hesitation. I knew I'd be better staying with Robert until after sunrise at least, before setting off for Thompson's to get my brother and sister away from Witherstone. There was no way I was going to try to get through the woods in the dark on my own, with the Sylvestre family searching for the wounded man.

I felt my back prickling at the thought of them creeping through the trees behind us, and I kept looking over my shoulder as I followed Robert's hunched shadow up towards the crags. He looked behind us often too, and I knew when dawn was coming as eventually I could see the worried expression on his face. As the shadows faded into dawn, the crows rose from the trees and wheeled across the grey sky with slow beats, their hoarse voices echoing in the woods around us.

I watched Robert making his way up the track in the rain, walking quickly despite his burden, and the strangest suspicions were in my mind about the wounded man, even though what I was thinking was impossible.

The dark figure who had attacked the intruder first must have been the Squire, as both Lady Sylvestre and the intruder had called him Henry. I'd recognised Lady Sylvestre's voice, of course, but still couldn't believe she had – had – stabbed the man. Yet I knew she had. His terrible cry and the sound of the knife driving into flesh kept coming back to me, making my skin clammy and my head spin.

It didn't seem possible, but I couldn't help thinking that the wounded man must be William Sylvestre, the old Squire's eldest son and Sir Henry's brother, who was believed to have been killed during the Civil Wars. Robert had been calling "William" to find his friend, not young Master William as I had first thought. I shook my head as I looked at Robert's burden. It couldn't be... could it?

Suddenly, Robert turned and spoke, his voice hoarse with exertion.

"We need to stop, now it's light enough to see. I just hope it isn't too late."

We climbed down towards the stream and Robert gently lowered the man to the ground. He listened to his friend's heart, and I knew it was still beating as the relief on Robert's face was immense.

Carefully, he untied the shockingly red neckerchief and lifted the sodden shirt. There was so much blood it was difficult at first to see the wounds, but Robert scooped water from the stream and washed away the blood, and I could see the thin gashes in his friend's side, seeming too small to be oozing such thick, dark blood.

Robert pressed moss onto the wounds like dressings, then he took out a knife and cut strips off his friend's shirt and bound the make-shift bandage around the wounded man, trying to pull the cuts closed as he tied the knots firmly. Then he bound the bloody neckerchief tightly over the bandage, and washed his hands in the stream. He wrapped his own cloak around his friend, and gave him some water, and the injured man mumbled something and tried to swallow the water, though he choked and spluttered. Robert sighed as he lowered his friend back down to the ground, then he drank some water himself.

I followed his lead. The water was freezing, but then I was already soaked through and shivering.

Robert took in my sorry state.

"We can't stop an' light a fire, I'm afraid. I'm goin' to try to get him to where we're camped. I need a needle so I can stitch his wounds up, though God knows I can do little to stop the rot settin' in, if it's goin' to. But you – well, what will you do, Eppie? An' how did you come to be there anyway, with – my friend?"

I looked at the wounded man, his face ghastly pale beneath his silver-grey beard.

"Is he William Sylvestre?"

Robert's breath whooshed out in surprise, and he shook his head, smiling suddenly.

"My God, you are a little witch, aren't you?" he laughed. "How on earth did you know?"

I surprised myself by laughing back, instead of being annoyed at him for using *that* word. I shrugged.

"I guessed."

He shook his head again, though his smile faded suddenly, concern for his friend setting his mouth into a thin line and his scar a deep shadow.

"Well, we can talk about that later," he said. "Right now I need to see to his wounds properly. I don't suppose you know of anythin' better than moss for stoppin' the blood an' keeping wounds clean, Eppie?"

I shook my head. Then I stood up, still shivering, and turned towards Witherstone, searching for that shadowy huddle in the bend of the river below - the river which I knew would be swollen and fierce with the rain.

My stomach was churning with indecision. I knew I needed to get to Richard and Catherine, and could walk to Thompson's from here in half a day. Then I looked at the wounded man. His breathing was shallow and he had a thin sheen of sweat on his face, and above our heads the raucous crows were still riding the wind.

"Although I know someone who might be able to help," I said finally, and I thought about Richard and Catherine, and my heart juddered, praying they were safe for now as I turned my back on Witherstone for the moment.

I tried to smile at the scarred man.

"But you'll have to carry him a long way."

He frowned as he tried to read my face, then he nodded.

"I trust you, Eppie," he said.

Robert heaved William Sylvestre back over his shoulder, and followed me as I set off up the path towards the wild wood.

~

Witherstone

Witherstone

Coming in 2012...

Witherstone
Book 2: The Hunt Begins

www.witherstone.com
www.jabrunning.co.uk

Witherstone

Made in the USA
Charleston, SC
10 October 2011